The Leaving

S.M. Elthen

Dedication

For my wife – who helps transform
my dreams into realities.

Prologue

Being the one to leave is never easy — even when it's best for everyone.

I could feel their little eyes watching me as I walked down the sidewalk. I had wiped the tears from their eyes. I had hugged them tight and made a promise that I would see them again one day. But I couldn't tell them when. I couldn't tell them how long I would be gone. As adults, my wife and I knew the truth was that I might not be back in this world — ever.

Pieces of my heart fell to the ground with each step that took me farther from my boys. I hoped that they would find those pieces. That they would pick them up and hide them away with their shiny treasures. I wanted them to never forget that the steps that took me from them were taken to keep them safe.

Being the one to leave is never easy — especially when it breaks everyone's heart.

CHAPTER 1

Tenja stood looking through the French doors into the studio and smiled. Her boy with bouncing red curls kept disappearing and reappearing in different areas of the room. She could tell he was testing his skill as he attempted to reappear standing on a brick, and then in a handstand. Conner was constantly pushing the limits of his magic. Her heart swelled with pride.

They had sound proofed this room when the boys were little. Learning magic can be loud – especially when that magic is music. But even sound proofed the glass of the French doors let out the quiet melody being played by another one of her boys. Graysen's magic let him play multiple musical instruments at the same time. It sounded like he was playing strings, wind, and percussion in the current piece. She closed her eyes and took in the beauty of it.

After a moment she opened the studio door. The room quieted and movement stopped.

"Hey momma!" Graysen said excitedly. "Did you hear my music?"

"I did! It was beautiful. Was it your composition?"

"Yep. I'm working on it for my final presentation," he explained.

"Well, it's coming along quite well!" she assured him. "And Conner, I saw that handstand you tried. You're really close to nailing it!"

"Yeah, I'm getting there," he responded like it was all no big deal.

"Where's your brother?" she asked them.

"Last time I saw him he was headed out back," Graysen shared.

"Okay. Well, dinner is on the table," she said as she headed out to find her third boy.

She did find Hodgens out back. She watched him for a minute, before interrupting.

"What are you reading?" she asked.

"About being a veterinarian," he said as he closed the book.

"Still leaning toward that career when you're out of prep?"

1

"Yeah. It just feels right."

She ruffled his hair – to his dismay. "Okay, bud. Well, dinner is ready. We should get in there before your brothers eat it all." They walked into the house together in companionable silence.

#

She expected to find Conner and Graysen at the table, plates heaping with spaghetti. But the room was empty and the food untouched. Hodgens looked at her, shrugged as he sat down.

"Boys?" Tenja called.

"In here, mom," Conner replied from the front door.

She walked in to find them standing at an open front door. "What's going on?" she asked.

They stepped aside to reveal a dog sitting on the front steps. Just sitting there. Looking at all of them.

"I – I think it rang the doorbell," Graysen told her.

"Well, that's just silly," she laughed.

"No. I think he's right," Conner backed his brother.

"How do you think – "as she spoke, the dog wiped its feet on the mat and trotted into the house like it had always lived there. It looked left and right as if it was trying to find something – or someone. Then it turned into the dining room and aroofed happily. It scurried around the table, sat down next to Hodgens, and extended a paw as if to shake hands.

Hodgens sat there looking confused as the others hurried into the dining room. Graysen and Conner dropped to their knees next to the dog.

"Go on," Conner said, "shake its hand – er – paw."

Hodgens look at his mother, who just shrugged in disbelief. Hesitantly, Hodgens reached down and shook the dog's paw.

"Is it me," Graysen asked, "or does that dog look like that stuffed animal you carried around for years when we were little?"

"Beagle Girl," Hodgens agreed and the dog aroofed again and nodded its head. All the humans in the room looked at each other in shock. "Momma," Hodgens began.

"I don't know," she responded before he could finish. "For now, get the dog a bowl of water and let's eat before the food gets cold."

There was little conversation during dinner. Which was unusual around their table. But no one knew what to make of this strange new visitor. She, they had determined the dog was female, had curled up next to Hodgens' chair and fell asleep. As he finished his dinner and sat back Conner asked, "are we keeping her?"

"Well, let's check her collar, see if she belongs to anyone," Tenja instructed.

Hodgens sat down next to the dog and inspected her, "there's no collar," he finally said.

"Interesting," Tenja replied, "Then I don't think it's a matter of keeping her so much as a question of 'how long will she be staying'?"

"What does that mean?" Hodgens asked.

"I sense magic," she began hesitantly. "It's been a long time since we talked about your Momma Raben, but she used to tell us stories of animals, of creatures, who could do magic."

"I always thought those were just stories," Graysen interjected.

"Well, they were. They were true stories."

"Wait, you're telling us that the fairy tales she used to tell us on rainy days were true? That can't be possible," Hodgens discounted her statement.

"It was always a stretch for me believe the tales about the dragons," she admitted. "But I've seen other animals do strange things, sensed a level of magic in them."

"What kind of strange things?" Conner pushed.

"I once saw a cat levitate itself from a tree into my friend's bedroom window."

"No way!" he exclaimed.

"Cross my heart," she nodded. "As the years have gone by, though, I've seen and sensed less and less animal magic. It's like it is disappearing from this land."

"What do you mean 'from this land'?" Graysen asked.

"She is saying that Draiocht does exist. That Easpach isn't the only land. And now, you sound mad, momma," Hodgens said in disgust as he shoved his chair back from the table. He startled the dog who jumped out of the way. The others sat in silence as he washed his dishes and put them in the drying rack. As he headed up the stairs the dog trotted after him.

#

Hodgens sat down on his bed. When the dog jumped up beside him, he bounded off. She looked at him, head cocked, obviously wondering what the problem was.

"Uh huh, no," Hodgens shook his head, "off my bed. That's my bed. I sleep alone in my bed."

With sad eyes the dog jumped down and sat on the floor next to the bed. Hodgens sat back down and stared at the dog.

"So, you really have magic?" He asked.

She nodded.

"This is crazy!" He exclaimed. "Dogs can't understand every word a human says. Dogs don't have magic."

Then she levitated and he just shook his head.

"I don't know what to do with you," he finally admitted.

She sat back down on the floor and nudged his hand with her nose. He rubbed her head and thought about how much she really did look like his old stuffed animal.

"I'd like to call you Beagle Girl if that is okay," he told her.

She aroofed and he took that as a yes. He didn't know why she had come to them or how long she would stay. But, for the moment, he was glad she was here.

4

"Why do they talk about Momma Raben?" He said to Beagle Girl. "Why do they bring her up? She left us ten years ago. Momma Tenja is the momma who loves us. If Momma Raben really loved us she wouldn't have left us."

Beagle Girl shook her head as if in disagreement.

Hodgens looked at the dog, "oh, like you know something I don't?"

He watched in shock as she shook her head yes and aroofed again.

"I must be tired," he said. "I'm getting ready for bed. You," he tossed an extra pillow on the floor, "you're sleeping there."

#

"I don't think you're mad, momma," Conner said softly.

"Me neither," Graysen added.

"It's okay, boys," she said as she stood up and began to clear the table. "We all know that the subject of Momma Raben is a touchy one for your brother."

They talked of school and finals as they cleaned up dinner. Once they were done Graysen asked, "will you tell us about Momma Raben and why she left?"

Wearily, Tenja looked at him and his brother. "You haven't asked to talk about that in years." She had anticipated this conversation. But now that it was here, she wasn't sure she was ready to have it with them.

"I know. But I just want to tonight. I don't know why."

"Let me make some tea then we'll all sit down in the family room."

Once Graysen, Conner, and she were all tucked into comfy chairs she asked, "what do you want to know?"

"Well," Conner began, "it's been almost ten years since she left. I remember her leaving, walking down the sidewalk. But I don't remember what she told us before she left. I just remember feeling so sad and not wanting her to go."

5

Tears filled Tenja's eyes as she thought to herself me too, kiddo, me too.

"I remember she told us something about the magic, but I don't remember what," Graysen added.

"What she told you was that the magic was breaking and needed to be fixed. That she needed to go help with the problem until the fixer arrived."

"But, since she hasn't come back, does that mean the fixer never arrived?" Conner asked.

"I don't know, son."

"Does it mean she's dead?" Graysen asked quietly.

"No, your Momma Raben is very much alive," she replied with certainty. "My heart and Momma Raben's heart are connected. Because we both have magic, our wedding ceremony was a magical one and during that ceremony we were bound by blood. My heart would know if Momma Raben's heart was no longer beating."

"And you don't think magic could have changed that?" Graysen nudged harder.

"No, Graysen. There is no magic that can change the blood bond."

"So, why do you not know as much as Momma Raben about magic?" Conner this time.

"Momma Raben and I were both born in Draiocht, but my parents came to this land when I was an infant. Being raised here I didn't experience magic all around me growing up like Raben did."

"Is that why we never met any of Momma Raben's family?"

"Yes, Conner. None of them are in this world."

"So, is that where Momma Raben is now? Back in Draiocht?"

"That I don't know, Graysen. I know she's alive. But I don't know where she is."

Before anyone could say anything else, Beagle Girl came down the stairs. The door opened and she went out closing the door behind her. A couple of moments later the door opened and she walked back in, not bothering to look at them she went back upstairs.

"That is going to take some getting used to," Tenja remarked.

The boys laughed and shook their heads.

#

"Why do you guys bring up Momma Raben?" Hodgens asked still awake and furious with his brothers when they came up for bed. "She left us! She chose the magic over us! She could have stayed! She could have let someone else help until the fixer arrived!"

"You remember the story about the fixer?" Conner asked.

"Of course, I remember it! Don't you remember why our mother left us?"

"No, actually, we didn't," Graysen replied. "We were just talking to Momma Tenja about it. She reminded us."

"Well, I remember. I remember how she broke our hearts when she packed a bag and walked down that sidewalk."

Graysen walked over to his bookshelf and took down a small brown box. Opening it he dumped the contents on his bed. "Do you remember these?"

Conner and Hodgens moved closer to the bed. "No, what are those?" Conner asked.

"I don't know," Graysen admitted. "But there was one on the sidewalk for every step that Momma Raben took. They were strewn from the front step to the street. When you two ran inside crying I picked them all up. I've kept them in this treasure box since that day. This is the first time I've ever taken them out."

His brothers just looked at him.

"So, Momma Tenja doesn't know you have these?" Hodgens asked.

"No."

"They're magic, Graysen. Don't you feel it?"

"Of course I feel it!" Graysen shot back.

"I can't believe you kept these to yourself for almost ten years!" Conner yelled angrily. "You had a part of Momma Raben this whole time and you didn't share it with us? That was selfish Graysen, even for you."

Graysen looked at Conner and saw pain in his eyes. "I'm sorry, I didn't think...you two were so upset that day. Hodgens, you haven't wanted to talk about Momma Raben since the day she left. I didn't figure you would care. And Conner, I thought they would just upset you that day. And the more time that went by, the crueler it seemed to bring it up again."

Shocking the boys back into the moment, Beagle Girl jumped on the bed and sniffed the gems. Then she started barking erratically and spinning in circles.

"Hodgens shut her up!" Conner yelled.

"Shhh!" Hodgens told the dog as he grabbed her. Just then the door opened. Conner and Hodgens spun around, blocking the bed with their bodies.

"What is going on in here?" Tenja asked with a raised eyebrow.

"We were just playing with Beagle Girl," Hodgens said quickly.

She crossed her arms and gave each one of them a suspicious look. After all these years she knew when her boys were lying to her. But, for some reason she felt the need to let them have their secret. "Well, you need to head to bed. You all have exams tomorrow."

"Okay, momma," Graysen agreed.

"I love you my favorite little people."

Conner rolled his eyes, "momma, we're not little anymore."

The words they exchanged every night. She would miss this when they were out on their own. She laughed and closed the door. They held her heart. Now and forever.

"Do you think she believed us?" Conner asked.

"No way. She knows something is up," Hodgens said. "I wonder why she didn't make us tell her the truth."

Beagle Girl wiggled in his arms, and he let her down. She returned to his bed and laid down, eyeing them all like they were criminals.

8

"Graysen, put those gems away," Hodgens instructed. "Tomorrow, we start on the business of figuring out what they are,"

"Again I say, why aren't we telling Momma Tenja?" Conner asked.

"I can't explain it," Hodgens shrugged. "It's a feeling I have."

The other boys looked at each other. After a moment's hesitation Graysen also shrugged and began scooping up the gems. Conner helped him put them all back in the box. Once they were safely back on the shelf the boys let out a collective breath and went to bed.

#

Feeling a bit of angst, Beagle Girl left the boys to their tasks. Tenja had just settled into her bed with a book when she heard a soft scratch at the door.

"Come in," she said to the dog. Why get up? She thought to herself.

The dog walked in, jumped on the bed, and extended a paw. Tenja looked at the dog inquisitively and took the paw in her hand. After three exact shakes the dog pulled back her paw and nudged Tenja's hand. She looked at her hand and gasped. In the center of her palm was a symbol. A magic symbol.

She looked at the dog and whispered, "Raben?"

CHAPTER 2

Tenja tossed and turned all night. Her dreams were filled with goodbyes, magic symbols, puppy dogs, and fear. Over and over, she woke with her heart racing and her hair matted with sweat. When the clock said 4am she gave up and stepped into a hot shower. She had so many questions. But it wasn't like she could ask a dog. Could she? No. She shook her head. All magic had limits. Maybe there was no deep dark meaning. Maybe Raben sent the dog just to let them know she was okay. Should she tell the boys what she saw? Not now. Not yet. They had final presentations and exams this week. And, she admitted, she needed time. Time to sit with what she had learned. Time to do some investigating of her own. The last thing she wanted to do was get everyone's hopes up and then have them crushed again. That would be more than any of them could handle.

She stood in front of the mirror French braiding her hair. The light brown was now mixed with strands of gray. It had been almost ten years since she'd worn a French braid. The morning Raben left had went much like this one. She hadn't slept. She'd showered early. She'd felt like she was going to battle. And the proper hair for battle was a braid.

The first few months after Raben left had been the hardest months of her life. She instantly became a single parent to 7-year-old triplets. The financial responsibilities fell to her. The academic responsibilities, the emotional responsibilities – she scoffed – all the responsibilities were suddenly on her shoulders. And she was alone. She'd never felt so lonely in her entire life. But somehow, they had managed - together. The months turned into years and those years were now a decade.

She put the ponytail on the end of the braid and stepped back from the full-length mirror. Her five feet eight-inch, well-toned body was reflected back to her. The green shirt accentuated her piercing green eyes. Her blue jeans and brown walking boots rounded out an outfit that made her look like a formidable opponent. She couldn't explain why she felt like she was going to battle. But as she took one last look in the mirror she thought yes, this will do nicely.

#

Hodgens finished putting school supplies in his backpack. "Are you guys ready for your exams today? We have to pass our classes to graduate."

"Puh-lease," Graysen laughed, "they don't want the three of us around any longer than we have to be. They aren't going to keep any of us from graduating."

"Besides, Professor Koarré and momma are friends. He'll make sure we get through," Conner stated with certainty.

"Well, I for one am not going to rely on handouts to get out of there. I'm going to keep my marks up and –"

"And make mommy proud" Graysen said in a sniveling voice.

"Whatever," Hodgens muttered as he rolled his eyes and grabbed his backpack. Just then, he heard a whistling sound outside the window. "Funny Graysen. Did you put a recorder out there?"

"I'm not doing it!"

They all looked at each other and then at the window. As if one person, they all jumped when something black smacked against the window.

"Was that a bird!?" Conner screeched in disbelief.

"What are you two up to?" Hodgens asked as he turned on his brothers.

As triplets they had pulled a lot of pranks on each other, and on others, truth be told. So, Hodgens was sure that his brothers were messing with him in that moment.

"Seriously, we aren't doing anything!" Conner exclaimed as he walked to the window.

The sound of flapping grew louder. Frantic even. "It looks like," Conner squinted, "some sort of – book."

"That doesn't make any sense!" Graysen said as he pushed past Conner. "Let's just open the window!"

"Graysen, no!" Hodgens yelped as he dove for the window. But it was too late. A strong gust of wind blew the object into the room. It landed with a thud on the floor in the middle of the room. Graysen looked out the window one more time and then closed it.

The three gathered around the book. "Is that the front or the back?" Conner asked.

"No idea. Turn it over Hodgens," Graysen instructed.

"You turn it over!" he told Graysen.

They watched, mouths agape, as Beagle Girl flipped the book over with her nose. The sound of their collective gasp filled the room.

"That symbol...it's..." Hodgens started to say just as they heard "Boys! Breakfast is ready!"

"Should we take this down to mom?" Conner looked at his brothers. After a moment of silence Graysen grabbed the book and shoved it under his mattress.

"Not now," he said. "Not until we know what it is."

#

"Are you all ready for your exams?" Tenja asked the boys as she set the milk on the table. They all gave her a grunt or a yeah. She glanced at them and saw them all looking around at each other. "What's going on?"

"Nothing!" Graysen responded a little too enthusiastically as Conner kicked him under the table.

"Uh," Hodgens added, "we're just a little anxious about today."

While there was a thread of truth in what he said, Tenja knew it wasn't all of the story. The years of being an attentive parent told her

12

she was definitely missing something. She sat down in her chair, crossed her arms, and leaned back.

"So, that's the story we're going with?" she asked as she looked them each in the eye. After a moment's silence Graysen finally cracked.

"Okay…" he began.

"Graysen!" the other boys yelled in unison.

"Mom, we're working on a surprise," Hodgens began. "Can we just keep it between the three of us for a little bit longer?"

She raised one eyebrow and studied him. He held her gaze without wavering. "Okay," she finally shrugged. "I'm going to trust you three on this. Now, pass the milk." The boys looked at each other and their shoulders visibly relaxed. She had no doubt that she would find out about whatever was going on with them. She always did.

"So, what exams do you each have today?" she asked as they all began eating breakfast. The rest of the meal was a typical family breakfast. Her boys were growing up. It was exciting and difficult to watch. She missed her littles but was so very proud of the young men they had grown to be.

She gave them each a hug, and, to their dismay, a kiss on the cheek as she sent them off to school. There wouldn't be many more chances for those moments so she planned to keep stealing them as often as she could. As they headed down the sidewalk, she saw Beagle Girl run to catch up with them. What are you up to little girl? she thought to herself while also feeling thankful that the dog was out of the house for the time being. Heading back into the house she locked the door and turned toward the stairs.

In her bedroom again, she sat down on her side of the bed and turned her end table so she could see the back. It looked ordinary. Until she laid her hand flat against it. Then, a rectangle the width of the table and about 5 inches tall swung downward to reveal a compartment. Inside of the compartment was a long, ornate box. She lifted the box and set it on the end table, closed the compartment, and moved the end table back into its place. She stared at the symbol on the box.

It was a magic symbol. It was her symbol, her real symbol. She turned over her right hand and looked at her wrist. The magic symbol there did not look like the one on the box. But, she knew the box would do as it was spelled. She laid the symbol on her wrist on top of the symbol on the box, counted to three, and heard the lock click open. She opened the lid and stared at the two items inside: a paint bottle, and a brush. Her hands shook as she took them out and set them on the table. She closed the box and relocked it. One could never be too safe with magic.

She couldn't remember the last time she had used the paint and brush. They had been made especially for her, to aid her in performing her special brand of magic. Prior to her birth, there hadn't been a finder born in centuries. That is why her parents had left Draiocht. The last known finder was a prized possession, wanted by a lot of people. Her parents wanted her to be safe, to grow up without fear of being held hostage for the control of her power. They had succeeded and left her to protect her, to try to ensure she would be okay. Now there was only one other person who knew what she was. And she hadn't seen her in ten years. Her mind drifted back...

"Raben, are you sure this is the only way?" she begged.

"Yes, Tenja. I wish it wasn't. I wish there was a way to restore Sa Lár from here, to keep you and the boys safe from here. But I just haven't found any way to do that. The only thing I know to do is to go there. I have to be physically in Sa Lár to buy us some time."

"I don't like this," she said, laying her head on Raben's shoulder.

"I don't like it, either" Raben agreed, "but we have to keep our boys safe. As hard as it is going to be on us, it's the only right thing to do."

"I know," Tenja sighed.

"Tenja, I need you to promise me something."

"What?"

"I need you to promise that you won't use your magic to find me. I need to know that you're here with the boys, that they have you, all of us. I don't want both of us at risk."

Tenja let out a sob. "I can't promise that Raben. I can't."

"You have to, Tenja. I have to know that we're both doing what we can for our boys. And for you, that is being here, being present. Not chasing after me. Please, Tenja. Promise me."

"Okay," she said through the tears, "I promise I won't use my magic to find you. I'll be the best mom that I can for the boys and wait for the day you are back with us."

Shaking her head Tenja forced herself back into the present, pushing down the emotions and focusing once again on the bottle and brush. Well, my sweet, figuring out where Beagle Girl came from is not the same as searching for you.

#

Hodgens turned and looked at Beagle Girl.

"You cannot come into the school building."

She looked up at him with stubborn eyes. Then she let out a demanding aroof and turned toward the door while nodding her head yes to communicate that she would actually go in the building.

He stepped in front of her and looked at her in disbelief. "Seriously, you have to wait out here or go back home. You can't come in here."

15

She gave him a long look and then sauntered over to a tree where she sat down facing the door. He shook his head and turned to go into the school.

"Dude, how did you get her to stay out there?" Graysen asked.

Hodgens shrugged, "I didn't really give her a choice. I told her she had to either stay outside or go home."

"And that worked?" Conner scoffed as the bell rang. "Gotta go. See you guys at lunch," he said and hurried off to class. Graysen and Hodgens gave each other one last look and turned toward their classes.

Hodgens always enjoyed school. It was a place where he felt he belonged. He could do as much or as little magic as he wanted, as long as he did enough to satisfy his teachers. So many of his free hours had been spent reading and learning everything he could about magic even though he only used his when he absolutely had to. He preferred to experience the world he lived in and felt that magic kept him separated from it.

"Okay class, attention here, please," Professor Koarré said as he rolled into the classroom. He was a commanding presence. Students didn't question his authority. Or his kindness. He was as genuine as they came. "I hope you all took my advice and got a good night's sleep. Had a good breakfast. And came prepared to nail this exam."

He handed out a stack of papers to the first student in each row. "You have two hours to complete this exam. It won't be easy. Do your best. That's all I ask."

When the last student received her exam, Professor Koarré turned over the hourglass. Then he sat in his wheelchair at the front of the class reading a book and looking over the classroom every few minutes. Hodgens was feeling pretty confident as he read through the questions. He set about answering them with enthusiasm.

About half-way through the exam the class was interrupted by a gasp from Sandra, a girl sitting by the window. As everyone looked up to see what was wrong, she pointed toward the window. There, hovering just outside, was Beagle Girl. Hodgens groaned loud enough for his classmates to hear. But, they were all now at the window trying to see the person who was magically levitating the dog. Everyone had their faces pressed against the windows...everyone except Professor Koarré. The professor was looking right at him. When they made eye contact the professor said sternly, "everyone back to your seats."

As everyone rushed back to their seats Professor Koarré opened the window. Beagle Girl nodded and trotted in like a dog entering a room through a second story window was the most normal thing anyone had ever seen. She hopped off the window ledge, walked over to Hodgens and curled up under his desk. Now everyone was staring at him.

"Everyone, finish the exam. Hodgens, I will see you and," he nodded toward the dog at his feet, "after class."

"Yes, sir," he said quietly and went back to his exam.

#

As he turned in his exam, Hodgens glanced out the door and saw some of his classmates lingering in the hallway. Great, he thought to himself, now she has a fan club. He went back to his seat and waited for the last student to finish the exam. When Professor Koarré called time there were still two students working on the exam. They wore long faces as they turned in their exams and left the room, joining the ever-growing throng outside the door.

With a wave of his hand Professor Koarré shut the door. Beagle Girl stretched and stood up from her spot under the desk. She jumped on a desk in the front row and extended her paw to the professor for a shake. Unable to control himself the professor let out a deep, belly laugh, and the dog howled.

Hodgens stared at them as Beagle Girl jumped onto Professor Koarré's lap. The professor turned to face Hodgens.

"Where did she come from?" he asked as he stroked the dog.

17

"We don't know. She just showed up at our house last night."

"And you thought it a good idea to bring her to school?"

"I didn't bring her. She followed me. I told her to either stay outside and wait or go home."

"Hodgens was right, little miss. You aren't allowed inside the school – magic or not."

Hodgens thought he heard the dog hrmpf as she jumped down to the floor. "You know she has magic?" he asked the professor.

"How else did she come in through the window? Besides, I can feel it. Can't you?"

"I can. I just didn't know if everyone could."

"Probably not everyone. One has to believe in magical creatures in order to feel their magic."

"That explains it," Hodgens said mostly to himself.

"Explains what?"

"When she first showed up Graysen, Conner, and I just thought she was, well, a dog. We didn't even consider magic. Momma was the one who recognized it in her."

"But," the professor started to say and then stopped, looking away.

"I know. Momma Raben used to tell us stories. But, after all of these years that is what they became for the three of us – stories. We didn't consider the possible reality of what she told us. It's not like we're taught about it in school."

The bell rang. "I'm sorry Professor Koarré. I have to go to my next exam," he said glancing at the door, the dog, and the man.

"Go, go," he said to Hodgens flipping his hand to shoo him out the door. Then he pointed at the dog, "but it's time for you to leave. Do as Hodgens said. Wait outside or go home little one," he said softly. As Hodgens headed out the door to his next class, confident the dog could take care of herself, she made her way back to the professor and once again extended her paw for a shake. She nudged his hand after she pulled her paw away. Then she strolled out of the classroom and left him staring in shock at the symbol he now saw on his palm.

18

CHAPTER 3

Tenja opened the front door and stepped out onto the porch. The fresh air cleared her senses. Taking a deep breath, she removed the lid from the bottle and dipped in the brush. She put the lid back on the bottle and shoved it in her pocket. Then she touched the now glowing brush tip to the door mat and whispered the words 'Beagle Girl' three times. Paw prints began to glow on the door mat, then down the porch steps and the sidewalk. Tenja put the brush in her pocket and said to herself Now, little girl, let's see where you've been.

She walked along, following the paw prints and trying to not look suspicious. After all, no one else could see them and she wasn't one to look at her feet when she walked. She preferred to look the world square in the eye as she faced it. Her neighbors knew her and would find any other demeanor odd. So, she tried to amble, wave at folks as she passed, and keep an eye on the prints.

Two blocks into the trace she came to a fork in the prints. She stopped and knelt, placing her hand on the spot where they went two separate ways. There was only one chance to get this right. She looked back to see that the paw prints she's already passed were no longer illuminated. If she picked the wrong direction, she would lose her chance to trace the dog's magic. That was the downside to finder's magic. A finder could only use it to follow a particular creature's magic one time. If she screwed this up, she wouldn't get another chance.

She stood up and looked in both directions. Right led downtown. Left was the direction of the school. Beagle Girl had left with the boys to go to school this morning. So, it was a good bet that the paw prints leading to the school were from today, not from last night. She turned right and contemplated downtown. Could she really have come from somewhere downtown?

She glanced up at the sun. Almost noon. She only had a couple of hours before the boys would be home from school. Glancing both directions one more time she began to follow the paw prints that led downtown. Pausing she looked over her shoulder, confirming that the paw prints leading to the school were gone. Her heart skipped a beat and she hoped she had made the right choice.

The prints took her past so many places that held memories of fun times with the boys. The library where they had spent so many hours with books. The deli and ice cream shop where they still went every Friday after school. The gaming arcade where they had won too many stuffed animals. This is a great town to raise three boys in, she thought as she followed the paw prints out of downtown and toward the city park.

She stood at the entrance of the park staring at the paw prints that led inside. I guess my boots were a good choice for this adventure she said out loud to herself as she continued following the prints. About 200 yards into the park, the prints veered off into the trees. Tenja stopped and said, "are you serious!?" in an exasperated voice. Now she was wishing she'd paired her jeans with a long-sleeved shirt. But she'd come too far to turn back and reminded herself that this was her only chance.

Raben, she thought, I really hope that Beagle Girl is from you and I'm not going to regret this.

The paw prints were harder to see in the woods. Luckily, she only had to walk for about 20 minutes. What was unlucky was that the paw prints came to a sudden stop. She stared in disbelief. She had made the wrong choice. "No!" Tenja cried and fell to her knees. "I was sure this was something," she said as she closed her eyes, suddenly feeling exhausted. Pull yourself together, she thought. Get home to the boys.

She stood up and dusted off her jeans. As she turned to leave a shiny red object caught her attention. She faced the spot where the paw prints disappeared and took in what was before her. To the untrained eye it would look like nothing more than the other trees they'd walked past. But there was something there. She took a few steps back so she could take in more of her surroundings at the same time. That's when it all came into focus.

Hidden in the brush of the forest floor, about 10 feet apart, were two objects. Between them was the slightest shimmer. So slight that even most people with magic would miss it. But she was a finder, and a finder could see just a little bit more than everyone else. She walked over to one of the objects and moved the grass and twigs off of it. There, staring up at her, was a ruby-eyed dragon. The second object was its matching partner. Standing between them she knew what she had found. She held her hand up close to the shimmering and reached out with her magic. Rather than penetrating the space, her magic bounced back to her indicating that she was not allowed to pass through. At least, not now.

Looking up at the canopy she checked the sun. She had to get home. Before she left, she covered up the dragons. On her way out she marked a trail that only she would be able to find. She knew in her gut that she'd be back.

#

"Momma, we're home!" Conner shouted as he tossed his knapsack on the foyer bench and headed for the fridge.

"Momma?" Graysen echoed his brother.

"I'm here," Tenja replied as she set a basket of folded laundry on the stairs. "Where's Hodgens?"

"Grabbing the mail," Conner said, a bite of apple in his mouth. "Wait until you hear what happened at school today!" he exclaimed with a laugh that had Graysen snickering.

"Do I want to know?" she asked.

"Hey mom, here's the mail," Hodgens said as he entered the kitchen. Looking at his brothers he rolled his eyes. "You told her, didn't you?"

Graysen threw up his hands. "We haven't told her anything...yet," he responded with a laugh.

"Why don't you tell me over dinner. Let's get ready to walk down to the diner."

"Hey mom?" Conner asked.

"Yeah, bud?"

"What's up with the outfit and the hair? I don't remember the last time you wore a braid."

That statement stopped Hodgens and Graysen in their tracks. They both looked at her.

"I woke up feeling spunky this morning. Thought I would do something different," she said nonchalantly as she grabbed her wallet. "Now come on. I'm craving some mint chocolate chip ice cream."

#

About a block from the house Beagle Girl joined them. As they walked, the boys took turns telling parts of the Beagle Girl at school story. It didn't take long for Hodgens to lighten up and join in the idea of how funny it must have been for everyone.

"What did Madifen say? What did he do?" Tenja said between laughs, referring to Professor Koarré by his first name.

"Well," Hodgens shared, "after he told everyone to go back their seats, he just opened the window like it was no big deal and Beagle Girl walked right in."

The dog aroofed and nodded. Tenja had to stop walking because she was laughing so hard. The humor in imagining her friend seeing a dog hovering outside his second story classroom was too much to contain. Tears were streaming down her face as she gasped for breath between laughs.

"Okay, okay," Hodgens grabbed her arm and hauled her upright. "I'm hungry can we get dinner now?"

She wiped her face with her hands and looked at her boys. Then she burst out laughing again. Graysen grabbed her other arm, and they directed her the rest of the way to the deli while she laughed it all out.

"I'm okay, I'm okay," she said as the waitress seated them. "I'm sorry, I just wish I could have been there."

"Can we talk about something else now?" Hodgens pleaded.

"Yes, please," the other boys agreed.

"Alright, alright," she conceded. "How did exams really go?"

They talked about exams and weekend plans as they enjoyed their dinner. Friday night diner and ice cream were something they had been doing almost every Friday for at least the last eight years. She looked forward to every week because it was then, no matter what had transpired during the week, they all came together in fun and laughter. After dinner, as they walked to the ice cream shop they talked about what board game they were going to play when they got home.

Just as they sat down with their ice cream Madifen came over to the table. Tenja began eating her ice cream and tried to avoid looking at his face. She just knew that if she did, she wouldn't be able to contain her laughter...again.

"Hey Araven family! How's everyone doing?" Madifen asked.

That was all it took. Tenja choked on her ice cream and burst out laughing. Her laughter was contagious, and the boys all busted out. Madifen folded his hands in his lap and waited patiently. When everyone was breathing regularly again and had wiped their eyes he dared say, "So, Tenja, I see you heard about Hodgens' visitor in class today..." and the laughter started again.

After about five minutes they settled down and Tenja said, "I'm sorry Madi. The whole thing just creates images in my head that crack me up."

At that, he finally laughed. "I imagine it was quite funny."

As a waitress brought him his order he said, "So you don't know where this little girl came from?"

"We have no idea," Conner said as Tenja looked at the table.

"She just showed up at the front door and rang the doorbell," Graysen added.

Madifen raised an eyebrow, "rang the doorbell?"

"Yep. She's an interesting little dog," Tenja added.

"That she is," Madi agreed holding his palm flat up and looking at Tenja. "That she is."

Tenja just looked at him and held her palm flat up as well. The boys were so busy talking about their weekend plans they didn't notice the gesture between the two adults.

They finished their ice cream with light conversation. The boys invited Madifen over for game night and he accepted. It was a rousing game of Apples to Apples with everyone winning a few rounds. When they were done playing the boys headed off to their own activities.

"Want to join me for some lemonade on the deck?" Tenja asked Madi.

"Absolutely," he replied.

Madifen had been a part of her life as long as Raben. He and Raben had been friends before she and Raben got together. In the time that Raben had been gone he had been an invaluable part of their lives. At first, he was a shoulder to cry on. Over time he became a trusted friend and someone who the boys respected and sought out for advice. But he didn't know why Raben had left. It had been Raben's choice not to tell him the 'why'. So, Tenja had kept her secret. Tonight, she would walk a tightrope of secrets.

"I shook paws with the dog today," Madi started.

"I guessed that was what you meant by the palm up gesture at the ice cream shop. And why I responded in kind," she stated. "She left Raben's symbol on your palm, didn't she?"

"What does it mean, Tenja? What happened ten years ago and why is there a dog, one that looks like a live version of Hodgens' old stuffed animal, in your house leaving Raben's symbol on our palms?"

"Those are some big questions," Tenja answered, "and I'm not sure how much I can tell you."

"Well, I know what she told the boys. Something is broken in the magic and she had to go help until the fixer arrived."

Tenja nodded and took a long, slow drink of her lemonade.

"So, Tenja, tell me what you two didn't tell the boys."

"There is a lot of the background information you know, just because you lived it. When Raben left here she was headed to Sa Lár."

"Wait, what? How could she do that? People haven't traveled between the lands for..."

"A decade?" Tenja asked, her voice holding a hint of truth.

Madi shook his head. "I don't understand. Why was she going to Sa Lár?"

"To help find a way to hold the magic together between Draiocht and Easpach."

"To do what!?"

"Madi, you know that magic has been fading in this world. And you know what happens if the link to Draiocht is broken."

He stared out into the night, a thoughtful look on his face. "Yes," he nodded, "we have had fewer and fewer new students with magic at the school. Since no one can move between the lands, no new magic families are coming to Easpach. And it doesn't seem that the magic is being passed down through bloodlines here as strongly as it used to be."

"I've noticed this, too. The boys' friends are a mix of magic and non-magic families. And it seems like the younger children don't have as strong of powers as their older siblings."

"And you're telling me that all of this has to do with something happening in Sa Lár?"

"I don't know for sure. That was Raben's thought," she paused for a moment. "Can you answer a question about the curriculum at the school?"

Puzzled, he looked at her, "Sure…"

"Why don't they teach about magical creatures as part of the overall history of magic? The boys still thought the stories Raben used to tell them were fairy tales."

"I've argued with the curriculum committee about this for years. It feels like the curriculum is getting us farther and farther away from the roots of our magic. When we lost the ability to travel between lands the committee decided that the curriculum should be geared toward teaching the students how to live in Easpach, how to survive in a partially magic land."

"Because it isn't in this land doesn't mean it isn't real!"

He nodded, "I agree, Tenja. But they think it is in the students' best interest to balance magical knowledge and skills with tools to be successful in the life ahead of them. I can tell you; all of my students were shocked and amazed to see that little dog hovering outside of the window."

"Her name is Beagle Girl, Madi. Might as well get used to it," she said with a chuckle.

He laughed, "so, where do we go from here? What's next?"

This is where the secret keeping has to start, she thought to herself, for now. "I don't know," she shrugged. "I was just going to see if something else happens that is outside of the usual."

She could feel him looking at her. "I just don't know what else to do at this point."

"But Beagle Girl has a link to Raben!" the shock was evident in his voice. "We have to do something! What if this is her reaching out for help?"

She looked at him, "I believe that if Beagle Girl is a cry for help, she'd do more than sleep at Hodgens' feet. She would be frantically trying to lead us somewhere, wouldn't she?"

He thought about this for a moment and then nodded, "okay, I see where you're going with that thought."

She saw his tears glimmer in the moonlight.

"She was my best friend, Tenja. My best friend and she made this decision without me. She included you, she included her 7-year-old boys. But she excluded me. Maybe I could have helped. Maybe if I had done something she would be back with us, could have been back years ago."

Her heart ached for him, "I know, Madi. I know this has been hard for you, too. But I think we have to be patient. Hold fast. Trust Raben."

He sighed and headed into the house.

#

She finished washing the glasses and set them in the dish dryer. The conversation with Madifen had exhausted her. It had been years since she and Madi had engaged in a conversation about all of this. Right after Raben left he brought it up every time he got her alone. But as the years moved on and Raben didn't come back he stopped talking about her and about why she left.

She wasn't sure why she felt it necessary to keep information from Madi. When he asked what they were going to do next, though, her heart skipped a beat and that told her that she needed to start tucking away what she knew. Raben hadn't included Madi in her decision to leave and at the time she told Tenja that she had her reasons for excluding him and asked Tenja to trust her. And she did trust Raben. So, she'd tried to keep what she shared with him to things that he already knew or could figure out on his own. Going forward, though, she would keep all new information to herself.

A yell brought her out of her thoughts.

"Beagle Girl, stop!" she heard Hodgens say, followed by his brothers yelling "get your dog!" and the sound of six teenage feet running down the stairs.

She turned just in time to see Beagle Girl run into the kitchen and jump on the table. The dog looked at her – and then looked up. She followed the dog's gaze upward. There, hovering above the dog, were two objects. She recognized one as a treasure chest that Graysen had had since he was little. The other object looked like some kind of book, but she didn't think she'd seen it before.

Hodgens skidded to a stop at the table. Conner and Graysen were moving so fast they couldn't stop in time and ran into him, knocking him into the table. The table shook and startled Beagle Girl who then lost control of her magic. The objects dropped with a thud onto the table, the box falling open and the jewels spilling out onto the table. The dog sat down with a disgusted aroof.

Everyone froze. The boys held their breath and looked at Tenja.

Her mouth was hanging open. She walked to the table and reached out cautiously. Slowly she laid her fingers over the symbol on the book. Raben's symbol. She closed her eyes and took a deep breath as if she was breathing in the scent of her wife. After opening her eyes, she reached over and gently touched a jewel.

After a few minutes she looked up. First, she pointed at Beagle Girl, "you, off my table. I'll allow a lot of things, but a dog on my kitchen table is not one of them." The dog held her gaze for one breath, two...then jumped down like it was her decision.

Then Tenja looked at her boys. "You three," she pointed at each of them, "I assume this," she pointed at the table, "is your surprise. Now, sit down and start talking."

Daring not to test their mother in that moment, they all sat down. And then they told her everything.

When they were finished, she looked at the clock. "It's two o'clock in the morning and I am exhausted. I'm going to keep the book and the jewels –"

"But mom!" Hodgens started.

28

"- for now," she continued. "I need time to examine them. I need to study the magic in them. I need time to think about everything that has happened in the last week."

She softened her voice, "boys, something has changed. I don't know what is going on, but the ebb and flow of magic is different than it has been for the last decade. My number one priority is always to take care of you three, to keep you safe. For now, this is how I do that."

"Okay, momma," Conner said.

"We trust you," Grayson added.

"Will you let us help? With whatever is going on?" Hodgens asked.

"I promise all three of you, if I can keep you safe while letting you help I will."

They all nodded.

She hesitated and then said, "there is one thing that you can all do."

"What is it?" Hodgens asked.

"Don't tell anyone about any of this. Not the jewels. Not the book. Not how much magic Beagle Girl has. None of it. This all has to stay between the four – she looked at the dog – the five of us."

The boys looked at each other and then at her.

"What about Madifen?" Graysen asked.

"Even from him," Tenja replied. She knew there was risk here but felt a greater risk if they let him in on everything.

"I don't understand," Conner admitted, puzzled.

Tenja sighed. How much do I tell them, Raben? "When Momma Raben left she explicitly told me not to tell Madifen any more than what we had told the three of you. I trusted her then, and I still trust her. All of this is more than what we told you back then. So, it stays between us," she said in a very direct tone.

After a moment, Conner held his hand out in front of everyone, "triplet strong!" he declared.

His brothers followed, placing their hands on top of each other and repeating the family mantra. Tenja placed her hand on top of theirs and added her voice to the decree.

"Now, go to bed," she laughed. "I don't expect to see any of you before noon at this rate."

In an atypical move each of the boys hugged her and told her they loved her.

"I love you my favorite little people," she said as she stood up.

Beagle Girl stretched and let herself out as the humans moved to get some sleep. Tenja put the jewels back in the treasure box and took it, along with the book, to her bedroom. Pulling her trunk out from under her bed, she released the spelled lock and lifted the lid. She added the book to the collection of items there. Before placing the treasure box inside, she lifted the lid and took out a jewel. She held it in her hand and pressed it to her heart. These jewels were literally the tears of her love. They were beauty born of heartbreak. They were a promise.

Suddenly feeling beyond exhausted she put the treasure box in the trunk, respelled the lock and pushed the trunk back under the bed. She crawled into bed, turned out the light, and fell into a deep, restless sleep.

CHAPTER 4

Graysen dropped an envelope on the kitchen table.

"Here are the tickets for tonight's showcase," he informed her as he sat for breakfast. His brothers strolled in behind him and took a seat.

"Thanks, bud. I'll be sure to bring them," she said after a long sip of coffee.

"I got four," Conner explained, "so when each of us finishes our presentation we can join you. We are in the second row, left aisle side of the middle when you're looking at the stage."

"I can't believe that you guys only have one week left of prep," she sighed.

"I know, right?!" Hodgens exclaimed. "Come on summer!"

The boys all gave a little 'hoot' and then settled into the business of eating.

After a few minutes Graysen broke the silence, "it's been two weeks since Beagle Girl gave you the jewels and book," he said hesitantly. "Have you looked at them yet?"

"I'm sorry, boys. But no, I haven't. The art gallery has been super busy with the new show. You know I've been working an extra day each week to ensure that the show is a success. All the events leading up to and including the moment Beagle Girl revealed the book and jewels were exhausting. So, I've had to build up some emotional strength to face whatever is next."

Three faces full of anticipation looked at her.

"I promise that I will examine them today," she finally conceded.

"Awesome, thanks mom!" Conner exclaimed.

She looked at Hodgens. He had been silent through the entire meal.

"Hodgens, what are you thinking about all of this?" she asked him directly.

He shrugged.

"I really want to know, son. Please tell us."

"I don't know. On one hand it's exciting, right? It's like a mystery, a puzzle. On the other hand, Momma Raben chose to leave us. I'm still so angry at her for leaving our family because she chose magic over us."

"Oh, Hodgens," she said softly, "she didn't choose the magic over you. She chose the magic for you."

She looked at the faces staring at her. They were still so young. How much to tell them? She wondered to herself. Before she could say anything else, Graysen jumped up.

"We have to go or we're going to be late," he told his brothers.

She looked at the clock and told the boys, "We'll talk more about this after the showcase tonight. Do you guys want to grab a bite to eat at the deli beforehand?"

"Sure!" Conner agreed.

She hugged and kissed them, "great, let's meet there after school. Dinner will have to be early since the showcase starts at six."

They waved as they walked down the sidewalk. She waved back and thought about what awaited her. Beagle Girl sat on the step beside her. She had perked up when Tenja promised to look at the book and jewels.

She looked down at the dog, "well, come on then. Let's get this done."

A chill went down her spine as she turned to go into the house. The feeling had her locking the door behind her. She didn't see anything out of the ordinary when she looked out the window. But with magic, not seeing something with your eyes didn't mean there was no threat. She shook it off and went on with the task at hand.

Items and coffee in hand, Tenja headed into the studio. This room was built to support and contain magic. It had been a safe place for the boys to experiment as they were learning about their magic. There had been a lot of laughter, tears, and anger in this room through the years.

She put the mug, book, and box on her worktable. Then she opted for coffee while she contemplated which item to examine first. After what felt like an eternity, she tipped the box over and the jewels spilled across the table. They were all the same size. Shaped like teardrops. She couldn't stop the artist in her from grouping the colors together and then putting the groups in the order of the colors of a rainbow.

She could feel the magic in each jewel. But there was something else. Like the magic in each jewel could be more than it was in its current state. It felt like potential magic, the kind that would evolve into something else when used correctly. She furrowed her brow and picked up the book. Turning it over in her hand she ran a finger over Raben's symbol.

A decade of emotional walls crumbled inside her heart as she pressed the book to her chest. Sobs erupted from her throat as the pain, loss, fear, anger, frustration, and loneliness crashed against her soul like waves on a hurricane battered beach. Beagle Girl whined and gently put a paw on her leg. Tenja let it all come flooding out of her. This was a big part of the reality that she had lived with since Raben left. A part that she hadn't let herself feel because she knew it would break open just like this.

Eventually she caught her breath, wiped her eyes, and blew her nose. She looked at the clock, unsure how long she had allowed herself to succumb to the storm of emotions. An hour and a half had passed since she had sat down at her worktable. Her coffee was long since cold. She looked at the book and decided to grab a bottle of water before she examined it more thoroughly.

Stalling, Tenja? She asked herself. Maybe. She responded as she walked into the kitchen. Grabbing the water, she took a deep breath and steeled her emotions. A promise was important in this family, so she had to examine these things today.

She was startled from her thoughts by Beagle Girl who began barking hysterically at the back door. Tenja ran to the back door just

33

in time to catch a glimpse of someone running out the back gate. The bottle of water slipped from her hand and the sound of it hitting the floor made them both jump.

"Raben, what is going on?" she asked out loud. Beagle Girl howled in response.

"Come on, little girl. We've got work to do." The dog nodded as if she understood perfectly. Examining the book was going to have to wait.

#

Tenja waved to the boys as they entered the deli. They were laughing about something, and she hoped she could keep that spirit going through the evening.

"How was your day?" she asked as they all sat down.

"It was really good!" Hodgens began. "We got all our exam scores back today. All that is left is our showcase tonight. I'm so ready to be done!"

"So...don't keep me in suspense!" she exclaimed. "How did you all do?" Like she had to ask. After all these years in prep she could guess how the grades turned out.

Hodgens said, "Conner got the highest overall marks!" as he high fived his brother.

"Conner that is amazing!" Tenja jumped up and hugged him.

"Come on, mom. We're in public!" he squirmed away from her.

She laughed and asked, "and you two?"

"You're looking at the top three students in the cohort, momma! Conner, then Hodgens, then me!"

"Holy smokes, guys!! We are so celebrating after the showcase!"

"Yes!" they all exclaimed and high fived each other again.

"Let's get you fed so you can get ready for the showcase. You all have your suits at school to change into, right?" she asked.

Dinner was lighthearted. Fun even. They truly enjoyed being with each other for the short period of time before the showcase.

"I still don't understand why we have to go to prep next week. We already know our final outcomes," Graysen said as they walked toward the school.

"It's tradition," Tenja said. "It's a week of fun and hijinks before you're off to the serious world of being an adult."

"Like you're serious?" Conner said jokingly.

They all laughed.

"You know I think life is too short to be too serious," she poked him with her elbow.

As they got to the school she asked, "what order are you guys performing?"

"They have programs at the door," Hodgens said, "but we are the last three. It's Conner, then Graysen, then me."

"Fabulous," she said as she hugged each of them. "I'll see you in a couple of hours."

#

The showcase was nothing short of amazing. The magic on display ranged from adequate to astounding. It was obvious that the students had put a lot of work and effort into their individual performances. She watched as they made plants grow, brought stories to life, and sculpted with water. It was all quite remarkable.

Then the lights went down, and music began blasting from the speakers. And she smiled. A stage light shined on an empty spot on the stage. One beat. Two. Conner appeared standing on one hand. And the audience went wild. He danced through the song, lights appearing around the stage and Conner appearing in various poses. It was mesmerizing. His final pose was front and center on stage in a magical salute to his classmates, who all jumped and screamed. It was quite an experience. She was taken aback when he ran off the stage

35

and grabbed her in a fierce hug. Then he thrust his fist high into the air and the crowd erupted again. She just laughed and wrapped her arms around her son's chest.

The stage curtain closed as the music faded away. The audience sat down and waited for the next performance. As the curtain opened Graysen walked out onto the stage and took his place at the conductors stand. He bowed to the audience and then turned to face the instruments. When he began to conduct, nothing happened. The instruments sat idle. She saw him stiffen. He placed his hands on the music podium and took a deep breath.

"Mom, what's going on?" Conner leaned over and whispered.

"I don't know. I've never seen that happen before," she responded.

When Graysen lifted his hands the second time and began to conduct, music flowed from the instruments. He moved through the composition with ease after that initial false start. Before it was over, he had every instrument in the symphony playing at the same time. As he brought the percussions to a crescendo, the trumpets bugled in time, as the strings sang their siren song. And then, Graysen dropped his arms, his jacket fell from his back as the instruments kept playing. On his back were the words 'I love you'. He turned to face the audience, a giant smile on his face. As he did, he spread his arms wide and held a sign that said, "Mom!" The music came down in a cacophony of sound as everything faded except the strings which played the last few measures of her favorite song before also waning. Again, the crowd went wild with students and parents alike rising to their feet and cheering. Graysen joined her and Conner, giving her a big hug as he took his seat. She looked him in the eye and patted her chest.

She took a deep breath as she watched the curtain begin to open. Hodgens was the last student to perform. The last of her boys to perform. It was the last act that any of them would have to take at prep. She swallowed the lump in her throat and watched as the lights came up on stage. Hodgens stood in the middle of the stage surrounded by a variety of objects. The audience remained transfixed as, without physically touching a thing, he built a physics defying structure from the objects on stage. A bicycle hung off of the tip of a broomstick by its tire while a teapot sat on the bristles at the other end. The middle of the broom was balanced on the top of a coat rack. When the structure would lean or shake the audience would gasp and some covered their mouths in anticipation of it coming crashing down. She smiled to herself because she knew that he made the structure do those things for the effect.

As the last object rose off the floor Tenja felt the magic drop out of the room and then surge up like a monster. Suddenly all of the objects on stage shot out from each other and were suspended in air as if caught in a snow globe...and Hodgens was in the middle of it all. A split second later the roof above Hodgens' head lifted off the auditorium and dust and building materials flew everywhere. Before she knew what happened, Conner was no longer standing beside her. One second, he was on stage beside Hodgens. The next second they were both gone.

"Momma!" Graysen yelled, bringing her back to the moment. She looked around. Everyone was on their feet screaming. Most were scrambling toward the back exits. She grabbed Graysen's hand and dragged him with her toward the front exit. Riskier. Closer to the stage. But a faster way out of the building.

As they hit the exit doors and exploded from the building, they heard what she assumed was the ceiling and all of Hodgens' objects come crashing down. Once outside she grabbed Graysen by the shoulders, "Together. We stay together. We find your brothers. We get home."

He just nodded and held her hand tightly as they ran yelling for Conner and Hodgens. When they heard voices yelling 'mom' they both turned. Conner and Hodgens were standing by a tree they used as a meeting place when the boys were younger. They started to run toward the tree just in time to see Conner drop to his knees, grab his wrist, and scream in agonizing pain.

"No! No, no no!" she said as she dropped to her knees in front of him. "Too soon! Too soon!" she said as she grabbed Conner's arm. She could see that his magic symbol was disappearing into his flesh.

"Okay. Okay," she said as she touched his shoulder. "We've gotta get you home, baby. We've got to go."

"Help me get him up," she said to Graysen and Hodgens.

They did as they were told. Without question. They each put one of Conner's arms around their neck and began to walk as fast as they could toward the house. A block from the school Beagle Girl came running up to them. She howled and then Conner was floating about a foot off the ground between his brothers. Hodgens and Graysen looked at Tenja who said, "Run!"

As they got to the sidewalk in front of the house Tenja grabbed Hodgens, who was in front, and said, "Wait a second." She reached forward, her hand flat in front of her, palm out.

"Alright, go, go! Everyone into the house," she said as she crossed onto their property, turned toward the street and repeated the gesture with her hand.

"I'm okay!" Conner was saying to the dog as she ran into the house. "Put me down!"

She noticed he looked pale and weak. But when Beagle Girl released her magic, he could stand on his own.

"Everyone to the basement," she instructed.

"What? Why —" Graysen started to ask.

"No questions right now. Go," she said sternly as she gently turned Hodgens toward the basement.

Beagle Girl led the way with each boy following in tow. Tenja brought up the rear, closing and spell locking the basement door. The more barriers the better, she thought to herself.

Once in the basement, Beagle Girl used her magic to move an entire shelf of boxes like it was a feather. Behind it was a blank wall. At least,

38

it was blank until Tenja placed her hand on it. When she did, a door appeared. In the middle of the door was a handprint. She laid her hand on top of it, and then said, "now each of you lay your hand on it."

Without asking any questions they stepped up one by one and placed their hand on the print. After all three boys had done it, Tenja placed her hand on the print one more time. They all heard a lock release and watched a door swing open.

"There, now the magical locks are keyed to your signatures as well. Anyone of you could lock or unlock the door," she explained to them.

As the boys stepped through the door their eyes widened.

"This is like an entire apartment!" Graysen exclaimed.

"How could we not know this was here!?" Hodgens asked.

"We, Momma Raben and I, had this built before we moved into the house. Then we spelled it so no one else could sense it or have access," she said as she secured the lock which also hid the door and replaced the storage shelf. (That was Raben's handy work, knitting basic spells together. Thank goodness.)

Graysen and Hodgens walked from room to room inspecting the place. Small kitchen, bathroom, bedroom that slept five, living room. It wasn't their beautiful, large house that sat above them, but it was livable.

Tenja turned to look at Conner just in time to see his eyes roll back in his head. She dove for him and yelled, "guys I need help!"

Graysen and Hodgens came running. She was barely holding Conner up when they got to her. "Get him to the couch," she told them as they each grabbed an arm.

As they laid him down his eyes flew open, he grabbed his wrist and began to scream. The boys jumped back and Tenja leaped forward.

She gently put a hand on each side of Conner's face. "Honey, look at me," she said as he screamed into her face. "I know it hurts. I know. Look in my eyes," she encouraged. "Look at me and try to take a deep breath. Come on baby, just try."

Conner fought back another scream and stared into Tenja's eyes. He took one deep breath. Two. Three. And then the tension in his body relaxed.

"Get him some water," she said without taking her eyes off of him.

Hodgens scrambled to the kitchen and returned with a tall glass of water.

"Here bud, drink," she told Conner.

"So tired, momma," he whispered between sips. "So tired."

"I know. You need to rest. It will help. We'll keep you out here and one of us will be with you all the time, okay?"

He nodded as he handed her the glass. Graysen covered him with a blanket as Tenja stood up. She watched Conner as he closed his eyes and then motioned the other boys to the kitchen.

They all sat at the table.

"Momma," Hodgens hesitated, "what is happening?"

"I think," she started and then looked at the frightened faces of two pieces of her heart. She reached out and grabbed their hands. "He's going to be okay. He'll get through this," she tried to reassure them.

"What exactly is he 'getting through'?" Graysen asked and glanced at Hodgens.

"When everything happened at the school and Conner saw you," she nodded at Hodgens, "in immediate danger, I think he triggered his magic evolution."

"He WHAT?!" Hodgens yelped.

"Shhh!" Tenja admonished him.

"You can do that?" Graysen asked with fear in his voice.

"But he isn't supposed to evolve for another year!" Hodgens added.

She pulled her hands back. "I know, guys. Yes, it can happen. It's rare, but it can happen. I know he isn't supposed to evolve until he's 18."

"But I don't understand," Hodgens said shaking his head.

"Conner has only ever been able to disappear and reappear himself. Tonight, he disappeared you with him, Hodgens. Together you both disappeared from that stage and reappeared by the tree. He forced his magic to do something it has never done in his entire life," she explained.

Graysen and Hodgens looked at her, their mouths hanging open.

"The first time Conner fell and started screaming I looked at his wrist. His single person magic symbol was fading. As you know, that's what happens when your magic evolves. The symbol fades from your left wrist and your new symbol appears on your right," she added.

"I thought the evolution was supposed to be painless!" Graysen fretted.

"When it happens on your 18th birthday it is painless. Typically, you wake up that day and your new symbol is there. Then you begin your next level of learning."

"But when you force it..." Hodgens trailed off.

Tenja nodded, "when you force it, the body fights the evolution. The magic always wins, but the body puts up a fight."

"People who force the evolution survive, thought, right?" Graysen asked.

She looked at their faces. They were growing up. "Most do," she admitted, "but there have been unfortunate situations where the person's body couldn't withstand the evolution."

The boys looked at each other and she continued, "but Conner is strong," she said without doubt. "He's physically strong. He's emotionally strong. And you saw his performance tonight. His magic is strong. We have every reason to believe he will get through this."

She got up and started to make tea, "I'm not going to lie to you guys. It's going to be a rough 24 hours. There will be more pain. Probably a fever. He'll hopefully sleep through a lot of it. We have to take shifts with him. He'll need to stay hydrated so lots of water. Broth if he can keep it down."

They nodded in unison.

41

"Well do anything, mom," Hodgens said.

"Yeah, just tell us what to do," Graysen agreed.

"I'm sure you have more questions...about a lot of things."

Again, they shared another look before turning their eyes back to her.

"I promise, after we get your brother through this, we'll talk about everything, and I'll tell you what I can."

#

She wasn't kidding about it being a rough 24 hours. The three of them took shifts sleeping. Conner's fever spiked at about 2am. She was glad it was her shift when it happened. Just like when he was little, she bathed her son in ice cold water. Coaxed him to drink cold water and Gatorade. And held him. The fever broke around 4:30am and he fell into a more restful sleep. When Graysen took over at 6am she caught a few hours of sleep.

"Momma," a shake on her leg. "Momma, wake up."

"Ugh. What time is it?" she groaned.

"It's noon. You need to eat something," Hodgens' voice.

She opened her eyes, looked around, and shot up out of bed.

"Woah, woah," Hodgens said, his hands up in front of him as if surrendering.

"What the...why are..." she stuttered out and then the events of the night before came rushing back.

"Conner!?" she exclaimed.

"He's okay. Momma, he's okay!" Hodgens reassured her. "He woke up in pain a little bit ago. His single person symbol is completely gone now. The new one is starting to appear, but we can't really make out what it is yet. His fever is completely gone. He drank some broth and went back to sleep."

She breathed a sigh of relief. "Okay," she sighed, "okay."

"I'm going to catch some sleep. You need to eat. You haven't eaten anything since the diner last night," he said as he sat down on a bed.

She ruffled his hair, which made him laugh, and said, "thanks bud. I love you."

"I love you, too, momma. You didn't get to see me display that in my presentation last night."

That stopped her. She leaned down and hugged him. He returned the hug and yawned at the same time.

"Okay, bud. Get some sleep," she said as she stood up.

She found Graysen in the living room reading a book. Conner was asleep on the couch. He was on his stomach and one arm was hanging off the couch. Looking at him know she wouldn't know that anything was out of the ordinary. She waved at Graysen who sat his book down and joined her in the kitchen.

"How are you doing?" she asked him.

"I'm okay," he shrugged. "Conner seems to be doing better."

"Thank goodness," she said as she opened the fridge. Gathering the items to make a sandwich, she grabbed a bottle of water and sat down at the table.

"Why is all of this happening?" Graysen asked pointedly.

"Once we are all coherent I will share my thoughts. Honestly, I don't know about last night. When Hodgens was performing it felt like,"

"The magic dropped out of the room," Graysen finished her sentence.

She nodded. "I've never felt anything like it."

"Would you mind if I take a nap? I'm really tired," he said between yawns.

"Go ahead, bud," she said gently. "It's been a rough night."

As he pushed his chair in she said, "I love you, Graysen."

He looked at her. "I love you, too, momma."

#

She finished her sandwich and checked on Conner. He had rolled over and was now curled up in the fetal position. He was shivering slightly so she touched his forehead. A little warm but nothing concerning. She covered him with the blanket. Then, she turned to the bookcase.

On the floor in front of the bookcase was the chest from under her bed. She released the spelled lock and took out the book with Raben's symbol. Respelling the lock, she took the book and sat down in a chair next to the couch.

She smiled when she opened the book and looked at the first page. When they were dating, Raben made up a secret alphabet so she could send love letters to Tenja that no one else could read. She recognized that alphabet on the first page. She flipped through the book. It wasn't long, maybe 30 pages. A lot of the pages were covered in drawings. Some of them looked like maps.

What in the world is all of this? She thought to herself. She went back to the first page and started reading.

The shimmer and the glimmer
Are fading from the sky
The tapestry is fraying
As the days go by
The creatures born of fire
Guard the relic in the dark
The one who can seek their help
Bears the origin mark
They say that tears can lead the way
To save the one who's lost
But the search to save just one
Comes at much too high a cost

She stared at the page. "What in all that is magic..." she mumbled semi-audibly.

"Momma?" a weak voice said.

She looked up to see Conner looking at her. Dropping the book on the coffee table she sat on the edge of it so she could be close to him. "Hey bud! How are you feeling?"

"Better I guess," he said as he sat up. "I have to use the restroom."

She stood up and gave him a hand. Once he was on his feet she said, "Can you make it on your own?"

"Yeah. I'm okay," he said as he shuffled toward the bathroom.

She headed to the kitchen to make him some broth. She was just about to open a can when he said, "Can I have something else. That stuff really isn't very good."

She laughed and put the can back in the cupboard. "Sure. What do you want?"

As she sat the toast and tea down in front of him, he held out his wrists. His single person magic symbol was completely gone from his left wrist. On his right was a dot with faint lines appearing around it. But it was still impossible to know what was emerging there.

"Momma what is happening to me?" he asked her.

"I think you triggered your magic evolution when you saved Hodgens," she said in her straight shooter voice.

He considered this and said, "how? I don't understand."

"You used your magic to do something you've never done before. I think your need to protect Hodgens was so strong, so fierce, that you bent your magic to your will to save him."

"I didn't know that was possible. I just knew I couldn't leave him up there on that stage alone."

"It was instinct, Conner. Love is the most powerful magic."

He flinched and grabbed his wrist. She moved toward him.

"It's okay. I'm okay. It just a burning now. Ebbs and flows. It's not the intense pain that I had most of the night."

"Then you've almost reached the end," she said looking at the clock. "You've got about five more hours. And it will continue to lessen as that time goes by."

"So..." he began but hesitated.

She just looked at him.

"Does bending my magic to my will mean that I changed the trajectory of the evolution? Will I have a different magic than I would have if I hadn't triggered the evolution?" he finished his questions.

"It's possible," she acknowledged, "but there's no way to know. All we will know is what you have once the evolution is complete."

"Huh," he said as he dug into his toast and tea.

She considered what all of this meant for him. Was it possible to protect him by hiding his magical reality from others? Was there an old spell that she could acquire to protect him that way? She shook her head and thought to herself, no, I won't do that to him. I've lived a life hiding who I am and never being able to speak my truth. I'll find another path for him.

#

Hodgens emerged from the bathroom showered and refreshed just as she set the frozen pizzas on the table. It was 8pm and her boys were all at the table. Conner had taken one more nap as his magic evolution completed the final stages. Now, they were all clean and mostly bright eyed. As she began cutting the pizzas Graysen said, "So, Conner, what is your new symbol?" They all looked at Conner's wrist.

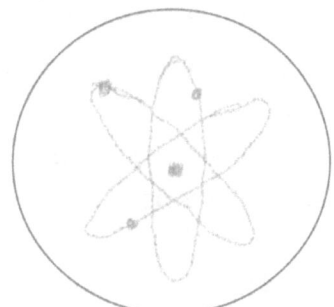

"What is that?" Hodgens asked looking at Tenja.

"I'm not sure. I've never seen a symbol like that before," she said with a furrowed brow.

46

"It looks like," Graysen started to say as he got up and walked around Conner, "like an atom"

Conner looked up at them. "What does that even mean?"

"I'll do some research tomorrow," Tenja said. "We have books on magic and symbols through the ages."

"Okay," Conner shrugged.

As Graysen sat back down Hodgens looked around and said, "has anyone seen Beagle Girl?"

Tenja looked at the clock and said, "she should be coming in any time now. I asked her to stay upstairs for the 24 hours of Conner's evolution. Then she was coming back in to let us know if it was safe to come out of here."

"You left her upstairs!?" Hodgens exclaimed. "She's just a little dog!"

Tenja gaped at him, "a little dog with a more extensive magic repertoire than any one of us has. If she was not comfortable being out there, believe you me she would have plopped her butt somewhere comfortable down here."

Graysen and Conner laughed at her last statement.

"She's right, man," Conner said. He reached over and patted his brother on the back, "she'll be alright. She hauled my sorry butt home, didn't she?"

"True," Hodgens said considering, "you were in a pretty sorry state," he added with a smile.

And in perfect timing, as if saying the name summoned the dog, the door swung open, and Beagle Girl strolled into the apartment. She didn't close the door behind her so Tenja assumed it was safe. But she waited for the dog's confirmation.

"All safe up there?" Tenja asked.

Beagle Girl let out one 'aroof' and jumped up on the couch.

They all looked at her and just laughed. Then they finished their dinner, gathered their belongings and headed upstairs.

Tenja retrieved Raben's book from the coffee table and took it upstairs with her. She needed to examine it more. As she stood, contemplating her trunk, Conner stopped beside her.

"Want me to carry that upstairs for you, mom?" he asked.

She shook her head, "I can get it, but thanks. I'm just not sure if I should leave it here."

He considered the locked trunk, "is there anything in it you might need access to quickly? Like if something weird happens again. If so, you wouldn't want to have to go through all the spells to get to it in here, would you?"

She looked at him. Preparing. He knew they were preparing. She patted his arm, "good call, Conner. Good call."

And with that, she picked up the trunk and headed up with her boys.

CHAPTER 5

She was headed downstairs when Beagle Girl starting barking at the front door. That's when Tenja remembered the boundary spell around the property. When she opened the front door, she saw Madifen sitting at the end of the sidewalk, and he did not look happy. She walked down the sidewalk, extended her hand, and released the spell.

"What in the hell, Tenja!?" he said as he rolled past her. "Why have you had this place spelled for over a day? Where are the boys?"

"Madifen, stop," she said in a direct tone she rarely took with him.

He ignored her and continued up the ramp.

"Beagle Girl!" she yelled.

The dog appeared in the doorway. Seeing the two of them she howled and Tenja felt the boundary shield go up at the front door.

Madifen spun on her, "what in all that is magic are you even doing right now?"

"I'd like to know the same of you," she retorted. "That was MY boy on the stage last night, Madifen. MY boy! What were you playing at?" she let the words fly from her lungs in anger and fear that she hadn't let herself feel before now.

"What do you mean what am I playing at?" he raised his voice. "Do you think I had something to do with this?"

"Did you do anything to try to prevent it? That sure as hell wasn't Hodgens' magic that caused the chaos!"

"What should I have done? How was I supposed to know that would happen?" he asked.

"You should have kept my son safe, Madifen! He was your responsibility. Instead, his brother saved him. Where were you?"

"I was stage left. Where I was for every performance, Tenja," he spat out in exasperation. "And when the power surged, I was knocked out of my wheelchair."

She just stood still. Arms crossed. Staring at him. She wanted to believe he had nothing to do with this. That Raben's mistrust didn't run to betrayal. That her mistrust shouldn't run to exile. But she just couldn't be sure. Beagle Girl had revealed to Madifen her connection to Raben. Was that a sign that he could be trusted? Or was it a warning? She didn't know anymore.

"Tenja, you've got to believe me. I've been trying to find all of you since it happened. When I couldn't get past your barriers and you didn't answer the phone, I didn't know what to do. I almost called Farlege to come break through your barriers."

She raised one eyebrow at him.

"I know. I know. I was worried out of my mind, but it didn't make me stupid," he let out a laugh, "I know what lines not to cross with you, Tenja."

"I hope it stays that way, Madi," she said directly.

She saw him flinch when she said it. But she couldn't care. She had to keep her focus on the boys and their safety.

Changing the subject, he said, "Tenja, they caught the guy who caused the destruction at the school Friday night. They have him in custody."

She frowned, "they what? A single guy?"

"Yes, a disgruntled student who was kicked out of prep a few years ago. Apparently, he's been planning an attack at the school for quite some time. He decided that showcase night would be best so he could show non-magic folks that we are a threat that should be exterminated."

"He said all of that, did he?" skepticism rolling through her voice.

"Talk to him yourself," he shrugged. "They're holding him in a magic cell down at the station."

They stared at each other. Beagle Girl held the boundary spell at the door. In her peripheral vision she could see the boys looking out the front window. What she said next would guide the boys in how to proceed with Madi.

50

"Well, you know how protective I am of my boys. I just wanted to be sure they were safe for a bit, until we figured out what was going on. The boundary spell kept out sound. So, we didn't know you'd came by."

"You didn't think I would?"

"Honestly, Madi, the evening was so terrifying that I just wanted to keep my boys close for a little while. Soon they'll be going out into the world, and I won't be around to shield them."

He looked at her for a minute and then finally said, "yeah, I get that. Can I see the boys? Are they okay?"

"Sure, why don't you come in for a little bit before we go to bed," she said as she nodded at Beagle Girl.

She followed Madifen into the house. At some point Conner had changed into a long-sleeved shirt, effectively covering his wrists. She was pleased to see the boys acted natural, like nothing had changed their view of Madi. It was quite impressive actually. They all had some tea and talked about what happened. He told the boys about the man they had arrested and reassured them that this as an isolated incident. They expressed relief and Tenja wondered if it was real or acting.

She walked Madi to the front door. After closing it behind him she turned to see three faces staring at her from the kitchen doorway. She held a finger to her lips indicating they should be quiet for the time being. While they waited for her to indicate they could talk, she engaged an undetectable oral shield around the house that would prevent anyone outside from hearing what they said.

"Okay," she said once she had finished. "We are literally in a cone of silence now. We can hear the outside, but the outside can't hear us."

"When do we learn to do those types of spells?" Graysen asked.

"After evolution," she said as she walked past them into the kitchen.

"So, I can learn now," Conner stated.

She looked at him thoughtfully. It would be helpful to have another protector in the house. "Yes, yes you can," she responded. "But you need to rest a few days before you start using your magic. Give yourself a chance to recuperate."

"Okay," he shrugged.

"Mom," Hodgens began as she rinsed her teacup, "I don't understand why you didn't tell Madifen about Conner. I thought we trusted him."

"You don't think he had anything to do with what happened at the school do you?" Graysen asked.

"Let's sit down in the living room," she suggested. "We have some things to talk about."

After they all, including Beagle Girl, had gotten situated she began, "first, I know it doesn't feel right to exclude Madifen, to not trust him. But right now, I don't know what else to do."

"But you're acting that way based on something Momma Raben said ten years ago!" Hodgens chimed in. "People change. He's been there for us, all of us, a lot over the last ten years."

"I don't know that he's been there for us as much as he's kept an eye on us," she amended his sentiment.

"What does that even mean?" Conner asked.

"I can't explain it, Conner," she shook her head, "but my heart and my gut tell me to hold fast to my promise to Raben when it comes to Madi. She knew him before I did. They grew up together. In the end, I will always trust her over an outsider of this family."

"Fine," Graysen nodded at his brothers, "we'll respect your wishes on this...for now." His brothers nodded in agreement. "What else did you want to talk to us about?"

"Wait," Conner interrupted, "what about my evolution. I can't wear long-sleeves all week. The weather is too nice. People will see that my magic has evolved. Madifen will see that it has evolved. Won't he know you lied to him about the last 24 hours?"

52

Tenja considered Conner's words. "People will know eventually anyway. Madifen will know. If he calls me on lying to him, I'll just tell him that it wasn't my story to tell. It is yours. You can tell your friends and teachers as much or as little as you want about the evolution, Conner."

He looked at her, just looked at her, "okay," he finally said. "I'll think about it."

"Now," Hodgens changed the course of the discussion, "what else did you want to tell us?"

"The book is from Raben," she stated.

"You're sure?" Hodgens moved to the edge of his seat. "You're really sure?"

"I am 100% positive," she assured him.

"What does it say?" Conner and Graysen asked at the same time.

"I had just started reading it when Conner woke up this afternoon. So, I don't know much yet."

"I want to read it," Hodgens demanded. "Does she say why she chose to chase magic?"

It took all of Tenja's patience not to roll her eyes. "First, I will show you once I finish going through it. You won't be able to read it because she wrote it in a secret alphabet that she and I have used for years. I will have to translate it for you. Second, she isn't chasing magic."

She crossed her legs and considered how much to tell them. Magic to the wind she thought and said, "Between Draiocht and Easpach is a place called Sa Lár. It is in Sa Lár that the worlds of Draiocht and Easpach meet. That is where Draiocht funnels a small amount of magic to Easpach. That magic feeds those of us here who have magic. It sustains our magic."

The boys looked at each other. Then back at her. They said nothing.

She continued, "ten years ago your Momma Raben received a message from her brother. Something was wrong in Sa Lár. They could feel it in Draiocht."

53

"But I thought Momma Raben didn't communicate with her family in Draiocht," Graysen furrowed his brow.

"She hadn't heard from any of them in years. So, the message was a shock and at first, she paid it no mind," Tenja agreed.

"Then one day none of our magic was working right. My brushes wouldn't hold paint. Raben's needles wouldn't hold yarn…"

"Wait!" Hodgens interjected, "I remember that day! Don't you guys remember?" he asked his brothers. Conner and Graysen just looked at him. "I couldn't pick up a block. Conner you couldn't disappear. Graysen, the bows of the violins wouldn't raise off the stand," he added.

"Oh yeah!" Conner's eyes lit up, "I do remember that day!"

"Yeah, me too, now that you said that" Graysen nodded.

Tenja also nodded, "yep, that was the day. You three came running to us telling us that nothing was working. The next day, though, everything was back to normal. That was when Raben got a message from Sa Lár. Whatever was holding the magic between the worlds together was breaking. Someone had to hold the magic together until a magic fixer arrived."

"Someone had to knit the magic together," Hodgens said softly.

"Yes. Someone had to knit the magic together," Tenja said gently.

"But why did it have to be her?" Hodgens spat out. She saw the anger and the hurt still boiling inside of him.

"She wanted to ensure that you, that we, were protected. She didn't trust anyone else to take care of all of us."

"What do you mean?" Conner asked. "How is leaving us taking care of us?"

And here is the sticking point, she thought, "If the magic breaks, if the connection between Draiocht and Easpach is destroyed," she took a deep breath, let it out, "then everyone in Easpach with magic will die. The instant the link is broken we will all die."

The boys sat back in their seats, their mouths hanging open.

They battered her with questions for at least 30 minutes and she had nothing left to give. She stood up, "it's almost midnight, guys. We're all exhausted. Let's get some sleep and we'll see what tomorrow holds."

Begrudgingly the boys stood up and followed her out of the room. Beagle Girl took the directive and let herself out to take care of business before bed.

"Goodnight my favorite little people," she said as they headed up the stairs and she switched off the kitchen light. She got three mumbled goodnights in response and couldn't help but smile. Beagle Girl walked up the stairs with her but veered off toward the boys' bedroom. Such power in such a little dog, she thought.

She finished up her nighttime routine and sat down on the edge of the bed. Raben's book sat on her end table waiting for her. She crawled under the covers and picked up the book. Yes, she was exhausted, but the book kept calling to her. All evening she felt as if it was drawing her to it. She read the poem on the first page again and then began to turn the pages. Each page had one drawing on it. Some pages had a tree, some a rock, some a stream. None of them had a sign of knitting, which is what she had expected. There were also no more words in the book. Page after page was blank except for the one drawn object. She turned each page individually and gaped at the mostly blank white space that stared back at her.

"What in all that is magic am I supposed to do with this, Raben?" she said out loud to the empty room.

CHAPTER 6

Tenja stretched and looked at the clock. 9:30. She had slept for nine hours. A smile crossed her lips as she let her ears take in the sounds of her boys talking downstairs. They had let her sleep in and boy did she appreciate it. It was unusual for them to be up before her, though.

She padded downstairs for a cup of coffee and some food. The boys were at the table, breakfast spread out before them. Hodgens handed her a cup of coffee and pulled out a chair.

"Thanks," she said, "I didn't expect you three to be up already."

"Hungry," Conner said between bites. She laughed.

"I hear that!" she agreed as she grabbed a banana.

"What are you guys doing today?" she asked them.

"Mark came by to see if we wanted to play some baseball," Graysen told her.

Conner elbowed Hodgens who let out a giggle.

"What?" Graysen asked.

"Of all the people to come by," Conner said, "it was Mark."

Graysen rolled his eyes, "come on, man."

Tenja looked from one boy to another, "what am I missing here?" She asked.

Then she saw Graysen blush and his brother smile.

She put up her hand, "okay, I get it. Stop teasing your brother about liking someone." She told Hodgens and Conner.

"All right," Hodgens told her. "We're all going down to the ball fields after breakfast. Everyone is meeting there around 10," Hodgens explained.

"Grabbing lunch with everyone?" she asked.

"Yeah, probably," Conner added, "if that's okay?"

"Fine with me," she said, "do you need money?"

"Nah, we're good," Hodgens said as he began to wash dishes.

She sipped her coffee and watched as they finished eating and cleaned up their breakfast. They had always been so helpful. Took care of their own messes when they could. She always wondered if they would have done so much around the house if Raben hadn't left. Life would have been different. Dynamics would have been different. They all would have been different people.

"Momma!" Conner said loudly.

She shook her head, "sorry, I was lost in thought."

"No joke," he snorted, "we're heading out."

"Okay, have fun. Be home for dinner." As they gathered up their baseball gear she put her arm around Graysen, "ignore them, their turn will come."

He smiled shyly and headed out after his brothers.

She watched as they made their way out the door. They were gifting her with an entire day to indulge in whatever suited her fancy. And she knew just what that was. First a bubble bath. Then some research.

#

Tenja moved the storage shelf and released the spelled lock to the apartment. Raben's magic history books were stored there for safe keeping. She perused the bookcase, selecting three she thought might be helpful. She wanted to look into Conner's new symbol as well as the teardrop jewels. Surely there was something about them in one of the books.

Back in the kitchen she set the books on the table and retrieved the box of jewels. She grabbed a bottle of water and spread the jewels out on the table. Opening the first book, she flipped to the index and looked for the term 'jewel' and then skimmed the list of subtopics under the word. Well, that was easier than I expected, she thought to herself when she saw the word 'teardrop' as a subtopic under 'jewel'. She turned to the page number listed and began to read.

57

Teardrop jewels resemble the shape of a raindrop or a tear that has fallen from a creature's eye. There are two main types of teardrop gems: deductive and inductive. The difference is the magic instilled within them during creation.

Deductive teardrop jewels are spelled to remove something from the one who triggers the magic within them. Throughout history there are documented instances of deductive teardrop jewels removing sadness, joy, knowledge, and even memories from a person.

Inductive teardrop jewels are spelled to give something to the one who triggers the magic within them. In the case of these types of jewels, there are documented instances of people receiving information, joy, sadness, and even nightmares.

If one is gifted a teardrop jewel from someone they know and trust, for a purpose of which they are aware and accept, then these jewels can be a fabulous gift. However, if they are found or given by someone who isn't trusted, the receiver should proceed with caution. If their purpose is unknown, using them could result in heartbreak or great danger.

She sat back in her chair. Well damn, Raben. You didn't make this easy, she thought to herself. Of course, Graysen retrieved these from someone they trusted with their lives. So, that in itself was not a concern. But was she giving them something to deal with? Taking away something she thought they didn't need? Who could trigger the magic in them? And how did Raben know ten years ago that they would need them? She had so many questions without answers.

She jumped when the phone rang. They didn't use the phone often, so it usually startled her when it did ring. The boys' friends all lived so close they were usually just in and out like the house had a revolving

58

door. She loved that about her boys. They didn't hesitate to hang out here with their friends and through the years she had grown to find comfort in the chaos.

The phone rang a third time and she scrambled to grab it.

"Hello?"

"Hey mom!" Conner's voice.

"Hey bud, what's up?"

"We are going to grab some burgers to bring back to the house. Is it okay if some of the guys come with us?"

"Of course," she replied, "thanks for the heads up, though. I need to put some things away."

"Yeah, we figured we should let you know," he paused, "want us to bring you dinner?"

"Sure! Burger, fries, and root beer," she said, "you know how I like it."

"Got it. We'll be home soon!"

She heard the click that told her he was off on the next leg of his adventure for the day. She hung up the phone, scooped up the jewels and books, and took them up to her room. There would be more time to research later.

The evening was spent in laughter and friendship. As she sat on the deck watching the boys play catch and talk with their friends, she wondered how life would change for them all after this week. She had always loved how the town didn't segregate the magic and non-magic students in school. Non-magic students could take the history of magic classes. Magic students could take wood shop. It was such a great balance and allowed the kids to grow up appreciating each other's strengths – magical or not.

The friends started to head out as the sky darkened and the lightning bugs began to blink. Conner joined her on the deck.

"Did you find anything out about my magic today?" he asked.

"No, I didn't get that far in my research. How are you feeling?"

"I'm good actually. I feel stronger than I did before the evolution."

59

She nodded, "that is to be expected. Your evolved magic has a deeper well. Later this week I'll start teaching you some of these shielding and defense spells. We'll start with basic ones."

"Awesome!" he replied with excitement in his eyes. "I'm going to go grab a shower."

She watched as the rest of their friends left. Hodgens and Graysen finished cleaning up the dinner trash.

"Good day?" she asked as the joined her at the table.

"Yeah," Graysen answered, "we had a good time."

"It felt - normal," Hodgens added, "like Friday night didn't happen."

Graysen nodded, "no one even talked about it."

"Well, they did a little when they noticed Conner's new symbol," Hodgens corrected.

"What did he tell them about it?" Tenja asked, curious how much of his story her son chose to share.

"Just that it happened when he saved me," Hodgens told her, "when they asked how he just shrugged and said he didn't know. That it just happened."

She nodded, "that's probably for the better. Forcing the evolution isn't common knowledge. We don't need a bunch of kids running around trying to do it on purpose."

"Ain't that the truth!?" Graysen exclaimed, "some kids I know would do it on a dare."

"And some could die in the process," she added.

The thought of kids dying from trying to force their evolution brought them all to silence.

CHAPTER 7

She sat at her desk in the art gallery looking over the layout for the next exhibit when Madifen came in. She watched as he shut the door and stopped just short of her desk.

"Why didn't you tell me about Conner's evolution?!" he strained to keep his voice down, his temper in check.

She leaned back and crossed her arms, "because it wasn't my story to tell," she answered in an unwavering voice.

They stared at each other for a good two minutes before Madifen broke eye contact. "What is wrong with you lately?" he asked. "You keep me out with barrier shields, you give me half-truths, don't tell me when something significant happens with one of the boys. It's as if you don't trust me!" he sounded angry rather than hurt.

She looked at the clock when her stomach growled. It was lunch time and she found herself caring more about what she was going to eat than about Madifen's feelings.

Feigning interest she asked, "what half-truth did I tell you?"

"The whole 'I shielded the house just to keep my boys safe for a little while' crap. You kept everyone out because Conner was going through his evolution!"

She shrugged, "true, he was going through his evolution. But the whole truth was that I needed to keep them all safe while it happened."

She got up and walked around her desk, sat in the chair opposite him.

"Madi, if there is one thing about me that you, of all people, should know to be true it is this: I will do what is best for my boys every time, without second thought, without regret, no matter who gets left out. Something is going on. Something has changed. And you can damn well bet that I am going to spend my energy making sure that my boys get to experience adulthood."

He looked at her and she felt like he was seeing her for the first time, really seeing her. She had made sure he knew the line. Now, she'd see where he decided to stand.

"Now, it's lunch time and I'm hungry. Are you joining me for lunch or are you going back to your office to pout?" she asked unapologetically.

They ate lunch at the café across from the art gallery. Madifen didn't talk about Conner's evolution anymore. Wise choice on his part, Tenja thought to herself as the conversation moved into easy territories of the current showing at the art gallery and his plans for the summer. She still didn't trust him but thought it best not to exile him completely. Keep your friends close and your enemies closer, she told herself.

When lunch was over and Madi had left, she stood looking at the art gallery. Then, she turned on her heels and headed to the police station. In this instance, she was going to take a piece of advice from Madi. She was going to see this guy who almost killed her son.

#

The door chimed as she entered the police station. Beth looked up from the receptionist's desk.

"Oh hey, Tenja!" she greeted, "how are you? How's Hodgens?"

"Hi Beth. I'm good. He's good. Things seem to be back to normal," she responded, "Is Farlege around?"

"Sure, he's in his office. Go on back," she gestured.

"Thanks," Tenja waved and headed down the hall. Living a smallish town had it's perks. She and Farlege had grown up together, been friends for as long as she could remember. She had stopped by the police station many times through the years and, if Farlege wasn't busy, Beth let her find her way to his office.

She knocked on the door and stuck her head in at the same time, "Hey friend," she said nonchalantly, "how are things going?"

62

He stood to greet her, "Hey Tenja! Come on in! Sit down, sit down! Can I get you some water or something?"

"No, I'm good. Just had lunch," she said, "and rather than sit, I'd like to see the guy you arrested for causing the destruction and chaos Friday night."

Farlege looked at her and swallowed hard, "I don't know if that's a good idea, Tenja."

"Why not? I just want to talk to him. Ask him a few questions."

"I know," he agreed, "but he's not exactly the chatty type. We haven't gotten him to say much after his initial dump of a confession."

"Really?" she asked suspicious of that fact, "why do you think that is?"

Farlege shrugged, "I don't know. He claimed responsibility and then clammed up."

"Then what does it hurt to let me try? You can stay with me the whole time," she pleaded, "come on Farlege, he could have killed Hodgens."

He rubbed the back of his neck and thought about it for a minute.

"Tenja, this request is pretty unconventional. We don't usually just let anyone talk to someone we arrest."

She looked him in the eye and said in a frighteningly quite voice, "he could have killed my son, Farlege."

They stayed in tense silence for at least five minutes.

Finally he got up, "okay, come with me. But, I have to document that you were here."

"Fine," she said, standing. "You can record the conversation if you want. I just want some time with him."

She followed Farlege down a long hallway and into the locked area that contained the jail cells. He nodded at a uniformed officer she didn't recognize. Then, they turned and faced a door that she sensed was spelled. He placed his hand on the door and she heard the lock release. They entered another hallway and here she saw three individuals she recognized. Bartray, Lancaster, and Jespen all

63

possessed magic that could maintain the spelled cells that held individuals with magic who had broken the law. The three tipped their hats to her in unison. She nodded at each man, thankful for his presence.

Farlege stopped in front of a cell. Tenja looked at the man inside the cell. He was small in stature, maybe four feet tall. His hair was the lightest blond she had ever seen and his eyes a shade of orange that was common in dwarves. He's a dwargic, she realized. She grabbed a chair she saw in the hallway and sat down outside the cell. The man looked at her but didn't move.

"I want to know the long game," she finally said, looking him directly in the eyes.

He let out a laugh and looked at Farlege, "where'd you get this one? She's no enforcer."

His attitude brought a growl from her. It was a sound she'd never heard herself make before – ever. Then she laughed, long and low, "you have no idea what I am, little one. So I suggest you tell me what I want to know."

The dwargic slowly moved his gaze from Farlege to her, and whatever he saw in her eyes made him shudder.

"Start. Talking. Now," she demanded.

And talk he did. Whatever he had seen in Tenja's eyes scared words out of him. No, he was not a former student of prep. No, he was not acting alone. There was a group made up of magic and non-magic people who wanted the connection between the worlds to be severed. They wanted magic in Draiocht and no magic in Easpach.

"What is their plan?" Tenja asked.

"I don't know," he admitted, "I was just a pawn. I was only given the orders for this one act. The guy said I was one cog in a big wheel."

"Tell us about this guy," Farlege interjected, "what did he look like? Where did you meet him?"

The dwargic threw up his hands, "I don't know. He was wearing a mask. I couldn't see his face."

"How convenient," Tenja rolled her eyes, "where did you meet him?"

"I didn't exactly meet him," the man said, "some guys put a bag over my head in the park. Next thing I knew I was deep in the woods. After he gave me the instructions, they bagged my head and took me right back to the park bench."

"But why did you do it? A strange man has you kidnapped and tells you to destroy the auditorium when it is full of people and you just say, 'sure why not!'?" Tenja stared at him, watched as he fidgeted, and just waited.

Finally, he said, "Kill or be killed. If I didn't do what he said he would kill my sister."

"Kill or be killed?" Farlege stated, "so you were trying to kill someone."

The dwargic nodded.

"But you didn't succeed," Tenja said slowly, "so what does that mean for your sister?"

"She's dead," he responded, "and now I have nothing to lose."

Farlege and Tenja looked at each other and then at the dwargic.

"Do you remember anything about the woods?" Farlege asked, "anything that would help us find that place to see if there are any clues? Anything that can help us get justice for your sister?"

The guy shook his head, "nah, it was all just green and brown like any woods anywhere."

"What about the park where they took you from?" Tenja asked, "where was that?"

"You know the trails that lead away from the gazebo in City Hall Park?" he asked.

"Yeah, I know them," Tenja acknowledged.

"I was sitting at the second bench you come to when walking the main trail."

Back in Farlege's office he offered her a bottle of water.

"Got anything stronger?" she asked.

He eyed her, "brandy."

She took the offered bottle of water and added, "I'll take a shot of brandy, too," as she sat down.

After they both threw back a shot they sat in silence for a few minutes. She watched as he got up and shut his office door.

"Tenja, we need to keep this between us," he began, "right now we have no idea how big this is or who all is involved."

"So, you do believe him," she stated.

"I do, yes. What he said and the way he said it sounded more genuine than at any other time I've dealt with the man."

"What are you going to do Farlege?"

He shook his head, "I don't know, Tenja. I'm not even sure where to start."

The phone on his desk rang, startling them both. "Hello?" he said as he answered it.

She looked at the clock. "I gotta go," she mouthed as she stood up.

He held up a finger indicating she should wait one minute. Then he held up a piece of paper on which he had written I'll call you.

She nodded and headed out. The boys would be getting out of school soon and she wanted to be home when they got there. She stopped by the art gallery quickly on the way home, just to make sure everything was going okay. Three works of art had sold. It was a good day for artist and gallery.

As luck would have it, she and the boys arrived home at the same time. They were laughing and talking about the day, the pranks people had pulled, and how even the teachers had gotten in on the fun. They talked and laughed through dinner and then were all off to their various evening activities. With homework over the boys were indulging in pastimes that entertained them.

Tenja got the history books, jewels, and Raben's book and spread them out on the kitchen table. She was searching through history books for Conner's new magic symbol when Graysen came in.

"Whatcha doing?" he asked as he filled a glass with water.

She sighed and leaned back, "trying to figure out what your brother's new magic symbol represents. But strangely, I'm not having any luck."

"That is odd," Graysen frowned, "how far back do the books go?"

"About 500 years," she explained, "I don't know if we have any that go back farther than that."

"Maybe you don't need to go back farther," he suggested, "maybe you just need a different perspective on magic history. A book written by someone else, maybe?"

She considered his words, "that's a good idea, Graysen. I'll check into that." She closed the book she'd been reading, "what are you up to?"

"I'm going to go play some instruments for a while."

"Have fun," she encouraged as she picked up Raben's book.

A few minutes later Hodgens came downstairs, Beagle Girl by his side. He grabbed a bottle of water and opened the studio door – and Tenja gasped. Hodgens shut the door and spun around. Beagle Girl jumped onto a chair to look at her.

"What's wrong?" he asked.

"Hodgens," she stammered, "open the door again!"

He did as he was told and they watched as jewels lit up, one at a time. Beagle Girl let out an 'aroof'.

There didn't seem to be a rhyme or reason for them lighting up. The humans glanced at each other and then at the jewels. When the music stopped the jewels lay as they were before, paperweights scattered across the table. Then Graysen struck the first note of a new song and the pages of Raben's book flipped open to the first page with a drawing. A blue jewel lit up and floated to the page. When it touched the page, it melded to it, becoming a part of the page. Tenja hesitantly reached out and touched the jewel. She couldn't separate it from the page.

"Momma?" Hodgens questioned.

She looked up at him. Saw the concern in his eyes.

"Raben," she said, "she created some spell that is using Graysen's magic to meld the jewels to the book."

"But why? And why aren't more melding?"

"I don't know, son," she shook her head.

"This is ridiculous!" he spat out.

She was shocked by his sudden anger, "Hodgens?"

"Why did she make this all some big mystery? Why didn't she just tell us what we need to know?"

"She had a reason. Maybe a lot of reasons. Raben was always a logical thinker. She didn't act impulsively. We'll understand one day. I believe that with everything I am."

He scoffed, "yeah, whatever."

She watched as he stalked back upstairs. Beagle Girl looked from her to the stairs and back again. Then she jumped down and headed upstairs after him. Raben's leaving created a chasm between her and Hodgens that Tenja wasn't sure would ever get completely closed. Oh, one day there might be a bridge across it. But the scars that her leaving had left on his little heart just seem to grow with him. While she had no idea what purpose Raben sent Beagle Girl to them for, she knew that his acceptance of the little dog's companionship was a sign of his continued love for his distant momma.

Her conscious came back to the present when Graysen walked into the room. He took one look at the book under her hand and said, "Momma! What did you do to the book?"

"I didn't do anything. You did," she started to explain. The revelation created an eagerness in him that was contagious. So, they moved everything to her worktable in the studio and Graysen experimented with instruments, sounds, notes, and tones until their eyes started to cross.

When Conner walked in and asked, "are you two ever going to bed?" Tenja finally looked at the clock.

"It's midnight?!" she exclaimed.

"Guess we should get some sleep," Graysen said, disappointed.

"What have you guys been doing?" Conner asked.

Graysen and Tenja looked at each other.

"I'll explain on the way upstairs," Graysen said.

"Goodnight, my favor little people," Tenja told them with a smile. "Don't worry, Graysen, we'll figure it out. Raben had faith we could, so we will."

The boys exchanged goodnights with her and headed upstairs. Exhaustion overtook her as she checked the door locks and turned out the last light. What happened to our normal life? she thought to herself.

CHAPTER 8

Beagle Girl's frantic barking had her practically falling out of bed as she rushed to get her feet underneath her. The boys were already in the hall when she threw open her door.

"You three, stay here!" she ordered as she headed down the stairs. They obeyed, staying at the top of the stairs watching as she disappeared around the corner toward the kitchen.

She found Beagle Girl in the studio, aiming her bark out the back window. She squinted to try to see what was causing the fuss. It was so dark out. There was no moon to light up the backyard. She saw a flicker at the farthest edge of the property. She watched for a couple of moments as a small light appeared and disappeared. It was a if...

"Oh, hell no!" she exclaimed emphatically as she threw open the back door, thrust out her hand and grabbed the boundary spell with her magic. Before the person on the other side knew what happened, Tenja shot a pulse of angry magic into the boundary. The boundary around the house lit up like a star. She heard the thumping of three teenage boys' feet coming up from behind her. She watched the person trying to breach her boundary fly high in the air and land with a thud in the alley.

"Call Farlege!" she yelled behind her. She held the no longer shining boundary with her magic and ran full speed toward the person who had tried to breach it. When she reached the edge of the boundary, she found a woman lying in the alley. She was moaning and trying to get up. Tenja reached through her spell and created a tight boundary around the woman, essentially putting her in a box.

"You aren't going anywhere," she told the woman. "There are some people who want to talk to you."

It was only a few moments later when Farlege's car came speeding into the alley. He jumped out and ran to where the woman still lay moaning on the ground. Pulling out his magic laced handcuffs he said, "you can let her out, Tenja. I've got her."

Tenja released the woman from the boundary spell and watched as Farlege rolled her over and secured the cuffs. Seconds later two squad cars pulled up behind Farlege's car.

She heard the boys run up behind her. They watched as Farlege ordered two of the officers to take the woman to the station and put her in a magical holding cell. He then instructed the other two officers to remain as security detail on their house for the remainder of the night. After all of the instructions were given and the officers were about their business, he turned to them.

"Can I come in?" he asked, pointing up at the boundary spell.

Tenja released the spell long enough for him to come in and then replaced it. They all walked to the house in silence, Beagle Girl leading the way. Tenja pointed toward the studio and the boys gave her inquisitive looks. She shook her head before they could speak and simply pointed toward the room. Once they were all inside, she shut the door and let out a frustrated sigh.

"Why are we in here?" Hodgens asked.

"Because this room saved us," Tenja began. "When I came downstairs, she was barking her head off," she explained gesturing toward the dog. "But that woman didn't hear her. She had no idea that we'd been alerted to her presence."

"The soundproofing!" Conner exclaimed. "But isn't there an oral shield around the house?"

"I removed the oral shield. I didn't feel it necessary all the time. But yes, it is because of Beagle Girl that we were able to capture the woman. So, for now, this is where we talk."

Farlege nodded, "that makes sense. How did you capture her?"

"Because the house was dark, she couldn't see me watching from in here. I saw the flickers of light on my spell. They were subtle. I couldn't really feel them. But it is so dark out tonight that they kept flickering. When I realized what was happening, I sent a gift of angry

71

magic into the boundary...surprise!" she pounded her worktable. "They really need to stop trying to get near my boys," she exploded and began to pace.

The boys looked at each other.

"Mom, what are you talking about?" Graysen asked.

She stopped moving and looked at her boys. At Farlege. Back at her boys. Then she dropped into her chair.

"We, Farlege and I, don't think what happened at the showcase was an isolated incident," she began, "we think there is more going on than what we see superficially."

"Why do you think that?" Conner asked.

Tenja drew in a deep breath. She had given Farlege a lot of thought since they had talked to the dwargic. He had been a friend for a long time. He'd never given her any reason not to trust him. He was the Police Captain, after all. If she couldn't trust him, who could she trust? Yes, Raben had advised her to not tell anyone about why she left. She had kept it from Madifen for all of these years, from everyone actually. But, things were happening and she needed an ally. Farlege seemed like the logical choice.

"Well, and Farlege you don't know a lot of this, but with all of the magic happening that seems to have originated with Raben – "

"Raben!?" Farlege interrupted, "you've heard from Raben?"

"Not exactly," she hesitated, "I'll back up and explain it all in a minute. Let me finish this thought," she patted Farlege's arm. "With all of that magic, then what happened at the showcase, and now this...there are just too many coincidences. And honestly, whomever is giving the orders isn't being very smart. Too many incidents so close together can raise suspicions."

"Maybe they are running out of time," Hodgens whispered, almost talking to himself.

"What did you say?" Farlege turned toward him.

Realizing he had said it out loud, Hodgens repeated, "I said maybe they are running out of time. Desperate people do desperate things. We have seen it happen over and over throughout history."

Tenja and Farlege looked at each other.

"That's true," she patted Hodgens leg, "and it's a bit unnerving because you never know what is going to happen next."

"Why don't you back up and tell me about the other incidents that have happened," Farlege suggested.

So, they did. The boys told him about Beagle Girl while Tenja retrieved the book and the jewels. Tenja explained how the music had caused the jewel to meld to the page. How they had kept trying but not had further success. They explained about Conner's forced evolution and how they were still trying to figure out what his symbol meant. And as the sun began to rise, they all sat in silence wondering what to do next.

Farlege broke the silence, "Tenja, is your boundary made to prevent outsiders from seeing magic that happens within it?"

She shook her head, "no, I didn't even know that was possible. It is just a basic boundary spell that Raben taught me. Meant to warn me if anyone tried to get in besides us. But I didn't feel what that woman was doing. It was so subtle that the spell didn't detect it. Without Beagle Girl I wouldn't have known she was there."

"Here's what I think. I think someone felt the magic of the jewels. I think they were trying to get them. And I think that little dog saved all of you," he said pointing at the sleeping beagle at Hodgens' feet.

"What are we supposed to do then?" Graysen asked. "We have to decipher the book."

"Yeah," Conner chimed in, "we have to figure out what Momma Raben needs us to know."

He looked at the three boys, took a deep breath and said, "boys, I need you to trust me. I need to talk to your mom alone. There are some things that you're just not safe knowing."

"But you want to put mom in danger!?" Hodgens exploded. "No. Absolutely not. Whatever Raben started I am not going to let her take Momma Tenja from us. Not gonna happen."

"Momma Raben," Graysen whispered, emphasizing the first word.

"What did you just say?" Hodgens shot to his feet.

"Whoa, whoa," Conner jumped between them, "we're all exhausted, Hodgens. Just let it go."

Tenja rubbed her hands over her face and said, "Conner is right. We're all exhausted. And hungry. Why don't you guys eat something and go to bed. I'll call you out of prep today."

"No thanks," Hodgens shoved past Conner, "I'll eat at the bakery and go to prep. I'll be home later."

As he slammed out of the studio Tenja looked at the other boys.

"I'm going to bed," Graysen said, "I'll eat later."

"Same," Conner agreed as they got up.

Graysen gave her a weak smile as he shut the studio door and turned toward the kitchen. Farlege laid a hand on her arm.

"Tenja," he started.

She pulled her arm away and wiped her eyes. "I'm okay," she told him. "This," she waved her hand over the book and jewels, "is hard on all of us. But Hodgens is struggling the most. He's still so angry with Raben for leaving."

Shaking her head she asked, "what did you need to tell me?"

This time he took a deep breath, "what I'm about to tell you is my secret, Tenja. No one knows. And I mean no one."

"Okay," she drew out in response.

"I guess the best thing to do is just say it."

She waited.

"Tenja, I'm a guardian."

Her mouth fell open and she stared at him.

"You're a what?!"

"A guardian," he said again.

"But I haven't heard of guardians outside of history books."

74

"There's a reason for that. There hasn't been one in Easpach in centuries. Guardians are in Draiocht."

"So why are you here?"

"I'm needed for what is starting to happen."

She nodded, "so why tell me?"

"Because I can put better wards around your house. Because I can protect all of you better than you can protect yourselves. If you'll let me."

She thought for a moment and then agreed, "okay. We'll take your protection. I'll do whatever it takes to keep my boys safe."

He smiled.

"How did you hide it from everyone all of these years? Your magic symbol is a defender, not a guardian. I've seen many symbols like yours through the years."

"Guardians have a unique set of defensive spells, old spells. They aren't even written down anywhere anymore I don't think. Except maybe in the depths of the Royal Archives somewhere. But, even if they are there they are behind some thick layers of defense," he told her.

"Okay, so you hide your magical reality through a spell?"

"Basically, when I became a guardian, I was taught a defensive spell to protect my secret. It could only be cast once, and I had to cast it on myself. It permanently changed my magic symbol to protect my true magic identity," he finished the explanation.

"Interesting," she hesitated, "there is something I want to tell you, too," she said with trepidation.

He raised one eyebrow, "oh?"

"But knowing it will be a risk for you. You knowing will be a risk for me. So, I must know that I can trust you completely."

"I'll carry risk for you, Tenja. You can trust me."

Moments passed as they looked at each other. This was a moment not to be taken lightly. She had only said these words one other time in her life. She finally sighed and said, "I'm a finder."

This time his mouth fell open, "you're a finder!? Tenja, does anyone else know this? Do the boys know? Does Madifen know?"

"The boys most definitely do not know. Madifen does not know. No one knows."

"Did Raben know?"

"Yes. And I think that is part of the reason she has entrusted me with solving this puzzle and figuring out what to do next."

He sat back in his chair, "why tell me, Tenja? Why now?"

"Because, like you, I feel I am needed for whatever is happening, for whatever is coming. And because we can help each other. I want to use my magic to see what we can discover about the guy from the showcase and this woman from last night. Maybe we can find something to help us understand what is happening."

He studied her for a few moments, "my turn to ask. How have you kept this secret all these years? How was your symbol changed?"

"My grandmother was a finder, I was told. I never knew her. She was kidnapped and passed around to the highest bidder after she had my mother. It's crazy what or who people will pay money to find. So, my grandfather took my mother and disappeared. When I was born and they saw my birth symbol grandfather just knew I had inherited my grandmother's magic. So, he bought an old spell that would permanently freeze my evolution spell, preventing it from making the final transition to finder. But my magic was so strong that the spell only froze the symbol. My magic still evolved fully."

"Old magic," he shook his head, "it's like we live with the spirits of our ancestors every day."

"In a way I really do," she looked at him, "the price to cast the spell was a life. The person who cast it had to die for it to work. They had to sacrifice themself for the person who received the spell. My grandfather died the moment he finished casting the spell on me. I was ten years old."

Farlege looked at her long and hard, "this is dangerous business, Tenja."

"I know. But I have to protect my boys."

After a few more minutes he said, "okay, we'll work together to see what we can find. Do not, for any reason, go looking alone. I won't risk you, Tenja. The boys need you."

"I won't" she agreed, "I promise."

He stood up, "I'm going to add wards to your boundary spell that will allow day-to-day sounds through but not magical essences. So, people could hear what goes on outside of the studio, but they won't sense any magic being used. I'm also going to add a notifier that will tell me if anyone tries to breach the boundary."

"Thanks," she said as she got up from the chair. "I need to get some sleep and then I have some things to take care of today. When are you available to go finding?"

"I'm off tomorrow. How about I stop by around 9 in the morning?"

"Great, I'll see you tomorrow."

She watched as he reached for her boundary spell, adding his wards to hers. They waved as he got into his car. As she crawled back into bed, she drifted off to the thought what in the hell is going on, Raben?

CHAPTER 9

Tenja sat at the kitchen table drinking a cup of coffee when Graysen and Conner came downstairs. She looked at the clock thinking it was later than 10am as she didn't expect them awake before noon.

"Not going into the gallery?" Graysen asked as he fixed himself breakfast.

"No. I called off. I am going to the library at prep. I want to do more research on your magic," she said to Conner.

"I want to come!" he responded.

"Me, too!" Graysen added.

She looked at them, "well, that's tricky since I called you both off of school today."

Their shoulders sagged.

She laughed, "I never thought I'd see you sad that I called you off school. Okay, you can come. I'll deal with the school. You only have a couple of days left anyway. What are they going to do to you?"

She got up and put her cup in the sink, "let's all get cleaned up and we'll head over."

#

When they arrived at the school, they found Beagle Girl curled up under a tree taking a nap. She must have sensed them and got up as they approached.

"Nope," Tenja told her, "we're going inside. You have to stay out here."

With a hrmpf she laid back down and watched as they entered the school.

After a stop at the main office, they headed toward the library.

"Any idea where the ancient magic history books are?" she asked the boys as they entered.

78

"Yes, actually," Conner said, "this way," and he led them to corner in the back of the library.

They spent a couple of hours poring over old texts and looking at different magic symbols. Tenja made notes and drawings in her notebook. Finally, she sat back in her chair and said, "okay, here's what I've pieced together."

The boys crowded around her and gave her their undivided attention.

"So," she began, "this was your original magic symbol, Conner."

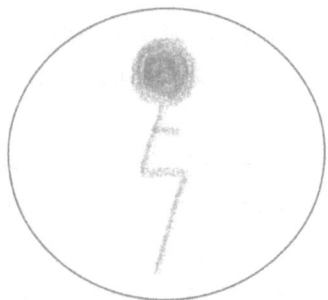

"We know that with your birth magic you could disappear and reappear yourself and anything you were wearing. But not anything you just held in your hands. Whatever went with you had to be a part of your person in some fashion."

"Right," he agreed, "anything I held just fell to the ground when I disappeared."

Graysen started laughing, "yeah, remember when you tried to take the cookies after momma told you no? Wasted a whole batch of mom's amazing chocolate chip and pecan cookies."

"Yeah, yeah. You are never going to let me forget that are you?" Conner rolled his eyes.

"Nope," Graysen punched him gingerly in the arm.

"Okay, okay," Tenja let out a laugh, "let's get back to this," she interrupted them and pointed at her notebook.

"I found this symbol that has been recorded as being able to transport objects from one place to another."

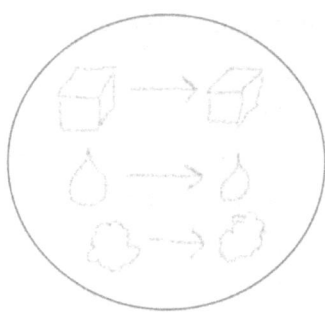

"I'm not sure I understand the symbol," Graysen admitted.

"If I had to guess," Conner answered, "those are the states of matter: solid, liquid, and gas. The arrows indicate movement. So, moving a solid object, or a liquid or gas substance from one place to another."

Tenja nodded, "that's exactly right. And we know that you can do that now. We've been working on that since the showcase. You've moved a solid object and a liquid substance. We haven't tried a gas but I'm assuming you could do that, too."

Conner pointed at the other symbol on the page and asked, "what about his one?"

"That," Tenja hesitated, "that is the symbol for the ability to transform matter."

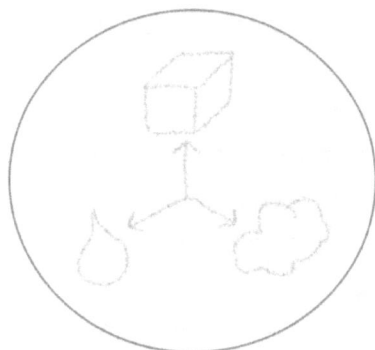

"Wait," Graysen said as he plopped into a chair, "you're saying that there are people whose magic allows them to change the state of matter?"

Conner followed his brother and plopped into a chair, "have you ever known anyone who could do it?" he asked Tenja.

She shook her head, "no. I didn't even know it was possible until I read this book."

The boys looked at the book where she pointed. Conner read, "Tales of Ancient Incants."

"What is an 'incant'?" Graysen asked?

"It's what they used to call people with magic," Tenja explained. "A long time ago magic was called incantations. Those of us born with magic symbols were called incants. I've only read of the use of the term. I've never heard it used in my lifetime."

"So, what does all of this mean for my magic?" Conner asked.

"Well, we don't know if you can change the state of matter. I think that is the next thing that we should try," Tenja suggested.

"Why don't I try taking a person with me again like I did with Hodgens?"

"No. Absolutely not," Tenja said too loudly and got looks from others in the library. Lowering her voice, she said, "that is a risk I am not willing to take with anyone's life just for practice, Conner. Yes, you saved Hodgens, and we are all really glad you did. But we are not going to test that magic yet. Not until we know more."

"Fine, fine!" he threw up his hands, "I won't do it."

Softening her voice, she looked at him, "Conner, I know you are desperate to understand your new magic. But without knowing what that symbol means we have to be careful."

Before she could say more, Madifen rolled up to the table.

"How's my favorite family?"

"Hey Professor Koarré!" Graysen said a little too enthusiastically.

Madi eyed him suspiciously. Conner gave a quick wave.

"Hi, Madi," Tenja responded to his greeting, "how are you?"

"Better than you guys it sounds like. What happened at your house last night?"

"How do you know about that?" Conner asked him.

81

"It's the big news around town," he explained. "Small town news always travels fast. So really, how are you guys?"

"We're fine," Tenja assured him. "Tired. But fine."

"Yeah, I saw Hodgens a little bit ago. He was basically asleep on his feet," Madi laughed.

She looked at her watch. "I'm going to check him out and feed us all. Then I think we all need a nap," she laughed.

#

Hodgens' temper had receded, she noticed as he joined them in front of the school. Probably dampened by exhaustion she thought as she looked into his tired eyes.

"You guys just want to grab a slice at the pizzeria?" she asked.

"That sounds great," Hodgens agreed first, his brothers nodding in agreement.

They walked in silence. Once they were seated at the restaurant Hodgens asked, "what were you all doing at prep?"

"Trying to figure out what my new magic is," Conner answered.

"We didn't have a lot of luck, though," Graysen added sounding dismayed.

"Really? You didn't find anything?"

"Well, we found some pieces to the puzzle," Tenja said trying to sound optimistic. She stopped talking as a shiver ran down her spine. It felt as if someone was watching her. She made a quick scan of the restaurant but didn't notice anything out of place or anyone she didn't know. A moment later the waiter walked up with their lunch.

"Let's talk about this more later. I'm starving and could really use a nap," she said with a forced chuckle.

"Me, too!" the boys agreed in stereo.

#

"Are you really sure you want to do this?" Farlege asked.

"Absolutely," she responded as she finished packing her knapsack. "We have to get on top of this, especially since convocation is in two days. It's the perfect opportunity for a large-scale disaster. Practically the entire town will be there."

"That had crossed my mind, too," he agreed. He let out a big sigh and said, "okay, where do we start?"

"Since we're here, let's start with the woman who tried to break through the boundary."

They headed out to the alley in silence. Once outside the boundary, Tenja opened the paint bottle and dipped in the brush. She bent down, touched the glowing brush tip to the ground where the woman had laid. Three times she whispered, 'woman who tried to break in'. Then she watched as a trail of footprints began to glow.

Standing she told Farlege, "okay, we're good to go."

"I don't understand," he said, looking confused.

As she put the bottle and brush into her knapsack she explained, "the magic in the paint illuminates the woman's footprints. All I have to do now is follow them."

"Fascinating," he responded with awe in his voice.

They walked along in silence. The footprints led them into town and then veered off toward the school.

"Well this isn't good," Farlege said through clenched teeth.

Tenja agreed, "no, it isn't. But the tracks don't stop here at the school. So, let's keep following them."

She found it disturbing that there was no other trail of these footprints. It's like the woman came from one place and went directly to their house. She hadn't been anywhere else in the town. There were no forks in the tracks, no turns, no choices to make. It was a direct path. The prints turned into the woods about a quarter of a mile from the school.

She looked at Farlege, "I don't like this one bit." She explained about the tracks, how there was a single trail and what that meant.

He rubbed his chin and thought for a moment. Then he asked, "do we keep going?"

"I don't think we have a choice," she told him stepping into the woods. She stopped just inside the trees, removed her bow, and nocked an arrow.

Farlege unholstered his gun.

They only had to walk about 50 steps into the woods to find an answer. The air shimmered in front of them. They looked at each other.

"Tenja, am I seeing what I think I'm seeing?"

"A working traversable."

"How do you know it is working? They can shimmer but still not allow someone to pass."

"Look up," she pointed, "in the trees you can see a faint blue glow. That indicates that the traversable is active; that people can move through it safely."

"I can barely see it," he admitted.

"Yeah, you have to know what to look for but once you see it, it's obvious."

"So here's the rub," he began, "if we disable it then they know we're on to them."

"Whoever 'them' is," she added.

"Exactly. But if we leave it active then we incur the risk of more people coming through. And right now, we don't know how many people are already here."

"I'd rather disable it," she stated as a matter of fact. "I'd rather face the risk of a limited number of people already being here than leave it open for magic knows how many to come through."

"I think I agree, Tenja. But I don't know how to disable it."

"Like this," she said as she chose a different arrow. Before he knew what was happening, she had fired the arrow into the blue illumination. A flash of bright orange followed and then the traversable stopped shimmering. She retrieved her arrow from where it had landed on the ground.

"The magic on the arrow will prevent the traversable from being fixed. But we may have another problem," she told him as they walked out of the woods. "I found another traversable a few weeks ago."

"You what? When? Where?"

"It's in the park. Hidden deep in the woods there. We need to check it now," she explained about Beagle Girl as they walked and how she had followed the dog's paw prints. She filled him in on everything that had transpired since then, stopping short of sharing her suspicions about why everything was happening.

When they got to the traversable in the park Tenja was relieved to see that it was in the same state it had been when she'd found it. It was not active.

"How do we prevent it from becoming active?" Farlege asked.

"We have to remove the rubies from the dragons' eyes."

"But" he hesitated.

She looked at him. "What?"

He swallowed hard, "what if Raben needs to send you a message? You think the dog came from her. What if she needs to send something else through but you've disabled the traversable from our side?"

Tenja looked at him. Just looked at him.

She pointed at the traversable, "this is a point of vulnerability – for everyone!"

"I know. I know," he threw up his hands, "but I can't help but consider that Raben may need our help. That she might need to communicate with us more. Then what?"

She paced back and forth in front of the traversable.

Damn it, damn it, damn it. Raben, I'm beginning to agree with Hodgens. Why couldn't you have just told us what we needed to know?! She thought as she walked. How am I supposed to know the right thing to do here?

She stopped pacing and sighed, "okay, here's what we're going to do. We're going to take the rubies —"he started to interrupt her, "- for now. Then, each Monday morning you and I will come out here and put them in their places. That way if something, or someone, is trying to come through we will be here and be prepared. But nothing will get through without us knowing about it."

He nodded, "I like that plan. We should each keep two rubies. Neither of us should have all of them. Just in case — both of us are needed to activate the traversable from this side."

"That's good thinking, Farlege," she agreed. They set to work removing the rubies.

On the way back to town Farlege asked, "should we track the dwargic now?"

She looked up at the sun, "yeah, I have time to do that."

"Okay," he nodded, "let's head to City Hall Park. He said he was sitting on the second bench you come to on the main walking trail that leads from there."

They walked in silence, both contemplating the reality they were discovering. When they got to the first bench Tenja sat down.

"Tenja, are you okay?" Farlege asked as he sat next to her.

"I'm fine. It has been a long time since I've used this magic. And I've used a lot of it in the last couple of weeks. I just need a drink and to sit for a minute," she said taking a bottle of water out of her pack. She offered it to him after taking a long sip.

"Thanks," he said between drinks.

"Let's make this quick," she nodded down the trail, "I'm starving."

In that moment Farlege's stomach growled and they both laughed.

At the bench Tenja repeated her magic steps, this time saying dwargic three times as she touched the bench and the ground with her brush. Then she watched as nothing happened. Frowning, she reached inward to feel for her magic. It was there. It's strength felt normal.

She frowned and asked, "can you use your magic here?"

"What? Why?" He asked looking around, "is something wrong?"

"Just try."

Farlege obeyed and easily put up a boundary spell around them. He took it down as he told her, "yeah, I can do my magic like usual. What's going on?"

She let out a sigh, "he lied, Farlege. The dwargic was never here."

"Wh-what? How do you know that?" He stammered.

"I know because my magic reveals nothing when I use it in search of him. There should be something here, Farlege, but the bench holds no dwargic presence and there are no footprints."

"I don't understand. I really thought he was telling the truth."

"I think he told us a partial truth," she stated. "I think there are others. I think someone else is in charge. But I believe he purposefully misled us in case we tried to find out more."

"Damn it!" Farlege erupted, startling her, "I want answers!"

"Me, too," she agreed, "but talking with these people isn't how we're going to get them. They aren't going to be straight with us."

"What about his sister? Do you think that was a lie?"

"No, I think he had a sister. I think she is dead. The haunted look in his eyes when he told us that wasn't fake. But I don't think her death was for the reasons he wants us to believe. We need to investigate her death. We need to find the truth about that and I think it will put us on the path to finding more answers."

He looked around as he considered her words, "okay. I can do that. I have his name. If it is his real name. I may have to call in some favors, Tenja. But before I do I will think about who I can really trust."

Throwing her pack over her shoulder and heading down the trail she said, "I understand. I have to get home. I do have a question for you, though," she added, "would you be willing to teach Conner some protection and boundary spells. Just the basics? I can do them. But Raben taught me and I'm not sure I'd be the greatest teacher of those kinds of spells."

"Sure, I can do that," he said happily, "have him give me a call and we'll set up a time to start the lessons."

"I appreciate it," she thanked him.

They headed separate ways when they got to City Hall Park. He to the police station and her to the house. She locked her artifacts and weapons safely in her trunk. Then she grabbed a glass of lemonade and sat on the porch steps waiting for her world to come home from one of their last days of prep.

CHAPTER 10

"Mom. Mom!"

Tenja woke with a start.

"Wh-what? What time is it?" She asked as she rubbed her eyes. Graysen was standing in the doorway to her bedroom.

"It's just after 8 in the morning. James is on the phone. He's kind of hysterical. You should talk to him."

She threw back the covers and raced down the stairs. She started talking as she raised the receiver to her face, "James, what is it? What's wrong?"

"Tenja! You have to come to the gallery! Now! You have to see this!"

"See what?"

"Just get here, Tenja. Fast!"

The next thing she heard was the click as James hung up. She placed the receiver on the base and turned to see the boys all staring at her.

"What's wrong?" Graysen asked.

"I don't know. I guess I'm going in early today."

"We're coming with you," Conner stated in his matter-of-fact tone.

"Fine. I'm not awake enough to argue."

They all threw on clothes and headed out the door, Beagle Girl leading the way. As they turned the last corner toward the gallery they found police cars, lights flashing, blocking the street so no one could drive in front of the gallery. At this sight, they all broke into a run. Police stopped them at the barricades.

"Let me through," she demanded.

"Let us through!" Hodgens corrected.

Just then Farlege emerged from the building.

"Farlege!" Conner yelled and waved.

"Officer Banderlacht, let them through!" He commanded.

Nodding, the officer moved aside and motioned the four of them through the barricade before stepping back to keep the growing crowd at bay.

They didn't have to reach the gallery to see that there was paint on the windows. As they got near the messages became clear.

"The end is near," read Hodgens.

"Enjoy the minutes," added Graysen.

James came running out of the gallery. As he grabbed Tenja's hand he said, "come on! You gotta see inside!"

"Oh god, what happened?!" She exclaimed as a zillion horrible thoughts flashed through her mind.

Her hand flew to her mouth to stifle her audible gasp as she crossed the threshold. All of the art they had was carefully moved to the sides of the gallery. On the back wall was a mural, the likes of which she had never seen.

"James," she whispered.

"I know," he nodded, "I don't know how this happened. I activated all the security when I left last night."

She made him let go of her and walked up to the mural.

"Tenja, don't touch it!" Farlege yelled and threw a boundary spell between her and the mural.

She ran into it and squealed, "what the hell, Farlege?"

"It's spelled," he explained. "If you'd slow down, you should be able to feel it."

"I do feel it," she agreed, "and that's why I have to touch it. Its magic is calling to mine."

"First, look at it. Step back and look at it," he instructed as he pulled on her arm to move her back from the mural.

Doing as she was told Tenja studied the picture before her. Wall to wall. Floor to ceiling. Draiocht was on the left full of beautiful green fields, fairies, dragons, and villages. Easpach was on the right and was filled with buildings, schools, people in the park doing magic, others playing baseball. Then in the middle was Sa Làr, and standing center mural was Raben! Her arms were outstretched. Magic was wrapped around her wrists and tethering the boundaries of Draiocht and Easpach.

Tenja sucked in a breath, "Raben!" The name caught in her throat.

"Momma!" Conner yelped. "Is that really what is happening?"

She turned at the sound of his voice. There, looking at her through confused and frightened eyes were the reason she would keep fighting.

"I don't know, boys," she acknowledged the truth, "give me a few minutes, okay?"

They nodded.

She turned to Farlege, "photographs. I want detailed photos of this before I touch it. I can't explain why, but it has to be done."

"I'm on it," he said as he turned. Within minutes there were three crime scene unit officers with large cameras taking pictures of the mural. After about thirty minutes they indicated they were finished and headed back to the lab to prepare the digital photos for her.

Taking a deep breath she looked at the boys and Farlege.

"Okay, I'm going to touch the mural. I can't explain why I need to, other than what I said earlier. The magic in the mural is calling to me. I honestly don't think anything bad is going to happen to me."

She touched each of the boys' faces, "I'm going to be fine. Trust me."

"We do, mom," Hodgens reassured her, "we do."

With that she turned and walked toward the mural. Where to touch it didn't even require contemplation. She didn't hesitate to walk up to the image of her love and lay her hand over her. One heartbeat. Two. And then everything started to change.

"Mom!!" She heard the boys yell as she felt herself falling.

#

Why is my forehead cold? She thought to herself reaching up to feel it. Doing so she found a wet washcloth on her head. Opening her eyes, she saw the faces of three very worried boys staring at her. Looking around she realized she was lying on the sofa in her office.

"Let me in, Farlege," she heard a voice yelling.

"Back it up, Madifen! No one gets in unless Tenja or the boys say it is okay!" Farlege held firm.

"Help me sit up," she said in a weak voice.

Hodgens and Conner each took an arm and gently raised her to a sitting position.

"Here, have some water," Graysen said handing her a glass.

"Thanks," she gave them a small smile. "How long have I been out?"

Hodgens looked at his watch, "about 20 minutes."

Her head shot up, "the painting!?"

She watched as the boys looked at each other and paled.

"Boys...?"

"It's...okay," Graysen drawled out.

"It's just, different," Hodgens tried to explain.

"What do you mean 'different'?" She asked.

"Well..." Graysen started, "it changed. When you touched Momma Raben it looked like the paint was wet and running down the wall. Then, as you fell, the image of the painting changed. It was still completely dry."

"If the painting wasn't so disturbing it would have been a really cool artistic thingy," Conner added.

She was too distracted by the continued argument taking place outside the office door. Slowly she rose to her feet.

"Mom, are you sure you should get up?" Hodgens took her arm.

"Yeah, I'm okay. But those two," she pointed toward the door, "are going to start throwing fists if one of us doesn't stop them."

As soon as she turned the handle on the door the voices outside silenced. Madifen tried to rush her when she opened the door.

"Tenja! By all that is magic, are you okay?!" He squeaked and tried to get past Farlege, who held steady.

She laid a hand on Farlege's shoulder, "it's okay. I'm okay," she stressed. "Let me out. I want to see the painting."

Farlege moved aside and she looked at Madifen, "I'm okay. Apparently, I fainted or something. But I'm okay."

Madi sighed, "I'm so glad, Tenja. But whatever is going on here is not okay."

"I need to see the painting."

All of the males around her looked from one to the other. She crossed her arms and stuck out a hip.

"Seriously? This," she pointed at each of them, "can stop now. When it's time to worry about me I will let you know. Now is not that time."

Madifen rolled out of the way and they all followed her to the painting. It was blocked off now. A giant screen had been erected between it and the viewing world. An unsettling feeling landed in her stomach. She stepped around the screen - and froze.

Raben lay in the middle of the Sa Làr, her arms having been violently ripped from her body. No magic was wrapped around her wrists. No magic was tethered to Draiocht or Easpach. She gasped. What had been Easpach was now an image of fire and smoke. Buildings, trees, grass, all of it burned. People were strewn all over the streets, dead, burned. It was an annihilation.

Someone slipped a chair behind her, and she sat. She stared at Easpach for a long minute before turning to look at Draiocht. It's glowing! She thought to herself. It's freaking glowing! It was as if magic overflowed from everything in the land.

The boys knelt beside her.

"Mom," Graysen hesitated.

She looked at him, "what baby?"

"Does this mean Momma Raben is dead?" He finished.

"No. This isn't now," she shook her head.

"So it is predicting what is to come?" Conner asked.

"Predictions aren't certainties, Conner," she explained. "They provide a possibility of what could come. Small changes can have big impacts on the outcome of an event."

"This depiction of the untethering of Draiocht and Easpach doesn't follow what I've always been told," she said as she got up and walked toward the painting.

"How do you mean?" Madi asked.

She gestured toward Easpach, "I was told that if the worlds became untethered the people with magic would die, leaving everyone else to live in a world with no magic. This," she waved her arms, "predicts the complete destruction of Easpach."

She spun around, "Hodgens, where is Beagle Girl?"

"She's outside. She's been guarding the door since you passed out. Madifen is the only person she has let through the door."

Stifling a laugh she said, "will you go get her? I need to ask her something."

They were back in a moment. Beagle Girl levitated so she was eye-to-eye with Tenja.

"If I activate the traversable and we go through, can you lead me to Raben?" She asked the dog.

With a sad look in her eyes Beagle Girl shook her head no. The boys groaned.

"She made sure of that didn't she?" Tenja slouched and Beagle Girl aroofed. The dog sat down on the floor and just looked at the painting. Then she walked over and sat right under the image of Raben's dead body and let out a mournful howl. Hodgens picked her up and carried her outside.

"Tenja, we took pictures of this one like we did the first one. I want this gone," Farlege stated as if giving an order.

"You'll have to nail boards over it," she told him. "The magic won't let you paint over it."

"What?!" Madifen interjected. "What do you mean the magic won't let you paint over it? How do you know that?"

"I could tell when I touched it," she began. "I could feel the magical seal in it."

"Why, in all that is magic, did you touch it? It could have killed you," Madifen expressed concern.

"Madi, I knew that it wouldn't. The magic called to my magic. I knew it wouldn't hurt me."

"But it did hurt you, Tenja. You passed out!" He shot back.

She rolled her eyes, "why are the males around me so dramatic?"

"I have to agree with Madifen on this one, Tenja," Farlege added and had her staring at him agape.

"Are you serious right now?" She asked.

"Yep, you're going to see Dahlia now," he directed.

Her eyebrows shot up, "you want me to go see the healer?"

"I'm telling you that you are going to see the healer," he responded.

"Please mom," Conner added, "just to make sure you really are okay?"

She threw up her hands, "fine. But, once I'm cleared, we have work to do," she said to her boys who nodded in return.

#

Madifen grabbed Farlege's arm, "what is going on, Farlege? What isn't Tenja telling me?"

Farlege stared long and hard at the man who had occupied a lot of time with Tenja and the boys over the years. Then he gave him an honest answer, "I don't know what is going on Madifen. I wish I did. As for Tenja," he hesitated and looked toward the door, "the only three people she really and truly trusts right now share her DNA."

"They are boys! What did she mean they have work to do?"

Farlege shrugged, "closer to men than boys now. As for work, it's a puzzle Madifen. The pieces are floating around in front of us. The

95

school, the attempted break in at their house, now this at Tenja's gallery. Her family is under attack. Have you ever seen her true, magic deep temper? I haven't. But I'm afraid that we are going to very soon."

The thought made Madi shudder and then sigh. "I want to help them, Farlege. I just don't know how."

"If you want to help don't let her keep you out. Show her you want to be there. Keep showing up. Try to help find answers. Don't just idly sit back and wait for her to come to you. That's not her style. You know that," Farlege recommended.

"You're right, it's not. But she came to you," Madi gestured to him.

"Because she wanted to talk to the dwargic. If we hadn't arrested him, I don't know if she would have come to me," Farlege explained. "Don't assume things, Madifen. It will get you into trouble every time."

"You're right," he agreed, "you're right. Okay, I'm going to head out. Sorry I yelled at you earlier," he added with a grimace.

"It's okay. No harm no foul," Farlege patted him on the back and the two men parted ways.

CHAPTER 11

Cleared by the healer, Tenja stormed into the house with the boys close on her heels. She tore up the stairs and into her bedroom. The boys opted to wait in the hall. They fidgeted nervously wondering as they waited. Within minutes Tenja emerged with her trunk and pack. She looked at their expectant faces.

"Bring any and all books and notes that you have on magic, magical history, anything of the sort. Meet me in the studio."

They nodded and headed toward their room.

"What do you think we're going to do?" Hodgens asked his brothers.

Graysen and Conner shrugged.

"She said we had work to do," Conner added.

"I for one am glad that we might be taking the offensive. This waiting around for the next thing to happen is nerve wracking," Graysen chimed in.

They entered the studio to see Tenja at her worktable. The book they believed to be from Raben and the jewels were spread out in front of her, along with her notes on Conner's new magic symbol. She didn't even glance at them when they came up to her.

"Okay," she began, "first I need to fill you in on some pieces that you don't know." And with that she told them about her talk with the dwargic, how Farlege was researching the dead sister, and about traversables.

"So, wait," Conner interjected, "you're saying that a traversable can be used to move between the three worlds, the worlds we saw in the painting?"

"Yes," she acknowledged his understanding.

"So, is that how Momma Raben got to Sa Làr?" Graysen asked.

"It has to be," she answered, "If there is another way to move between the worlds, I don't know what it is."

"But they have been closed since Momma left?" Conner again.

"As far as Farlege and I are aware. At least, until recently."

She looked at Hodgens who was staring at the jewels. After a few minutes of silence he said, "okay, now that we're all caught up, what is the plan? What are we going to do?"

"I'd like to try a few things with Conner's magic first," she told them. "Based upon what I have been reading, Conner, I think that you can now make an object disappear from where it is and reappear in another spot without having to touch it or take it with you."

"What?!" Conner squeaked, "are you serious?"

"Totally serious," she replied, "let's practice with this ball," she suggested as she picked up the blue ball and set it on her worktable. "If I'm understanding this correctly," she pointed at her notes, "you need to close your eyes, picture the ball where it is now, and then picture it in a different spot."

He took a deep breath, "okay. Let me see what I can do."

At first, nothing happened. He tried over and over for about thirty minutes with no progress.

"This is so frustrating!" He exclaimed.

Hodgens got up from his seat, "Momma, can I see your notes?"

She handed them to him and watched as he studied what she had written.

"Conner, what are you picturing in your head? Be specific," he instructed his brother.

"I imagine myself picking up the ball and moving it to a different spot," Conner told him.

"Ah, that is a problem. You aren't technically moving it," Hodgens said thoughtfully.

"What do you mean?" Graysen asked.

"Well, if I'm reading Momma's notes correctly, what you're doing is making it disappear into like a magical void, and then reappearing some place different."

They all looked at each other.

"Conner," Hodgens began, "when you disappear and reappear, where are you during the in between time? The time when you're not where you left but haven't appeared in the new spot."

"Uh," Conner began, "it's hard to explain because I'm not there long."

"When you saved me from the stage, you disappeared me and reappeared me. I didn't feel like you were moving me from one place to another. I felt like you wrapped me in magic, made me invisible on the stage, and then visible at the tree. It was a quick shift, but I felt like we were floating in magic."

"That is an interesting assessment, Hodgens," Tenja said. "Conner, disappear and reappear somewhere else. But this time, try to understand the in between without losing site of your destination."

"That sounds easier said than done," he huffed out.

The three of them watched as Conner disappeared. Tenja had expected he would just go across the room, but moments passed and no Conner.

"Uh, momma?" Graysen sounded concerned.

"Just give him a few minutes," she encouraged.

Fifteen minutes passed before Conner reappeared in the studio.

"Dude! Where have you been?" Graysen yelped.

"Kind of all over town. The farther away I choose to reappear the longer I'm in the in between. So, I went to the school, then to the baseball fields, then..."

"We get it," Hodgens waved a hand, "did you figure anything out?"

"I think so, but I still don't think I can explain it," he answered.

"That's okay," Tenja patted his shoulder, "magic is in the doing, not the telling."

Just then the blue ball disappeared and reappeared like it had been shot out of a cannon, ricocheting around the room so forcefully it had Graysen diving to protect his instruments. Hodgens intercepted the ball and set it back on the table.

"I think you might need to work on your control there, brother," Hodgens laughed.

Conner blushed, "sorry about that."

"Sorry!? Don't be sorry!" Tenja hugged him. "You did it, Conner! But" she said with a smile, "I recommend you practice with things that aren't breakable for a while."

"I need some water," he told them. When he opened the studio door, they all heard the ringing phone.

Conner answered it and said, "Momma, it's for you. It's James again."

Taking the receiver she said, "Hey James, what do you need?"

"Instructions," he replied, "you left and didn't tell me what you want me to do with the studio."

"Oh gosh, I'm so sorry! Call the handyman and have him cover the mural with paint resistant boards. Keep the gallery closed until that is done. Then rearrange the exhibits in a way that directs traffic far away from the mural wall. Once all of that is taken care of you can open the gallery again."

"Okay. Okay. I can do that. Tenja?"

"Yes?"

"Are you guys still going to matriculation tomorrow?"

The question stopped her thoughts.

"Uh, it actually slipped my mind. With everything going on...I don't know. I just don't know."

"Well, whatever you do, be safe," he said.

"Thanks, James. We will," she said and hung up.

"You okay, mom?" Graysen asked.

"Convocation," she simply stated, "boys, come sit at the kitchen table."

Drinks in hand they took their seats and just waited.

"We need to make a decision as a family," she started. "Tomorrow is convocation. It's in the park. There will be a lot of people there. Practically the whole town. It's a perfect opportunity for a large-scale incident. You have all three earned to be there. You deserve to be honored for your achievements. What do you want to do?"

The boys looked at each other. Then Beagle Girl startled them all by levitating so she could be a part of the conversation.

"Dang it!" Graysen spat out, "I'm never going to get used to that!"

Beagle Girl aroofed at him.

"I think we should skip it," Hodgens opined.

Beagle Girl nodded in agreement.

"I don't know," Conner shared, "I want to go."

"But is it worth the risk?" Graysen asked him.

Then they all looked at her. She let out a sigh.

"I'm honestly torn. If we are here, I can protect you better. We can protect each other. If we stay home and nothing happens at convocation, I will feel bad you missed it. If we go and something bad happens, I'll regret not keeping you at home."

The ringing phone startled them all. Tenja jumped up and grabbed the receiver.

"Hello?"

"Hey Tenja,"

"Oh, hi, Madi. What's up?"

"Can I come over for dinner? I'll bring pizza. I have some information that I need to share with all of you."

She turned and looked at the boys.

"Just a sec. Let me check with the guys," she said as she placed her hand over the receiver so Madi couldn't hear her.

"He wants to know if he can come over for dinner, bring pizza. Says he has information to share with all of us. What do you think?"

The boys looked at each other.

"I say yes," Graysen finally spoke. His brothers and Beagle Girl, all nodded yes.

She removed her hand from the receiver and said, "sure, why not? About 5:30?"

"Sounds good," he agreed, "see you all soon."

101

She hung up the phone and returned to her seat. "Okay, we have a little less than two hours before he will be here. We really need to decide what we're doing about tomorrow."

"I'll be honest," Hodgens said, "I think we are the magnet in all of this."

"What do you mean?" Conner asked.

"Beagle Girl comes to us. The dwargic waited until I was alone on stage, the woman tried to get through our boundary spells, the painting was put in mom's gallery...everything keeps happening to us."

"I hadn't thought of that," Conner looked at his brother with big eyes, "had you Momma?" He asked of Tenja.

"It had crossed my mind, yes," she admitted.

"But, then if we're here and the whole town is there, we're sitting ducks," Graysen said in a small voice.

"I know, son," Tenja laid her hand on his arm, "but, if we decide to stay, I will work with Farlege to ensure we are safe."

"I think we should stay, too," Conner said. "Taking everything Hodgens said into consideration, we need to be here and defend us without putting everyone we know and care about at risk. It just doesn't seem right."

"Yeah, I have to agree with Conner and Hodgens," Graysen concurred.

"Okay, then," Tenja agreed, "I'll call Farlege after Madi leaves and ask him to come over so we can make a plan."

With that, they all got up and went off to their various activities while they waited for Madi to arrive. Tenja went into the studio to put the book and jewels away. As she picked up the book she thought, Oh Raben, so many moving parts and no straight answers. Did we make the right decision?

CHAPTER 12

"Hey Madi," Tenja said as she opened the door. "Here let me take those for you," she said taking the pizzas from his lap.

"Thanks. Where is everyone?"

"Around. Boys! Madi's here with pizza!" She yelled up the stairs.

Three sets of teenage boy feet came tromping down the stairs.

"Excellent, I'm starving!" Conner bounced into the kitchen.

Hodgens moved a chair to the corner so there was a place for Madi to pull up to the table in his wheelchair.

"Thanks, bud."

"No problem," Hodgens gestured to the table. "What can I get you to drink?"

"Milk would be great," Madi replied.

"Ugh!" Graysen groaned, "I will never get used to you drinking milk with pizza!"

Madifen laughed as Tenja set a glass on the table in front of him.

Once they were all seated and their plates were full Madifen asked, "how are you all doing after everything that has been going on?"

They looked at each other and then all three settled their eyes on Tenja.

She let out a sigh, "it's been tough," she admitted. "The events of the last couple of weeks have really rattled us."

Truth. Truth weaved with caution. She hoped the boys felt it.

"I can only imagine," Madi said sitting back.

Tenja saw the strange look in his eyes. Caught the hesitation in his words.

"What is it Madi?" She prodded him.

He cleared his throat, "well, I was doing some thinking this afternoon. It seems like all of you are being targeted."

Hodgens nodded in agreement, "yeah, we came to that conclusion, too."

"Oh," Madifen seemed disappointed that this wasn't a new insight.

"Yeah, it's hard to think anything different," Conner chimed in, "I mean every incident has happened in some relation to us."

Madi nodded, "I had that realization today." He looked at Tenja, "do you have any ideas why someone would be targeting you? Do you think it's tied to Raben? Or that you have something someone might want?"

Tenja looked at him, long and hard. He held her gaze.

"I honestly don't know why someone is targeting us. Do I think it has anything to do with Raben? Yes, I'd put money on the fact that it has something to do with her. This all started with Beagle Girl's arrival."

She purposefully did not address his question about having something that someone might want. She was curious if he would push the question and was relieved when he left it alone and instead changed the subject.

"What I really came over for was to tell you that I made some progress in figuring out Conner's new magic."

"What?" Conner almost choked on his pizza. He quickly chewed and swallowed the bite in his mouth. "What did you find out?"

"I've got a couple of ancient texts in my backpack. When we're done eating, I'll show you what I found."

"Where did you get these texts?" Tenja asked. We were at the prep's library and looked through the oldest ones they have there."

"They are mine, passed down through generations. I've been going over them since I saw Conner's new symbol. It took me awhile because they are written in ancient Draiocht."

Tenja eyed him suspiciously. Remembering the story Raben had told her about her move to Easpach with Madifen, they came with nothing but the clothes on their backs basically. How did he have texts that were passed down through generations?

"What, you can read ancient Draiocht?" Hodgens jumped in the conversation. "How did you learn to read that?"

104

"Well, they used to teach it at prep. I studied it there, but my parents also made sure I could read, write, and speak it."

"Why don't they teach it anymore," Graysen asked.

Madi shrugged, "I don't know, Graysen. Every year I push to get it back on the scheduled curriculum and every year the board refuses."

"It's like they don't want us to know where we come from," Hodgens muttered before taking another bite.

They finished eating and cleared the table. Once everything was washed and put away Madifen got out the texts.

"Okay," he flipped open the first book, "this symbol means that someone can move objects. It's much like my magic."

"Yeah, momma found that one today," Conner acknowledged.

"This one," Madi turned the page, "means that someone can change the state of matter."

"You were right, Momma!" Graysen exclaimed.

Madi looked at her, "you knew that?"

"Well," Tenja gestured at the book, "we found both of those symbols in the books at prep. The first made sense because, yes, it is similar to yours. I guessed on the second one."

"Conner started working on moving objects today," Hodgens told Madi.

Graysen nodded, "yeah, he made good progress, too!"

"Thanks brother," Conner said as he lightly punched Graysen on the arm.

"Can you change the state of an object?" Madi asked Conner.

"I haven't tried," he replied.

"We wanted to take it one step at a time," Tenja explained.

Madi nodded, "that seems safest. So, I assume you haven't tried to disappear and reappear another human being again."

"Momma said I should wait on that," Conner laughed.

"Have you figured out anything else?" Tenja asked Madi.

At the question Madifen got excited and bounced in his chair. I've never seen him this excited, Tenja thought to herself.

Opening the second text, Madi pointed to a symbol in the middle of the page.

"That looks like my symbol!" Conner jumped toward the book.

"I know!" Madi shared his excitement.

"Wait," Hodgens said as he picked up the book. "It's not exactly like yours, Conner."

"What do you mean?" Madi asked.

"What's different, Hodgens?" Tenja asked.

"Look at it," he handed her the book. "It's really close but it's missing the electrons moving around the nucleus."

"Huh?" Conner inquired.

Hodgens grabbed Conner's arm, "see the little balls on the lines? Those represent electrons moving around the nucleus in the atomic symbol. The nucleus, the dot in the center, houses the protons, the positive energy, and the neutrons. Your symbol has the negative, the electrons, and the nucleus. The one in the book only has the positive."

Tenja sat the book on the table, "that is a really good observation, Hodgens. Madi, what does the text say this symbol represents?"

Madi picked up the book and started to read, "this symbol is one of the rarer symbols in Draiocht magic. Individuals who have this magic can stabilize objects, people, weather, etc. that are behaving in a seemingly unsteady, changeable, or unstable manner."

"Wait, what?" Tenja cut in, "are you saying it is possible to control things that aren't acting right?"

"Let me read more," Madi suggested and continued, "This magic has been proven to stop food from spoiling, prevent weak buildings from falling, stopping sickness, and dissipating storms. The rarity of this magic leaves one vulnerable to being hunted and misused."

Conner got up from his chair and started to pace. Tenja watched him and saw thoughts racing through his mind.

"But wait," he finally said, "this symbol isn't exactly like mine, though. Hodgens pointed out that I have electrons, too. So, if the symbol in the book allowed people to stabilize stuff, what does mine allow me to do?"

They all just looked at him. Finally, Tenja got up and went to her son. She put a hand on each of his shoulders and looked up into his ocean blue eyes, "we don't know, son. But I promise you with all that I am, we will figure it out."

His shoulders sagged and he laid his forehead on hers, "I'm scared mom."

A big admission made in a small voice.

She wrapped her arms around him, "I know, baby. I know. We all are."

"We got your back, brother," Graysen said coming to them.

"Yeah," Hodgens added, "triplet strong."

Madi said nothing. After a moment Tenja broke away and looked at the clock.

"I need to call Farlege," she said. "Madi, you're welcome to stay for this meeting if you'd like. You should probably know what is going on tomorrow."

With a furrowed brow he looked around the room, "Okay...sure. I can stay."

#

Farlege arrived thirty minutes after she called him. She let him in and pointed toward the studio.

"Madifen, boys," he nodded to the men in the room.

Men, Tenja thought to herself. My boys have grown into men.

She shut the studio door behind her and they all stopped talking, turned to look at her.

Graysen had moved some of his instruments off of chairs, so they all had a place to sit. She took her seat by her worktable and looked at each of them.

"It has become painfully obvious," she began, "that whatever is going on in town right now is targeting this family."

"We can't be certain of that," Madi started.

She held up a hand, "when there are too many coincidences, the fact is, they aren't coincidences."

The rest of the men nodded in agreement.

"Farlege, what is the latest on the dwargic and the woman you arrested?" She asked.

"The dwargic remains in custody until he goes before the judge. The damage he did and the lives he put in danger make his crimes substantial enough to hold him," he cleared his throat. "The woman, whose name we still don't know, was released today. She was charged with attempted breaking and entering. But it wasn't enough to hold her."

"I figured that would be the case," Tenja's shoulders sagged.

"Why do you not know her name?" Madi asked him. "Didn't you have to know it for the police report and record?"

"We know the name she gave us," Farlege explained, "but like the dwargic, I don't trust her. I don't believe it is her real name. She's trying to prevent us knowing the truth."

"And how do you know the dwargic was lying?" Graysen asked.

Farlege and Tenja looked at each other.

"He gave conflicting stories," Farlege shared. "He told me he was working alone. He told your mom that there was a group behind the attack."

They sat in silence for a minute.

"The boys and I have decided that we are not going to convocation tomorrow," Tenja told Farlege and Madifen.

Madifen's reacted to this news, "what?! You must go to convocation."

108

Hodgens shook his head, "no, we don't. We finished prep. This is just a party. It's for show."

"Pretty much the whole town will be there," Conner added.

"And we are not going to put everyone in danger again," Graysen finished.

Tenja looked at Farlege. He sat, a thoughtful look on his face, considering the three boys. Finally, he said, "that is a very grown-up decision."

"No, it's a reckless decision!" Madi spat out as he wheeled his chair away from them.

"What do you mean, Madi?" Tenja genuinely wanted to know his reasoning.

"If you aren't at the convocation then you're sitting ducks," he stated. "We can't protect you if we're there and you're here."

"I understand what you are saying," and she did. "But the boys and I talked about this at length. We won't risk our friends and others in the town. We won't use innocents as a shield."

He spun back around, "as a shield? Don't you think that is a bit dramatic?"

"Is it?" Farlege interrupted, "they are right, Madifen. The potential for casualties increases in such a public event."

"You don't care about this family like I do, Farlege. Why are you even here?"

"I'm here because Tenja asked me to be here, same as you. If you've got a problem with it, take it up with her!"

Tenja looked at the two men. Farlege was shaking with anger even though he was keeping his voice even. Madifen had wheeled up to him, toe-to-toe so to speak. She admired Farlege for not leaning over into Madi's face. Being able to stand upright made Farlege seem so much larger than Madifen. Over six feet tall, Farlege was the tallest person in the room. His brown hair was trimmed short and as the police chief, he kept his body in fighting form. If he could stand, though, Madi would match him inch for inch. He had once commented

109

that his height made being in a wheelchair even more difficult as he felt like his knees were always in the way.

Shaking her head to get in the present, she got up and stepped between them, "guys, come on. We don't have time for arguing. You're both here because you care about the boys, about me. Farlege, will you work with Conner to reinforce and enhance the boundary spells around the house?"

Stepping back he said, "of course. Conner let's go on outside," and the two left the studio.

"Do you need anything else from us?" Graysen asked and pointed at Hodgens.

"Not at the moment," she told them, and they headed out, too.

She looked at Madi and said, "I know you don't like this because you can't be in two places at once. But at the showcase I was too far away to help Hodgens. The moment when the roof shot off the auditorium and Hodgens stood there surrounded by so much danger," she breathed out a big sigh, "Madi, I've never been so frightened. They would be out of my sight at convocation. They would be too vulnerable."

He studied her for one minute, two. Then he said, "but Tenja, being here puts a target on all of you."

"And together we'll deal with that, if anything even happens," she assured him. "We don't know that anything will. By the time whoever is behind this realizes that we're not there it might be too late to switch plans."

"Or maybe they have two plans. One for you going and one for you not," he suggested.

"Why would you think that?"

"Why wouldn't I? If they really want to get to you guys, they would be prepared for any option, right?"

"Well, I guess we will see. Our decision is made, Madi. And now, between us, I'm asking that you don't tell anyone about this decision."

"But the school will need to know if the boys aren't coming. They will need to know not to read their names at convocation."

"Then you pull their name cards at the very last minute, Madi. If you want to help us, then do that for the boys."

She stared at him, watched his hazel eyes fluctuate between brown and green. He finally broke the eye contact, threw up his arms, and said, "fine, Tenja. I'll do what you ask. But I don't have to like it."

"Thank you, Madi," she patted him on the shoulder, "I know that it looks like we are the target, but I can't help but feel that this is bigger than just getting to our family."

"What do you mean?" He asked. "What else could it be about?"

"The reason Raben left us, Madi. The reason she hasn't come back to us. It has to be connected," she told him.

"What proof do you have," he leaned toward her.

Now I've got your attention, she thought.

"Nothing concrete," she shrugged, "it's just a gut feeling."

He sighed and leaned back in his chair, "well, I for one hope you're wrong."

CHAPTER 13

It was 9 o'clock when Madifen and Farlege finally left. After she closed the door behind them, she went to find the boys. They were in their bedroom talking. She walked in and showed them a piece of paper on which was written one word 'studio'. They nodded and followed her out of the room

Once they were all in the studio and the door was shut Hodgens asked, "okay, mom, what's up?"

"What's up is that now we need to finish preparing for whatever comes next," she told them.

"How do we prepare for something when we don't even know when or where it is going to happen?" Graysen asked looking at his brothers.

"I'd bet my magic that someone is coming for us tomorrow night," she responded to his question. She saw a flash of fear in all their eyes. But it was gone quickly and replaced with hot anger. Excellent, she thought to herself. That's what I was hoping to see.

Conner nodded, "all right, then. What do we need to do?"

She took a deep breath, "well, we aren't going to be sitting ducks. Conner you helped make sure of that by working with Farlege to enforce and enhance the boundary spells. I'm going to make a grocery store run to stock the fridge and cupboards in the apartment. I want each of you to think about what you hold most dear and do not want to lose. Gather those things and take them down to the apartment."

Hodgens looked at her and asked, "you don't think we're coming back to live upstairs, do you?"

She looked at the three of them, at her world, her heart, and said, "no, I don't. I think our lives are going to change dramatically tomorrow evening. I think that the reality we've lived for the last ten years is going to be shattered."

"And if it's not?" Graysen asked, "if nothing happens?"

"Then we were over prepared," she told him. "But I'd rather be over prepared than under prepared."

"Graysen, we need you to bring one instrument from each of the categories of instruments. We can't fit them all in the apartment. But we need them to keep working on the book Raben sent to us. It's a key to what is happening."

"Okay, I can do that," he agreed.

"Hodgens, we need all your texts and notes on magic. You were meticulous in your studies, and I believe that is going to come in handy."

"Got it," he acknowledged.

"What about me?" Conner asked.

"We are going to need your magic. So, you're going to keep practicing once we are settled downstairs."

"Understood," he nodded.

"I'll take care of some of my things when I get back from the store. Oh, and you should pack some clothes. Be sure to bring down some for a variety of weather. We have to be prepared for anything. Bring your leather knapsacks, too."

They all made notes on paper they found on her worktable.

"Now, we're going to move all these things tonight. But tomorrow we're going to live a normal day. Do the things we would always do."

"So, we're going to our last day of prep?" Hodgens asked.

"Yes, and I'm going to the gallery," she agreed.

"Is it possible that we won't see these people again?" Conner asked.

She looked at their faces and saw the boys whose hearts broke when their Momma Raben left them. Here she was, ten years later, about to tell them that now they were the ones who may be doing the leaving.

"Yes, it is possible that after tomorrow you may not see some of these people for a long time, if ever," she was honest.

"So now we're doing the leaving," Hodgens said sadly.

The boys all hung their heads. She tapped the table, and they looked up at her.

"You've made a tough decision to protect people that you care about. There's no shame in that, but there is sadness. We'll get through this like we've gotten through everything else in the last ten years - together."

She extended her arm, palm down, in front of her, "triplet strong," she said.

The boys placed their hands on top of hers, "triplet strong!" They shouted.

"Now go. Take care of your tasks. If something goes down tomorrow night, we only have one chance to get this right."

As the boys headed out of the studio Tenja said, "not you, Beagle Girl. I need to talk to you."

Conner shut the door behind them, leaving mother and dog to talk.

#

Upstairs the boys sat on their beds looking at each other but saying nothing. Finally, Hodgens broke the silence.

"Are either of you feeling angry about all of this?"

Conner jumped up and clamped his hand over Hodgen's mouth.

Hodgens pushed him away, "what in all that is magic are you doing?!"

"Messing around like we always do," Conner said playfully as he scribbled something in a notebook and handed it to Hodgens.

With a huff Hodgens read the words to himself - this room isn't soundproof people with magic could hear what we're saying - and he paled.

"Yeah, I'm pretty angry," Graysen jumped in, "it is silly that we have to go to prep all day tomorrow. It's convocation. We should get to sleep in and hang out with our friends."

"I agree completely," Hodgens admitted.

114

"I'm going to finish up and call it a night. It's kind of surreal that tomorrow is our last day of prep," Conner said,

"Yeah, then it's off to be adults," Graysen added.

They looked at each other one last time and then started on their task lists.

#

Tenja pulled into the grocery store parking lot. When the weather was nice, going to the grocery store or on long trips were the only times they really used the car. The town was small enough they all preferred walking places. She was thankful for it tonight, though, as being in it made her feel safer. It was strange to be out and about in a town where she'd felt so safe for her whole life, but now be completely uncertain of who she could trust.

"Just get the groceries," she said out loud.

The fridge and cupboards in the apartment were still pretty stocked up from a few weeks ago. But there were a few things that she wanted to add to the supplies, and they could use fresh milk and things. After all, she didn't know how long they would have to lie low before the situation would be resolved. And by 'lying low' she really meant finding the resolution to the situation. It was on them. She knew that much.

"Tenja! How are you feeling?"

Tenja turned to see Dahlia coming up behind her. Instinctively she turned and positioned the shopping cart between them. Then grabbed some oranges and put in the cart, acting like it was her plan all along.

"I'm good, Dahlia. Feeling one hundred percent," she replied.

"Good, good. I didn't get a chance to ask the other day. I saw the boys with you. They are really growing. What are they going to do after prep?"

"Hodgens wants to be a veterinarian. So, he'll go off to college. Conner is going into rescue services. Graysen is headed to the symphony," she was so making this up on the fly. If nothing went down tomorrow, she'd have to remember to tell Graysen and Conner what she had said.

"That is fabulous. You must be so proud!"

A truth she could state without hesitation, "I am, Dahlia. I really am."

"Well, take care, Tenja. Come by if you ever need anything," Dahlia said and turned to leave.

Tenja wanted to trust Dahlia. She wanted to trust all the people she'd trusted all her life. But the nagging at the back of her mind told her that there were enemies among them. They just haven't made themselves known yet.

She finished shopping and got home without incident. As she parked the car she thought, we're sitting ducks right now, and she jumped out of the car and ran in the house.

"Boys!? Boys where are you?" She tried to keep her voice normal. Like nothing was amiss.

"We're here mom, just finished up our stuff," Hodgens said as they came upstairs.

"Okay, grab the groceries out of the car, please," she said and ran upstairs to get a few things.

They did as they were told and once the house was locked up, she pointed to the studio. Looking confused they all entered, and she shut the door.

"As I pulled in the driveway, I realized that right now we are sitting ducks. Tomorrow, in broad daylight, I don't expect anything to happen. Tomorrow night, maybe. But point of fact is that two people know our plan. Which means they know we're preparing tonight and not paying attention to other things."

The boys looked at each other and then her. Beagle Girl growled.

"So, now you don't trust Madifen OR Farlege?" Hodgens asked.

"In all honesty, I don't know who to trust anymore," she stated. "I've lived in this town my entire life. I've trusted these people my

116

entire life. I just went grocery shopping and was watching over my shoulder the entire time."

"What do you want us to do?" Graysen asked.

"We go downstairs tonight. I held back about the apartment with both Farlege and Madi. No one knows about it except us and Raben. Everything we need is there now. It's the safest thing. No prep tomorrow. No gallery. We work on the book and jewels. We stay safe and try to solve this puzzle."

"Okay," Conner said, "we're with you."

His brothers nodded.

"Beagle Girl," Tenja knelt down to talk to the dog, "we'll go downstairs. You do what we talked about and then join us. I won't risk you. I want you with us in the apartment."

Beagle Girl aroofed and trotted out of the studio. The three of them headed for the apartment to solve a puzzle and wait for what was going to happen next.

#

Once the five of them were settled in the apartment and safe behind the magic, Tenja let out a breath that she didn't realize she'd been holding. Once again it was almost midnight. She used to be in bed by ten o'clock every night. There used to be routine in her life. For the last few weeks her routine had been broken up by episodes of chaos. Now it just felt like every moment was uncertain.

"Momma?" Graysen finally spoke.

She shook her head, "sorry, what?" She answered.

"We were just wondering what we should do now," Hodgens told her.

"Yeah, should we work on the book or something?" Conner asked.

"You all look exhausted," she admitted. "I am anxious to work on the book, but I think we all need to get some rest. We can think clearer when we're rested."

The boys all looked at each other. After a moment they stood up.

"Good night, momma," Hodgens told her as he kissed the top of her head.

"I'll be in in a few minutes," she told them, "I love you my favorite little people."

They all gave her small smiles and padded off to the bedroom. She headed into the bathroom to wash her face. As she dried her face, she studied herself in the mirror. She and Raben made a great team. They had their own strengths which offset the other's weaknesses. Raben was musical but couldn't draw a stick figure. Tenja was artistic but couldn't carry a tune. Raben was as bold as Tenja was timid, with a laugh that came from her toes. She was spontaneous and wild. Tenja liked plans and keeping things even keel. But given all of that there was one quality they both shared - strength. Paired with the fierce love they both had for the boys, no matter what they were up against, they would not go down without a fight.

She hung the hand towel on the ring and grabbed some pajamas off the shelf. As she lay in bed she listened as each boy took his turn using the restroom before bed. Once they were all settled, Beagle Girl jumped on Hodgens' bed and made herself comfortable. Her last thought before drifting off to sleep was thank you for her, Raben. She's like a guardian angel.

CHAPTER 14

"Okay, we're all settled on the plan, then?" he asked the other three. They all nodded. Standing at the end of the alley, they could just make out the gate at the back of the Araven property. He had made sure they waited until dark of night to make a move. There had been typical movement around the house during the evening, friends over, grocery store run. Then they had all settled in, been in different rooms around the house. The last person turned out a light around eleven thirty. But he had wanted to be sure they were asleep.

"It's two in the morning," she finally said, irritated, "are we going to do this or not?"

"Yes," he said, and began moving toward the gate.

"I don't know how you think we're even going to get to the house," she mumbled as she walked, "I couldn't get through her shields, and I have mad skills!"

"Because I'm not going to attack the shield. I'm going to create a doorway in the shield. As I said before, I'll only be able to hold it for ten minutes. So, you three have to be fast. If you don't make it out in ten minutes, you'll be stuck inside the boundary shield, and they will find you tomorrow."

He had told them all this at least four times but wanted to make sure they really understood.

"And there's no preference?" the little man asked, "you're sure?"

"I'm positive," he rolled his eyes. At this moment he was very thankful that the fourth and largest member of their team didn't talk. He just did what he was told, no back talk, no questions. Why couldn't they all be like him?

They stopped a few feet before the gate. He could see a nightlight in the kitchen. The car was parked in the driveway. If they did this right, they would incapacitate that dog first. Then it was just a matter of cloaking, silencing, and snatching.

He took a deep breath, closed his eyes, and with what seemed like no effort, opened a doorway in the shield. The edges of the doorway were visible white lines, making it easy to see the way through. He watched as the three opened the gate and strolled right into the yard and up to the house. Then he smiled.

"Come on!" She urged the men forward, "we don't have a lot of time here. Go, go, go!"

They ran toward the house. Touching the handle of the back door, the big man easily used his magic to bypass the locks. He opened the door slightly and the little man took out a dog whistle. They heard the dog bark inside the house.

"Damn it!" She muttered.

"Wait for it," the little man said, straining to hear. Then, there it was, the glorious sound of little paws padding across the floor. The door opened and dog slipped out. And she blasted it with magic. The hit knocked the dog across the porch. They all watched it for a moment. One breath, two, then nothing.

"Yes!" She high fived the big guy then they all headed into the house.

She held a finger up in front of her lips to indicate they needed to be quiet. Then she pointed up the stairs. As they got to the staircase the little man grabbed the newel post and gasped. Visible lightning shot through his arm. The other two watched as his eyes rolled back in his head and he fell to the floor.

"Crap," she whispered. Then she pointed from the big man to the little one and mimed a carry motion followed by pointing toward the back door. The big man simply nodded and did as she indicated, hoisting the little man over his shoulder, and heading back outside.

She continued up the stairs, being careful not to touch the rail. Once at the top of the stairs she opted for the boys' room. Sure, there were three of them in there, but they weren't trained fighters. Their momma could hold her own and would be a tougher catch.

As she stepped into the doorway of the boys' bedroom, she caught the faint sound of snoring and saw them all lying in their beds. Closest one to the door she thought to herself. Get it done. She pulled the spelled rag from her pocket and moved stealthily toward the closest bed. Leaning over, she put the rag close the boy's head with the intent of covering his mouth. But when she pressed down her hand landed on the pillow.

"What the..." she began to say as she pulled her hand back. She could see the boys, the blankets over their sleeping bodies. She could hear snoring. Aggravated she reached for the boy again, attempting to put her hand on his shoulder. But the blanket just deflated, and her hand was on the bed.

Angry, she flipped on the light...and she was the only person in the room. She ran to the other bedroom and flipped on the light. No one.

"Ahhhhh!" She screamed and ran toward the stairs. As she got to the top, she felt something at her feet, but it was too late. She was going too fast. The momentum was propelling her. She rolled and bounced down the stairs like a rubber ball, arms and legs flailing, trying for purchase, trying to stop the fall.

At the bottom she rolled to her hands and knees. So much pain. She spat blood on the floor. She had to get out. How long have I been in here? She thought to herself. Through cries of pain, she forced herself to stand up and make her way to the back door. As she made her way across the yard, she saw the three men on the other side of the boundary.

"They knew we were coming," she yelled, "that something was coming." She stifled a sob as the pain shot through her. Two strides away from the doorway she watched in horror as it disappeared.

"What are you doing?" She cried out. "Let me out of here!"

"Sorry," he shrugged, "I can't hold the doorway any longer."

"You said ten minutes! It hasn't been ten minutes!" She demanded.

"Oh, it's been long enough," he told her. "Come on, gentlemen. We have to come up with a new plan."

"No!" She dropped to her knees, "please, please, don't leave me." Then she watched as the three men left her there to face the consequences. Unknown consequences.

After a few minutes of sobbing, she struggled to her feet.

"Fine. If this is how it is going down, then I'm going out with a bang," and she watched as the roof of the house went up in flames.

#

As if an alarm went off in her head, Tenja's eyes flew open. She looked at the clock, 2am. She sat up and saw that Conner and Beagle Girl were also awake. That told her what she needed to know. She held one finger up in front of her mouth to indicate they should be quiet and then pointed to the bedroom door. The three of them quietly got up and left the room.

Once they were in the living room Conner said, "someone breached the boundary."

"I know. I could feel it," she agreed.

Beagle Girl nodded but then sat, seemingly unconcerned, on the sofa.

"What do we do?" Conner asked Tenja.

"Nothing. We stay put. Stay safe."

"And you're sure we're safe?"

"I am, without a doubt. I also know that there is a chance whoever has breached the boundary is not safe."

"What do you mean?" Conner said as he, too, took a seat on the couch.

Tenja dropped into a chair and said, "Beagle Girl and I made a bit of a defensive plan. If an intruder gets into the house," she paused, "let's just say there are some presents waiting."

"But there's no way for us to know what is going on up there. What if they make their way down here? If they breached the boundary, can't they get through the spells protecting us here, too?"

"I know it's hard to understand," she said, "but no. What protects us down here isn't a basic boundary spell. It isn't even an advanced boundary spell. Its multiple spells woven together, some of which Raben created. So, there's no way to even detect us here, which is the first thing someone would need to do."

Conner relaxed a bit, "okay. You're right, I don't understand it all. But I trust you."

Beagle Girl jumped off the couch and raised an ear, straining to listen. Then she let out a howl that sounded just like a fire truck.

Tenja sagged, "well crap."

"What? What is it?" Conner worried.

"If I had to guess, I'd bet that the roof of our house must be on fire," she told him.

He jumped up, "what?! Shouldn't we get out of here?!"

"Sit down," she almost laughed, "Raben ensured that nothing below the roof of the house could catch flame."

Conner gaped at her for a minute. Then he sat down, nothing to say. Beagle Girl's howl brought Graysen and Hodgens stumbling from the bedroom.

Rubbing his eyes Hodgens said, "what is going on?"

Conner responded, "someone breached the property boundary and now momma thinks the roof of our house is on fire."

That brought Graysen and Hodgens to a full state of awareness.

"What?!" They exclaimed at the same time.

"Why are you just sitting there!?" Hodgens asked her.

"Because we are still safe. The spells and protections Raben put into this house are beyond anything I can explain. But I can tell you that nothing below the roof will burn. I can also tell you that no one can detect us here. There is no safer place in Easpach than right where we are."

"So, what do we do now?" Graysen tossed out.

"Anyone want some tea?" She asked as she got up and headed toward the kitchen.

After they all finished a cup of decaf tea, she ushered them back to bed.

"There is nothing we can do right now. And we really should get some rest. I want to try to stay on a daytime/nighttime schedule. It would be easy to get our daily rhythms out of whack down here."

"When will we see daylight again?" Hodgens asked as they all crawled into bed.

"I'll think about how we can do that safely," she told him. "For now, everyone get some sleep."

Tenja looked at the clock. An hour had passed. It felt like the first of many hours that would chain together into this experience they were all having. It's not an adventure, she thought to herself, I look forward to those. This is a nightmare. She drifted off to sleep wondering when they would all wake up from it.

#

Farlege pulled into the alley and ran to the back of the Araven property. His brain registered two things: the roof engulfed in flames and the woman lying in the yard close to the boundary.

Well hell! he thought to himself.

He quickly placed a magical confinement around the woman and then dropped the boundary around the property so the fire fighters could extinguish the flames. He watched as the roof burned but the flames failed to ignite the rest of the house. If it wasn't such a frightful sight, he'd think it was fascinating. He heard someone walking up to him.

"Hey captain," Jespen said, "what brings you hear?"

"The fire captain called, said they had a house on fire, and they couldn't get through the boundary to put it out," he responded still watching the firemen work.

"How did they get through?" Jespen nodded to the house.

124

"I brought down the barrier. Tenja had asked me to enforce the spells after that woman tried to break in the other night. So, I was able to bring it down."

"Make sense," Jespen said thoughtfully. Then he gestured toward the woman, "she still alive?"

"I have no idea and don't really care," Farlege admitted.

"How did she get through your boundaries? I didn't think there was anyone in town who could get through a boundary that you construct."

"I don't know. But you can bet that I'm going to find out!"

"Have you seen the family? No one has come out of the house that I've seen," Jespen expressed concern.

"No, but now that the fire's out I'm going in," Farlege said as he took off toward the house, "take care of that," he said in disgust and pointed at the woman on his way by her.

"Captain," the fire chief acknowledged Farlege.

"I want to go in," Farlege said.

"Go ahead. It's completely safe. There is no structural damage, no smoke, nothing."

That stopped Farlege in his tracks, "what do you mean?"

"I mean, from the inside, it looks like nothing happened. It's the darnedest thing. I've seen spells to protect from fire before, Farlege, but I've never seen anything as extensive as this. Look at the roof," he pointed up.

Farlege did as he was told and stumbled back a step, "what in all that is magic!" He whispered.

"Right? We all saw the flames. We all smelled the wood burning. But there isn't a single charred shingle on that roof. Not one spot that looks burnt on the wood in the attic. Whoever spelled this house is powerful and knows spells that are not common knowledge," the fire chief said in awe.

Farlege considered this and thought of both Tenja and Raben. I know Tenja's secret...don't I? He thought to himself. But then he considered Raben. What did he really know about her?

"You okay, Captain?" The fire chief asked.

Shaking his head Farlege said, "yeah, yeah. Just thinking." Gesturing toward the house he asked, "did you find anyone inside? It's the middle of the night."

"Not a soul," the fire chief commented. "The car's in the driveway. The night lights are on. Everything inside looks like a family should be bunking there tonight. I'm tellin' ya, Farlege," he said scratching his chin, "this whole thing is very odd."

CHAPTER 15

Farlege jolted awake at the sound of someone banging on his front door. He threw his legs over the side of the bed, grabbed some nearby shorts, and wriggled into them as he ran to the door. Tenja? He thought to himself.

As he threw open the door he was greeted with, "where are they, Farlege!?" and he looked down to see Madifen angrily staring up at him.

Although anyone could knock on his front door, no one could get through the boundary spell without his permission. Knowing this, he was half tempted to slam the door in Madifen's face and go back to bed. But instead he sighed, released the spell at the door, and gestured for Madifen to enter.

Madifen rolled through the doorway and turned, "tell me where they are, Farlege!"

Farlege considered the man. Even in the chair he would be a formidable opponent, his mahogany skin rippling over his muscles. The man's upper body strength would definitely match his. Magic to magic, though, Farlege wasn't sure who would win.

"Stop yelling and come in," Farlege said rubbing his face. "Do you want something to drink?" He asked his guest as they headed toward the kitchen.

"No, I want to know where they are," Madifen said in a barely controlled tone.

Farlege grabbed a bottle of water from the fridge and moved a chair at the table for Madifen. Then he sat down and looked at the man.

"The fact is, Madifen, I have no idea."

"I don't believe you," Madifen crossed his arms.

Farlege shrugged, "well, that's up to you. But I was really hoping that the person banging on the door at," he looked at the clock on the stove, "five in the morning, was Tenja."

"Damnit!" Madifen banged a fist on the table.

The two men sat in silence, staring at each other for a long minute.

"What do you want from me, Madifen?" Farlege asked.

Madifen's shoulders sagged, "I don't know. I really thought you would know where they were. I was hoping they were here. Safe."

"Yeah," Farlege agreed, "wouldn't that be nice."

"Can you tell me anything?" Madifen asked.

Farlege stared at the man sitting at his kitchen table. They were friends, well that might be a stretch. They had always been civil to each other. Never had a beef with each other. But Tenja had made it clear that she was not trusting Madifen with any new information.

Farlege got up and went to the sliding doors that led to the deck. Staring out at the night turning to morning he finally said, "No, Madi. There is nothing I can tell you."

"Why not?"

"Would saying it is an ongoing investigation get you to leave my house?" Farlege turned and looked at Madi.

"Yeah, no. That's not good enough. Farlege we both care about Tenja and the boys. We can help them better if we work together," Madifen told him.

But do you want to help them? Farlege thought to himself. He had to decide, in that moment, what his gut was telling him about Madifen. There were a lot of firefighters at Tenja's house. They all saw what happened. Rumors and facts would start to spread through town soon, if they weren't already. So, he decided to tell Madifen what he'd soon find out from someone else anyway.

"I can tell you what the fire chief told me. But this stays between us, Madifen. If this gets out there could be a whole lot of trouble."

"You have my word. I won't tell anyone," Madifen put his hand over his heart.

"There is old magic spelling the Araven house, Madifen. Like, really old," Farlege shared.

"What do you mean?"

"I mean, the fire chief, in all of his years as a fire fighter, has never seen magic like what protects that house. We all saw the roof in flames. We smelled the word burning. Saw the smoke. But when the firefighters put out the fire there was no damage," Farlege explained.

"What do you mean no damage?" Madifen asked.

"Just that, Madifen. None. The roof was completely intact both inside and out. The house was like nothing had happened. There was no fire damage. No smoke damages. No water damages. The house was pristine."

Madifen's mouth hung open, "I think I'll take that drink now," he said. "Do you have anything strong?"

Farlege set a bottle of brandy and two shot glasses on the table. After each man had knocked back two shots Madifen finally said, "so what are we going to do now?"

"I'm going to do my job," Farlege responded.

"How can I help?" Madifen asked as he grabbed the brandy and poured the men another shot.

#

Tenja was sitting at the kitchen table making some notes in her journal when she heard raised voices. Then she watched as Hodgens came falling through the doorway and landed on the kitchen floor.

"What is going on?" She asked.

Hodgens jumped and ran back toward the bathroom, yelling at Conner who had apparently locked himself in the bathroom. She got up from the table and ran into the hallway just in time to see the bathroom door come floating toward her.

"Hodgens!" She yelled.

The door fell to the ground.

"What in all that is magic is going on here!?" She exclaimed.

Conner and Hodgens looked at each other. Then at her.

She crossed her arms and demanded, "explanation. Now"

Then the two boys started talking at the same time and she couldn't make out a single word that either of them was saying. When she held up her hand the talking stopped.

"You," she pointed at Conner, "to the kitchen."

Then she pointed at Hodgens, "and you, put that door back on its hinges and get your butt into the kitchen, too."

Graysen was sitting at the kitchen table eating cereal like nothing was going on.

Once everyone was seated Tenja said, "Hodgens, explain."

"I had just got up from bed and was headed to the bathroom. Conner knew it. He appeared in the hallway in front of me to beat me in there. When I tried to stop him, he threw me into the kitchen!"

"Yeah, but then you took the door off the bathroom! You know you're not supposed to do stuff like that with your magic," Conner retorted.

"Enough!" Tenja raised her voice slightly to get everyone's attention. "We have no idea how long we'll be living in this apartment. We barely all fit, but we're safe. I need you guys to try to get along."

Hodgens and Conner looked at each other.

"Sorry, momma," they said at the same time, hanging their heads.

"Get some breakfast and we'll talk about the day," Tenja said after giving them a moment to feel bad about what had transpired.

They grabbed something to eat and joined her and Graysen at the table.

After a few minutes of shoveling cereal in his mouth Conner finally broke the silence, "so, what is the plan for today?"

"Well, there are some things that I need to explain to you. So, I'll do that first. Then I need to show you something as part of a plan," she told them.

"Sounds intriguing," Hodgens added.

She laughed and said, "the first thing I want to tell you about is a traversable." And she told them everything she knew about traversables. While she didn't know how one was made, she knew how to use them and, obviously, how to break them.

"So, you've found two of them near town?" Graysen asked.

"Yes, one was close to the school. I broke that one from this side so nothing and no one can get through it."

"But can't it just be fixed?" Hodgens asked.

She nodded, "sometimes they can be fixed but there are certain conditions. One, a traversable can only be fixed on the side of the journey where it was broken. And two, the same magic that broke it has to fix it," she explained.

"What about the second one?" Conner this time.

"That one Farlege and I deactivated by removing the magical rubies from their casings," she told them. "And this is where the plan comes in."

They all looked at her expectantly.

"Farlege thought it was a good idea for each of us to keep two rubies. That way no one could get to one of us and have all the rubies to activate the traversable. At the time I thought it was a good idea but now I wish I had just taken them."

"Because you don't trust Farlege anymore?" Hodgens asked.

"Because I don't know who to trust anymore," she stated.

He nodded, "okay, so how are we going to get the rubies?"

She explained that she and Farlege had agreed to meet on Mondays to activate the traversable in case Raben tried to send anymore messages through. Then she said, "so, Conner and I are going to be there waiting for him."

Conner squeaked, "what? Why me?"

"Because you are going to travel the two of us there," she told him.

He choked on his milk. "I'm going to do what? But you said I shouldn't try to do that!"

"We are going to spend the next three days practicing your magic. As quickly as you picked up those boundary spells and moving objects, I'm certain we can make this happen," she reassured him.

Hodgens and Graysen looked at each other and then at her, fear in their eyes.

"But mom," Hodgens said quietly, "what will we do if something happens to you?"

She patted his arm, "nothing bad is going to happen by doing this. I can feel it in my gut. But I will promise you this, if it doesn't seem like Conner's able to do it by Monday, we'll put it off for a week and keep practicing. Does that sound good?"

The boys all nodded.

"One thing," Conner tapped on the table, "I've only ever traveled to places that I've seen before. I don't know where this traversable is."

"I've got that covered," she told him. "Tonight, when everyone is at the commencement we will go there so you can memorize it."

"How are we going to do that?" He asked.

"Magic, of course," she told them with a wink. "Your old mom's got a few more tricks up her sleeve."

Beagle Girl aroofed and trotted around the kitchen table.

"Yes, you can go with us tonight. We'll all go. But you are not going on Monday," Tenja said. "I want you to stay here with Hodgens and Graysen while we're gone."

This time the dog barked, like really barked, at Tenja. They all looked at the dog.

"Mom, I think she knows something," Hodgens finally said.

"Or senses something," Graysen corrected.

She aroofed at Graysen.

"You're sure about this?" Tenja asked.

Beagle Girl let out one more bark.

Tenja sighed, "okay but this will be tricky. Conner will have to learn to travel all three of us."

Beagle Girl shook her head and then left them all in shock when she disappeared. Two breaths later she reappeared in the doorway to the living room.

"Have you been able to do that all along?" Hodgens asked her.

The dog shook her head no, again.

"An absorber?" Tenja whispered, dumbfounded by the thought. Her words were barely loud enough for the boys to know she had said something.

"What, mom?" Hodgens asked.

Tenja motioned for the dog to come to her. Beagle Girl happily trotted to Tenja and levitated so they were eye to eye.

"Beagle Girl, are you an absorber?" Tenja asked.

The dog aroofed, wagged her tail and spun in a circle. Then she dropped back to the floor and headed toward her water bowl like nothing out of the ordinary had just happened.

"Mom," Hodgens began, "what is an absorber?"

"An absorber is someone, or in this case a creature, who can absorb some of the magic of a person or creature with whom they come in contact," Tenja explained.

"So that's why she could travel?" Conner asked. "She has absorbed some of my power?"

"Exactly," Tenja agreed.

"I've never heard of that," Graysen chimed in.

"It's really, really rare," Tenja told them. "I've only known of them. I've never known anyone who had the power."

"How does that change the plan?" Conner asked.

"It doesn't, really," Tenja thought about it. "She will travel herself while you take me."

"What is the point of meeting Farlege? Are you going to activate the traversable?" Graysen asked.

"No. I just want to get the rubies from him," Tenja said. "I want to have all of them in case we need that traversable."

"What do you mean in case we need it?" Hodgens asked.

"If things go really wrong in Easpach, we're going through it," she told them.

They all stared at her, their mouths hanging open.

"But you don't even know where it goes!" Graysen exclaimed.

"True, but if it is even close to Draiocht then there is magic. The deeper the well we draw from, the stronger we become," she explained.

They were quiet for a moment.

"Well that is just plain frightening," Conner finally said.

"How so?" She asked.

"Because if we, with our good will, are stronger, then our enemies are stronger, too," he looked at them all.

Tenja nodded, "that's true. But I have to believe we'd have allies if we did cross through."

"What do we do for the rest of the day?" Hodgens asked.

"Conner, I want you to practice moving objects made of different matter. Move liquid and solid. We don't really have a gas you can practice with, so you'll have to start with those. Start small and then move larger objects as you feel confident. Move combinations of objects, like a glass with water in it. I'm a combination of different matters so the more mixing of matter you can do the closer you will get to moving me," she explained.

He nodded.

"Hodgens, I'd like you to help Conner. You sit in the bedroom. Conner move the objects to the bedroom. That way Hodgens can be there to manage any mess that might occur," she laughed.

"Sure thing," Hodgens said as he stood up. "Just give me a heads up when you're sending something my way, brother," he told Conner and headed toward the bedroom.

"Graysen let's go work on the jewels some more," she said as she rose.

CHAPTER 16

"Okay," Tenja told the boys and dog, "everyone should be at the commencement now. So, let's go to the traversable and get back here where it's safe."

Beagle Girl aroofed and headed toward the bedroom.

"Why is she going into the bedroom?" Hodgens asked.

"That's where I'm going to open the portal," she told them. They all just looked at her perplexed.

She led them into the bedroom and opened the closet door. Then she touched each of the four corners of the doorway and said dragon traversable three times. The boys let out a collective gasp when the closet disappeared, and they were looking at the park. Beagle Girl pranced through the portal and into the park. Then she turned back and aroofed for them to follow.

Tenja stepped through and motioned for the boys to join her. They looked at each other, shrugged and walked through. Beagle Girl led them to the traversable.

"I don't see anything," Hodgens said as he stopped beside Beagle Girl.

"That's because it is deactivated," Tenja told them all. "See the dragon head here," she pointed down, "and there," she pointed to the second one. "If I were to place the rubies in the eyes of the dragons it would activate the traversable. But I would need all four."

"I see," Graysen rubbed his chin, pondering her words and looking at the dragons.

Conner leaned down and touched one, "that's interesting. They look like rough stone but feel really smooth."

Intrigued, the other boys touched one, too. When Conner stood up Tenja said, "okay, Conner, I want you to look around and memorize this place. I would like for us to travel to this spot exactly," she said moving about twenty-five feet away from the traversable.

He followed and stood beside her. She turned them so they were facing the traversable.

"I'll be on your right. I need to be able to use my bow and arrow. So I need space for my right arm to draw my bow."

"Why will you be using your bow and arrow?" He asked.

"I'll have it up in case I need it to protect us. Hopefully I won't."

"Got it," he nodded.

"Okay, let me know when you've got the memory stored and we'll head home," she told him.

Conner stood for a few minutes taking in the sights, sounds, and smells around him. When he finally said, "okay, I'm good. I can travel back here," Tenja was the one to nod.

"Good. Let's all head back home," she said.

Once again Beagle Girl led the way through the portal. Tenja sent the boys through next, choosing to bring up the rear for safety's sake. As she turned toward the portal the hair on the back of her neck stood up. It was a feeling of being watched. There and gone. She turned around to take one last look at the forest. She couldn't detect anything. Quickly she ducked into the portal and closed it. When the closet returned, she let out a sigh of relief.

"Everything okay, momma?" Conner asked, concerned.

"Yeah, I just had a weird feeling," she patted his arm, "we're okay."

"So, why can't you just use a portal on Monday like you did today?" Hodgens asked.

"Because, as you saw, a portal allows two-way travel. We would be able to get into the forest, and other people would be able to go back through to here. I won't risk that."

"That makes sense. So, what's the rest of the plan?" Graysen asked.

Tenja led them to the kitchen and took a seat at the table.

"I don't expect Farlege to show up at the traversable until after 9am. He's not a morning person and while we didn't set an exact time, I expect if we're there by 8:30 we will beat him and can be cloaked."

"What do you mean, cloaked?" Hodgens asked.

"I'm going to use a cloaking spell," she told them, "Farlege won't be able to see or sense us as long as I have it up."

Graysen's looked shocked, "you can do an invisibility spell?!"

"It's not really an invisibility spell," she explained, "it's more like a refracting spell. It refracts the light, sound, and smells away from us." She thought for a moment, "the way it was explained to me was that it's like bending light, so it goes in a different direction."

"How do you know how to do all of these spells?" Hodgens asked.

"When I came into my full power at eighteen my parents felt it was important that I know them to protect myself," she said.

"Why did they think you needed to protect yourself?" Conner asked.

She looked at them. She was torn about explaining her magic to them. On one hand it would be nice for them to know the whole story. On the other hand, it would increase the danger to them. The second thought was stronger and won the argument for continued secrecy.

"I really, really wish I could tell you," she said in all honesty, "but there are some things that will put you in more danger simply because you know them. I promise that one day I will tell you everything. But for now, I just need you to trust me. I have to keep this one secret," she pleaded with them for understanding.

All three of them just looked at her. Then at each other.

"We have no reason not to trust you, momma," Hodgens finally said. His brothers nodded in agreement.

She let out a sigh of relief, "thank you. Now, Monday," she changed the subject. "My hope is that Farlege will hand over the rubies without much fuss."

"Do you really think he will?" Graysen asked.

"Well, when I drop the cloaking spell, I'm going to have an arrow nocked and pointed at his heart. So yeah, I think there's a high probability he'll give them to us," she stated.

"You're what?!" Conner exclaimed.

"We won't have time for a debate after I drop the spell," she looked at Conner. "We need to get the rubies and get out as fast as possible. I don't want to risk any of us any longer than I have to."

She watched as Conner considered her words, "okay," he finally said, nodding.

With that agreed Tenja said, "we need a break from all of this. Why don't I make some kettle corn and we can play a game to relax before bed?"

"That sounds great," Graysen said.

"Yeah, I could use a break from practicing magic for a bit," Conner said.

"I'd love to beat you all in a game of Catan!" Hodgens added as they all started to clear the table and make room for a normal family evening.

#

Farlege woke on Saturday morning to the sound of silence. Nothing had happened the night before. The commencement went off without a hitch. There were no fires. No break ins. He actually slept all night without interruption. When he rolled over to check the time, he was shocked to see the clock display 10:21am. He hadn't slept that late since…heck he couldn't remember the last time he'd slept that late.

He sat up, swung his legs over the side of the bed and rubbed his face. He had one plan for the day. But he needed a shower, breakfast, and coffee before he could even consider fulfilling that plan.

As he was just finishing off his pancakes, Madifen rolled up to his table.

"Do you know anything more?" Madifen asked Farlege.

"About what?" Farlege asked after a swig of coffee.

"About Tenja? The boys? Anything?" He whispered.

"No, Madi. I haven't learned anything new in the last twenty-four hours," Farlege said with a sigh.

"This is frustrating," Madifen growled.

"I agree. But, at this point all I can do is keep doing my job," Farlege told him.

"You don't look suited up to do your job today," Madifen said, crossing his arms. "Are you actually taking the day off when Tenja and the boys are still missing?"

Farlege sighed and sat down his coffee mug, "The uniform doesn't make me a cop, Madi. Nor do I have to be in said uniform to do cop work."

"They could be kidnapped! Someone could be torturing them!"

Customers were staring at them now.

"Madifen," Farlege said, lowering his voice, "we'll find them. But you know as well as I do, if they are missing because Tenja wants them to be, we won't find them until she wants them to be found."

"We'll see about that," Madifen spat out. "People were whispering last night. Speculating about where they'd gone. They think Hodgens did the damage to the school. That Tenja created the painting at the gallery."

Farlege sat back in his chair. Tapping his knife on the table he looked at Madifen and asked, "now who would have given them those ideas?"

#

Farlege put his car in park and looked up at the sprawling building. I hate this place. He thought to himself. He got out of the car and walked up the sidewalk. The sign on the door read Must be cleared for entrance". He pushed the buzzer and waited for someone to answer.

"Name please," a voice said.

"Captain Farlege," he responded. The door opened and the antiseptic smell of a hospital wafted out. He gagged a bit and walked into the long hallway. At the end was a glass window and he saw

Althea there waiting to verify his identity. He gave a small wave and walked toward her.

"Hi Althea," he said as he showed his badge.

"Hi Captain," she replied as she slid the sign in sheet across the counter. "Who are you here to see today?"

"The woman who was arrested for the incident at the Araven house," he told her. He heard the door release buzz and pulled it open.

"Okay, let me get her into a room for you. You wait here," she instructed.

He checked his watch again. It was had been about ten minutes since Althea left to secure the patient. Another five passed before she came back.

"She's ready in room 4. Sorry it took so long. She really doesn't want visitors," Althea apologized.

"It's no problem," he told her and headed down the hall.

Room 4 was one of the larger visitor rooms. It was also the one with the strongest magical protections. Between those shields and her magic absorbing bracelets Farlege was not worried about his safety. He'd been in the room before, so he knew the code. He punched it in, swung open the door and found the woman handcuffed to the table. She looked up at him and laughed.

He sat down and stared across the table at her. Once she had finished laughing, he said, "what is so funny?"

She tilted her head and looked him in the eye, "how did you pull off getting a cop's uniform?" She finally asked.

Confused, he furrowed his brow and replied, "well, they typically give you one when you are hired as a police officer."

"Wait, when did they hire you?"

Still confused he said, "over fifteen years ago."

Now she studied him. She looked at his hair, his eyes, his hands. She even looked under the table to see his legs and feet.

"So, what's the plan? How are you getting me out of here?" She asked him.

Now he laughed, "and why would I do that?"

"Stop playing with me!" She screamed and kicked the table.

Calmly he said, "I think you have me confused with someone else."

He watched as his statement took her breath away. She physically looked like a deflating balloon.

"I don't understand," she murmured, "you look just like him."

"Like who?" He really wanted to know.

She didn't answer.

"What's your name?" He asked.

Silence.

"Okay, let me tell you what I know about you," he started. "You came through the traversable close to the school. Once you were here you tried to break through the shields at a house in town but were unsuccessful. After being released you joined up with some people to try it again."

"I work alone," she muttered.

"Lie number one," he said. "It was a male that made the doorway in the shield at the house."

She eyed him suspiciously, "how do you know that?"

"They were my shields," he stated as a matter of fact. "Shall I continue?"

She shrugged.

"So this man got you past the shields. But something went wrong. Either his doorway through the shield didn't hold," he saw the flicker in her eyes, "or he closed you in on purpose," he drew out. He saw the second the truth registered in her eyes.

"You're the scapegoat!" He told her.

"I am not!" She exploded. "They're coming for me, just you wait and see!"

"They?" He inquired. She shrunk again.

"No one's coming for you. If they were, they would have done it before you got in here. You're ours now," he told her.

"Praelox belongs to no one!" She erupted again.

"Praelox? Is that your name?" He asked.

She looked away. He spent another twenty minutes trying to get more information out of her. Then the nurse came in and said it was time for her medication.

As he stood, he said, "we'll talk again Praelox. I'll be back in a few days when you realize no one is coming for you."

CHAPTER 17

Farlege sat at his desk in the police station looking over pictures of the paintings placed in the gallery during the break in. James had reported that nothing was taken or even broken. All of the artifacts were treated with care when they were moved out of the way.

"That should tell me something," he said as he made a note in his case book. He wished that he knew where Tenja was, that he could talk to her about all of it. There were things he just couldn't piece together. But it was Monday and...

"Oh crap, it's Monday!" He piled up the pictures and grabbed the jump drive. He shoved it all into his leather satchel and headed out the door.

"Hey Beth, I have to run an errand. Then I'm going to the hospital to talk to the woman who was found at the Araven house. You can reach me on the radio if you need me," he gave her a small wave.

"See you later!" She replied in a cheery voice.

#

The weekend had passed quickly. He had spent most of Saturday at the gallery. He talked to staff, inspected the space, and looked at the security footage. Whoever had broken in either had help with the technology or was tech savvy. That in itself was a clue because few businesses in town used security technology. Tenja's gallery had a sterling reputation because of that security. She had never had anyone even try to break in.

Farlege pulled into the lot at the park. It was empty. He had half expected to see Tenja's car parked there and her waiting for him. He threw his satchel over his shoulder and headed into the woods. Finding the traversable again was easier than he thought it would be. Again, he was hoping he would find Tenja waiting for him. Again, he was disappointed. He looked at his watch; 9:30am. Taking out his water bottle he decided to wait for thirty minutes.

As he waited, he applied his detective skills to the area. He didn't know what he was looking for exactly. Something, anything, that was different from the first time he had been here with Tenja. He was bent down looking at one of the dragons when he heard a soft whistle. Slowly he stood and turned around. At first there was nothing there and he thought he had imagined the sound. Then, suddenly, Tenja appeared.

"Tenja!" He exclaimed. "I'm so happy —" he broke off when he realized she had an arrow aimed straight at his heart.

"Don't move, Farlege," she said in a low but firm voice.

"Tenja, I don't understand," he said holding his hands up as if in surrender.

"Where are the rubies?" She asked.

"In a leather pouch in my pocket," he replied, "I keep them with me all the time so no one can get to them."

"Take them out…slowly, and toss them over to me," she instructed.

He did as she said without taking his eyes off hers. When the bag hit the ground Conner appeared beside her and picked them up.

Farlege gasped. How had they both managed to be behind him, cloaked, and he didn't know they were there?

"Tenja, again, I don't understand. We're friends," he pleaded.

"I don't know who our friends are anymore," she told him. "There are too many coincidences. And as I've said before, when there start to be too many of them, they aren't coincidences at all."

"What are you talking about?" He asked.

"How did someone get through the boundary, Farlege? Knowing what you are, I have to wonder how that happened," she pulled the arrow back a little further.

He glanced at the arrow and back at her face, "whoa there. You know I'm shielded."

144

"And you don't know what my arrow can do," she tipped her head slightly, "wager a bet? My arrow against your shield?"

"Momma?" Conner said in a concerned voice.

Farlege paled, "no, I have no desire to bet against you, Tenja. I'm not an idiot. Just tell me what you want."

"I want to know how someone got through the boundary."

"I don't know, Tenja. I'm still working that out," he said.

"Wait, how do you know about that? You weren't at the house," he said slowly.

"I didn't have to be there to feel someone breach the boundary spell. I changed my magic in the spell and added a notification."

She looked at him and they all stood silently while the minutes passed.

"Momma," Conner whispered, "we've got the rubies. Let's get out of here."

"Do you know anything helpful?" She asked Farlege.

"I have things in my satchel for you. It's a jump drive of information and pictures of the paintings from the gallery. I thought, if you were here, we could talk about them. Work on the case together."

"The boys and I will work on the case alone," she retorted, "we've had enough help. Toss the satchel to Conner," she nodded to her right.

Before the humans could react, Beagle Girl revealed herself and jumped chest high in front of Conner. She let out a howl of pain and Tenja realized that she'd been struck by an arrow. As Conner reached out and grabbed the dog Tenja pivoted and released her arrow in the direction the other originated.

As Tenja reached back to her quiver she saw the woman who had shot the first arrow. And she gasped.

"Go, Conner! Go! Go! Go!" She yelled. The last thing she saw before they disappeared was her own arrow hit Farlege squarely in the center of his chest.

#

Hodgens and Graysen jumped up when Tenja and Conner appeared in the living room. They reeled back when Tenja started shouting orders.

"Hodgens, grab a bath towel! Graysen, grab the first aid kit!" She yelled as she stripped off her quiver and dropped all of her gear to the floor.

"Spread the towel on the couch and then lay Beagle Girl on it," she told them as she grabbed a medium sized box out of her trunk. The dog's eyes were glassy, and her breathing was labored.

Damn it! Damn it! She yelled in her head. Why did I hesitate? We should have gone when Conner said to go.

"What the hell happened?" Hodgens asked as he spread the towel on the couch. He watched as Conner gently laid the dog down and stepped back.

"She saved my life," Conner whispered in awe.

"Quiet!" Tenja told them. "Be quiet or go to the bedroom until I tell you to come out."

The boys backed up and silently watched as Tenja worked.

"Oh sweet girl," Tenja whispered. The dog whined in response. "I've got you. I'll take care of you. First, we have to get this arrow out. Are you ready?" Another whine.

Fortunately, the dog had taken the arrow in her shoulder. So, no internal organs were struck. But, what was on the arrow was the concern. Tenja shielded her hands then placed one hand on the dogs shoulder, with her thumb around the arrow.

"Okay, girl. One, two, three and then I'm going to pull it out," Tenja told her.

As the arrow came out the dog let out a shrill cry. Tenja placed a shield around the entire arrow.

"Conner, shield your hands and take this. Lay it on the tile floor in the kitchen," she instructed without taking her eyes off Beagle Girl. He did as he was told without uttering a word.

146

Tenja watched as the dog's breathing evened out. Then she turned to the box she'd retrieved form her trunk. Unlocking the magic that secured it, she opened the top to reveal nine vials with various substances and six empty vials. She selected one and removed the dropper. The blue liquid inside the dropper almost sparkled. Then she took an empty vial from the box.

Turning back to Beagle Girl she said, "three drops and the worst will be over." Then she squeezed the dropper three times and watched as the blue liquid slid into the wound made by the arrow. Quickly she laid the dropper on the towel and uncorked the empty vial. Holding the vial upside down over the wound she watched as purple smoke floated out of the wound and into the vial. Once the vial was full the smoke stopped coming from the wound. Tenja corked the vial and set it back in the box. She put the dropper back in its original vial and resealed the magic lock on the box.

Then she let out a big sigh. She gently ran her hand down the dog's back and said, "okay, girl. Now we bandage that wound." And with speed and efficiency she used the medical kit to clean the arrow wound and bandage it.

"Hodgens," she said as she stood, "she needs water, and to rest. Carry her to your bed. She'll rest easiest there."

With those instructions given Tenja hurried to the bathroom and closed the door. She stripped as fast as she could get out of the clothes, turned the shower on as hot as she could stand, and climbed in. As the water flowed over her, tears streamed down her face.

#

She didn't know how long she'd been in the shower when the tears finally subsided. Pull it together she thought to herself. The boys need you. So, she finished up and headed out to deal with the aftermath.

As she walked by the bedroom, she stuck her head in to check on Beagle Girl. She was resting peacefully in Hodgens' bed - with Hodgens. When he saw her, he got up and headed out.

"How's she doing?" Tenja asked quietly.

Hodgens shrugged, "okay, I guess. She drank some water and has been sleeping."

"Good," she said and nodded, "that's good."

"What happened? Conner won't tell us anything," he asked.

"Come on," she said. "I need some tea. Then we'll all sit down and talk."

Once she had her tea they all moved to the living room. They had taken care of the towel and the regular medical kit. But she saw her box sitting right where she had left it.

Conner shrugged when he saw her look at it, "we didn't know if we should touch it."

"It's fine," she told him as she picked it up and put it on the coffee table.

After a moment's silence Hodgens finally said, "are you two going to tell us what happened?"

Tenja and Conner looked at each other. Then Tenja spoke, "everything was going as planned. Farlege was there. He had brought the rubies and Conner has those now."

"He just gave them to you?" Graysen asked.

"After she basically challenged him to a duel," Conner let out a small laugh and told them about the threat of Tenja's arrow against Farlege's shield.

"Could your arrow really have broken through Farlege's shield?" Hodgens asked.

Tenja looked at her boys, "honestly, I don't know. The spell on my arrows was passed down to me. I was told that it had been in my family for many generations. So, maybe?" She shrugged.

"Would you have really fired an arrow at him?" Graysen asked.

"If I felt he was threatening your brother or me? Absolutely. Without a second thought," she stated as a matter of fact.

Conner looked at the floor. Tenja knew that move.

"What Conner?"

"Well, it's just..." he started.

"Just what?" She pressed him.

"Right before I got us out of there I saw an arrow strike Farlege in the chest. One of your arrows," he said shyly.

The boys all looked at her.

She nodded, "so did I. But I didn't fire that arrow."

"What do you mean?" Conner asked.

"I never got a second arrow out of my quiver. Look," she pointed at the bow and quiver where she'd dropped them when they got back. "I took ten arrows. How many do you see?"

"Nine," Graysen said.

"Then how did your arrow hit Farlege?" Hodgens asked.

"Because there was another person in the woods, the person who shot Beagle Girl," they all looked at her.

"I fired an arrow in the direction from which the arrow that hit Beagle Girl originated, hoping to hit something. My guess is that I missed and the person used my arrow to shoot Farlege," she explained.

"Why would someone do that?" Graysen asked.

"The only reason I can think of is to frame me," she stated. "My arrows are unique, and they have my magical signature on them."

"Oh, this is bad," Conner said as he got up and began to pace the room.

"It is," Tenja agreed. "It's an issue that will cause problems for us, that is for sure."

The room fell silent again and Tenja stared at the tea mug in her hands. Finally, Hodgens said, "momma, is there something else?"

She raised her head and looked at them with shock. The boys looked at each other and then back at her.

149

"Momma, what is it?" Graysen asked.

She swallowed hard and said, "the person who fired the arrow that hit Beagle Girl was Raben."

CHAPTER 18

Conner stopped pacing. Hodgens and Graysen erupted from their seats.

"What?!" They yelped in unison.

"Then why did we leave?" Conner asked.

"Because when she dropped the cloaking spell and we looked at each other she mouthed one word - go. So, we did," Tenja explained.

"Momma Raben shot Farlege with your arrow?" Hodgens asked bitterly.

"I don't know," Tenja admitted. "I didn't see where it came from, I just saw it hit him."

"This doesn't make any sense," Graysen said shaking his head.

"The arrow that hit Beagle Girl was a message arrow," Tenja started to explain.

"A what?" Hodgens asked.

"A message was magically attached to the arrow. The purple smoke that came from the wound is the message. I just have to transform it," she told them.

"So do it!" Hodgens exclaimed. "I want to know what she thought was so important that she wounded Beagle Girl!"

"And would have wounded me if Beagle Girl hadn't been there!" Conner added.

She looked at their faces. She was exhausted - physically and emotionally. Raben was here. She was in Easpach and not with them. She had fired an arrow at them. It was almost too much to take. But her boys needed to know. So, she got up and went to her trunk. From it she collected a brown, leather bound journal, and a fountain pen. On the way through the living room she grabbed the box of vials off the coffee table.

As they entered the kitchen Tenja picked up the shielded arrow and placed it in the sink. I'll deal with that later she thought to herself. They all sat down at the table and the boys watched as Tenja put the contents of the vial into the fountain pen. Then she opened up the journal and laid the pen on a blank page.

"Uh, now what?" Hodgens asked.

"Just give it a minute," Tenja told them.

And they watched as the pen floated above the page as if someone was holding it. Then it began to write a message in purple ink.

"What does it say?" Graysen asked when the pen stopped and floated down to the table.

Conner leaned forward and read out loud, "I'm not the woman you've known me to be. But imagine if me and you could find a way."

"What?" Hodgens asked, "what does that even mean?"

Tenja leaned forward and read the words for herself.

"It's a riddle," she told them. "Another small part of the big picture." Frustrated, she slammed the journal shut and shoved everything back in her trunk.

"I don't understand any of this," Hodgens spat out. "If she's in Easpach why isn't she with us?"

"Yeah," Graysen added, "doesn't she want to be with us?"

"She didn't even say anything to me when we were in the same place," Conner interjected.

"I wish I had answers," she told them. "I wish I knew why all of these things were happening. I want to know why Raben was in the park but isn't with us. Believe me when I tell you that trusting her is getting harder and harder."

"Then why do you still trust her?" Hodgens asked what they all wanted to know.

"Because of this," she waved her arms indicating the apartment. "Because of the book, the jewels, you three, love. I'm not ready to give up on all of this."

"Yes, it is frustrating. Even sad at times. But I have to remember that there is something bigger than us going on out there. There are other worlds that impact ours and there are things going on there that we know nothing about."

The boys followed her to the couch, and each took a seat.

"We have pieces to a puzzle, and I believe it is important that we solve it. So, we will."

A few moments passed before Graysen finally said, "okay, mom."

His brothers nodded in agreement.

Just then Beagle Girl came walking out of bedroom. The bandage and the wound were gone. Hodgens jumped to his feet and scooped up the dog. As he examined her he said, "wow, Mom! Your healing magic is amazing!"

She shook her head in disbelief, "I don't have healing magic. I bandaged it the old-fashioned way."

After a moment of all of them giving Beagle Girl attention, Conner reached into his pocket and pulled out a small leather pouch. He tossed it on the coffee table.

"What's that?" Graysen asked.

"The rubies," Conner told him. Then he got up and walked to the bookshelf. "I also have this," he said and handed Tenja the satchel that had been over Farlege's shoulder.

She looked from him to the satchel and back again, "how did you get this?" She asked.

"I traveled it from his shoulder to mine," he said with a smile.

"But you don't know what's in it," she said.

"Well, he told us a little, so I used what he said to make it work," he told her.

She got up and threw her arms around his neck. When she finally let go, she looked at all of her boys and said, "you three are the reason we will survive whatever is going on."

They all smiled at her.

"So, what's in the bag?" Hodgens finally broke the silence.

Tenja dumped the contents onto the coffee table. Graysen grabbed the file folder. Hodgens grabbed the jump drive.

"We don't have technology in the apartment," he said turning the jump drive over in his hand. "What are we supposed to do with this?"

"Well, Farlege has no idea where we're staying or what we have access to. He just brought what he could," Tenja took the jump drive. "He thought that we would work with him to solve the case."

Hodgens laughed, "what did you say to that?"

"She told him that we don't need his help," Conner shared.

"And we don't," Graysen added, "triplet strong!"

They all smiled and then Conner said, "you have your computer at the gallery. I could get you in there."

"Tricky," Graysen added, "because of the security."

"But your cloaking spell is amazing!" Conner interjected. "Couldn't we just do that again?"

"The problem with that is we have to arrive first, then I cloak us. We'd be on camera before I could get the spell up," she told him.

"Aren't there any blind spots in the security?" Graysen asked.

"Maybe," she considered his question. "I'll have to think about it, Conner. For now, let's study the photos and book," Tenja patted his hand.

"I have an idea for the photos," Hodgens said. "I'm thinking it would be helpful if they were arranged on the wall so we can see them as whole images, not just small squares."

"That's a great idea!" Tenja agreed.

"I'll help you," Conner said.

As the brothers got up and headed to the biggest blank wall in the living room Graysen asked, "do you want to work on the book more, mom?"

"I really, do, bud," she said. She watched as Conner and Hodgens sorted out the pictures and Graysen grabbed an oboe. She opened the book on the coffee table and dumped out the gems.

"According to my list," Graysen told her. "This is the last instrument to try."

"Okay, play something beautiful," she said and looked down at the book. After a few minutes of playing Graysen stopped.

"Nothing?" He asked.

"Nothing," Tenja acknowledged. Graysen plopped down in a chair, obviously disheartened.

"I don't know what else to do," he said sadly.

"Well, what we know is that no matter what instrument you played, there was always one note that caused the first jewel in the book to glow," she thought for a moment, "then other jewels took turns glowing, but none melded to the book."

Hodgens spun around, an excited look on his face, "so the notes were right, but they weren't being played in the right order!"

"What?" Graysen and Tenja said in unison.

"It's like a puzzle," he was bouncing now, "the notes. They have to be played in the right order! Here," he grabbed a paper and pen, and handed them to Graysen, "draw music staffs on the paper."

"Why?" Graysen asked taking the items from his brother.

"Just trust me," Hodgens told him.

Doing as Hodgens suggested, he filled the page with music staffs. Once he had finished, he looked at his brother expectantly.

"Now, fill in the first note that lights up the jewel in the book," Hodgens pointed at the paper and watched as Graysen filled in a note.

"Mom, you take another piece of paper," Hodgens pointed at the stack on the table.

She did as he instructed.

"Okay, now, Graysen, start playing something. Mom, when a jewel lights up, stop Graysen. Lay the jewel on the paper and write down the note. Once we have all of the notes, then we can put the song together like a puzzle," he smiled at them.

"Hodgens, this is genius!" Tenja squealed, jumped up, and threw her arms around him.

#

"Captain? Captain!" Farlege moaned as the voice echoed in his head.

Where am I? He thought to himself as he opened his eyes. He furrowed his brow as he realized he was looking at trees. The sun was high in the sky. It must be noon.

"Captain are you alright? Do you need backup?" The voice said again.

He reached for his radio and a pain shot through his chest. He let out a scream and reached for his chest. It was then that he realized his shirt was unbuttoned. There was a bandage in the middle of his chest and an arrow lying across it. Shit! He exclaimed. His first attempt at sitting up was a failure as pain once again shot through his chest. On his second try he took a deep breath and pushed through the pain. He sat, each breath painful, his head spinning.

"Captain! Where are you?" Beth's voice broke through the silence again.

He took a deep breath and reached for his radio. Sound fine. Don't let her know anything is wrong. He gave himself a pep talk.

"Farlege here. I'm okay, Beth. I lost track of time," he clicked off the radio, took few deep breaths. "Do you need me at the office?"

"Nothing out of the usual here, Captain. I was just worried when you didn't come back or answer the radio," Beth responded.

"Okay," he acknowledged her, "I'll be back in the office in about an hour."

"Roger that. Out," Beth closed the call.

Farlege reached down and picked up the arrow lying on his legs. As he held it in his hands he said, "Tenja. You freaking shot me!"

Now he was just angry enough to stand up. Once on his feet he stood for a minute to let the pain dissipate and his legs to stop wobbling. He buttoned up his shirt, took another deep breath, and made his way to his car. He tossed the arrow on the passenger seat and got behind the wheel.

None of this makes sense, though. Who bandaged my wound?

He made his way back to his house. After tossing the arrow on the kitchen counter he went to the bathroom to look at his wound. He stood staring at the wound in the mirror, his mouth agape. Her arrow had penetrated his shields. His strongest shields. Sure, based on the fact that the arrow hadn't made it through his sternum, the shields had obviously slowed the arrow's force. But it had gotten through. He put a new bandage over the wound and headed back to look at the arrow.

He grabbed a bottle of water and sat at the table with the arrow. It was then that he saw the words burned into the arrow. "Know who you are and who you trust", he read out loud. A warning. But from whom? Was I left alive just to be killed later? He wondered.

He was roused from his thoughts by Beth's voice again, "a pedestrian has been hit by a car in front of the diner," she said.

"I'm on my way," he said and got to his feet. He had prepared to feel pain his chest when he stood, but there was none. He reached up and touched the bandage. Then, out of curiosity he removed it. The wound was gone. Only a white scar remained, marking his light-brown skin. He glanced at the arrow and saw that the message was gone. He stumbled back a step. In all that is magic, what is going on?

CHAPTER 19

Madi set down the dumbbell and stood up. Grabbing a towel, he headed to the kitchen for a glass of water. As he leaned against the counter, he looked around the room. He loved his house. It was his sanctuary. This was the one place in Easpach where he could be wholly and completely himself.

A photograph on the refrigerator grabbed his attention. He couldn't even count the number of times he had stared at that same photo over the years. Two kids, barely twelve years old. One in a wheelchair and one standing beside him.

He had loved Raben since the moment he met her. They were about five years old and she was living with her mom in a little shack in the middle of nowhere in Draiocht. He was on his own; his parents having been killed by raiders while he was at school one day. The day he met her he was filthy and starving. He'd been walking for days, living on berries and water. When he saw her, he stopped in his tracks. Even at five he knew she was the most beautiful girl in the world.

At first her mom was suspicious of him. They didn't get many visitors in the woods. She grilled him about where he came from, where his family was, why he was wandering around on his own. When she was satisfied with his answers, she took pity on him and brought him into their home. She gave him food, a bath, and a blanket to sleep on. He cried himself to sleep that night in the safety of Raben's home.

He stayed with them, helped them fix up the house, gather food and wood. He even learned to grow some basic food. As he and Raben grew so did the house and the farm. Together they added rooms to it, got a few farm animals. Her mom made sure they knew how to read, write, and do math. At first, he hated it, but Raben's enthusiasm for learning was contagious and soon they made trips to town to trade eggs and vegetables for books. He always thought it strange that her mom also insisted that they know how to defend themselves with clubs, knives, and a bow. She always told them it was in case they ran into an animal in the woods.

Then, one day, just after they turned eleven Raben found him in the woods. Her knapsack and bow were over her shoulders, and she was carrying his. She was panicked. A visionist had visited the farm. She had said that Raben had to leave Draiocht. That she had to go to Easpach. He had told her that was crazy, that visionists were crazy. But her mother had gotten very upset and insisted that they had to do as the visionist said. So her mother packed their knapsacks as quickly as possible, hugged her, told her she loved her and sent her to find him.

He had hugged her and took his stuff. Then he grabbed her by the hand, and they ran for the closest traversable where her mother would meet them. He remembered wondering how they would get through, that they didn't have the proper paperwork to go through. By the time he understood her mom's plan it was too late to stop the events that were about to unfold. As they ran toward the traversable her mom began to scream and yell at the gate guards.

When Raben had sensed him slowing down she grabbed his hand. Always the brave one she dashed toward the traversable, practically dragging him with her. One of the guards saw them and yelled. Also a smart one, Raben threw a shield around each of them. She made it through safely, but as she pulled him through the traversable began to close and prevent the guards from coming through after them. The traversable magic closing smashed into the shield Raben had put around him. The impact against the shield threw him to the ground.

To this day he could still hear the sound echo up his spine and reverberate in his head. He remembered lying on his back looking up at the blue sky. There was no pain. No sound. No feeling below his waist. Then Raben was there, at his side, like she had been since the day they met. She knew they had to get away from the traversable. It was only a matter of time before that traversable reopened and the

159

guards came for them. Then she put him over her shoulders and carried him until they had found this town.

The guards never came that day. Instead, two very nice families had taken them in. He had tried to convince Raben that they should stay together. But people did eventually come looking for them. Because he was now in a wheelchair, he couldn't be the boy that ran through the gate. And Raben cut her beautiful, long hair so she didn't have the braid that would give her away. The townspeople had rallied around them. They told the searchers that he and Raben couldn't be the children that illegally came through the traversable because they had been born here. There were even fake birth documents to support the story.

Now, here he stood, living in a gorgeous home, maintaining the illusion of immobility. He hadn't planned to keep up the facade. But then, one day when they were fifteen, Raben came to see him. She was happy, giddy. Her news shattered him. She had met someone. She had kissed someone. She was in love. She was so thankful that Madi was her friend and that she could tell him about a girl named Tenja.

Shortly after Raben and Tenja got together the feeling started to come back in his feet. He told no one. Instead he allowed everyone else to believe he had given up. He pretended that he wasn't making any progress. Eventually his parents accepted that he would remain in the chair and built the house he now lived in. But in reality, he continued to hone the healing magic that he had kept hidden from everyone. The day he found his birth parents dead he had decided that he would never let anyone know he could heal, that he didn't want to help anyone. At first, he used make up to cover his real magic symbols and let everyone believe that his magic was about moving objects. Then, when he turned eighteen, he bought a spell on the black market to change his symbol from healer to builder. It didn't change his magic; just what others thought his magic to be. Meanwhile he honed that healing magic and fixed his spine.

He had spent his life alone, watching Raben and Tenja build a life. Sure, they included him, let him be a part of the boys' lives. But it wasn't the same. Loving someone who would never love you back was a lonely road. Then she left and he was stuck with the love of Raben's life and their boys. But now everything was changing and where they would all end up was, as of yet, undetermined.

The ringing of the phone brought him out of memories.

"Hello?" He answered.

"He came to see her today," Althea stated.

"How long was he there?"

"About forty-five minutes," she told him.

"Did he get anything out of her?"

"Only that her name is Praelox."

"Okay, thanks. Keep me posted."

"Will do."

He hung up the phone and headed to his office. On the chalkboard he wrote the name Praelox.

#

"Mom?" Conner said.

"Yeah, bud?" She responded. She was staring at the photographs of the paintings, tea in her hand.

"I have some questions," he told her. "A lot of questions actually."

She turned and looked at him, "yeah, I imagine you do. Why don't you get your brothers, and we'll all talk for a bit. If you have questions, they probably do, too."

As she sat on the couch Beagle Girl jumped up and joined her. She absentmindedly ran her hand over the dog's back. She watched as each of the boys grabbed a drink and found a seat in the living room.

Looking at each of them she said, "okay, who wants to start?"

"I will," Conner began, "I want to know how you and Momma Raben can do all this magic. I thought her magic was knitting and yours

161

is art. But" he waved his hands, "this seems like a lot more than knitting spells together and creating art."

"Yeah," Graysen added, "it doesn't make sense."

She let out a sigh, "starting right in with the hard questions, I see." She took a long drink of tea. "I'll be honest and say that I find it all quite interesting. I knew that Raben's magic was advanced. I also knew that we both have multiple sets of magic skills."

"What do you mean multiple sets?" Hodgens asked.

"Well, I knew she could knit spells together. I also knew that she had a gift with protection spells, like the cloaking spell you learned, Conner. I can do them, but she had a knack for embedding power into them that was way more protective than anything I could ever do. Securing this apartment was a combination of her knitting spells and her protection spells," she paused.

"What?" Conner asked.

She hesitated.

"The other spells, the arrow, Beagle Girl, whatever is hidden in the book...I can't explain those," she admitted.

"But you knew the arrow held a message," Graysen pointed out.

"I did, because I, too, am trained in some alternate magic."

"So, what does this mean?" Hodgens asked.

"It means that we have to be open to anything that Raben might send our way. We can't discount something if we feel Raben's magic in it."

"You can tell if her magic is in a spell?" Hodgens leaned toward her.

She furrowed her brow, "yes, can you not?"

The boys all shook their heads.

"But you can tell if my magic is in something?"

They nodded.

"And you can feel if each other's magic is in something?"

Again, they nodded.

Has it just been so long that they can't sense her anymore? She asked herself the sad question.

"You need to be able to sense her magic. We may be in situations where there isn't time for me to interpret for you," she thought for a moment.

"Graysen, go get the book and jewels," she instructed. When he brought them to her, she spread them out on the coffee table.

She opened the book to the page where Graysen's music had attached the gem. Then she told them, "reach out for Graysen's magic in the gem."

She watched as each boy looked at the gem. When they all nodded to acknowledge they could feel it, she then instructed them, "now, reach over to the book and find the magic there."

Again she watched. One by one their brows furrowed. Hodgens finally gave up and threw himself back in the chair.

"There's nothing there," he told her.

"What do you mean there's nothing there?" she asked.

"There's no magic to feel," Conner shrugged.

Her mouth agape she reached for the book and threads of Raben's magic flowed back to her.

"Well, damnit," she rubbed her face, "she spelled it so only I could feel it. This is frustrating because I need you three to be able to identify Raben's magic."

Beagle Girl jumped on the table and aroofed. Then she sat and held her paw out to Hodgens. Sitting up again he took her paw in his hand. One heartbeat. Two. Then Tenja watched as the boy's eyes filled with tears. He dropped the dog's paw and went into the bathroom without saying a word. The dog repeated her action with Conner and Graysen and like their brother, their eyes filled with tears. But they simply wiped their eyes on their shirts, cleared their throats and took a drink. Her work done; Beagle Girl curled back up on the couch beside her. Tenja said nothing.

"Okay," Conner finally said, letting out a deep breath, "we all know what Momma Raben's magic feels like now."

Tenja looked up as Hodgens rejoined them, "good. We'll leave it at that, then. What other questions do you have?"

"What is the difference between a traversable and a portal?" Graysen asked.

"Ah, good question! The simple answer is that a traversable is stationary. It is always in the same place when it opens, and it always allows passage between the same two places."

"And that's different from a portal how?" Hodgens chimed in.

"A portal is learned magic. Traversables are constructed for passage between two given points. Portals are created as needed," she tried to explain.

"So, when you created the portal in the closet," Graysen started.

"I used the closet doorway to access a place that I knew, the forest. Portals can be created with just about any opening and can allow passage to wherever the creator wants to go,' she told them.

"Then why do any of us walk anywhere or use any type of transportation if we could just create a portal?" Conner asked.

"Because not everyone can create a portal. In fact, there are only a few magic skillsets that include being able to create a portal," she said tentatively.

"And artistry includes that skill in its set?" Hodgens asked in disbelief.

"What?" Tenja asked.

He gestured toward her wrist, "your magic skill set, artistry, it includes being able to create portals? I don't see the logic there."

She paled. She felt cornered by this line of questioning. Raben, and now Farlege, were the only people who knew about her true magic. If she told the boys she'd put targets on their backs. She just couldn't do that.

"I'm sorry, guys, but I can't fill in that blank for you right now."

When they started to protest, she raised a hand, "I promise that as soon as I can tell you, I will."

"You don't trust us," Graysen said dismayed.

164

She shook her head, "oh Graysen, that's not it at all. It's just that knowing some things would put you in more danger. I'm trying to protect you in the ways that I can, the ways I can control."

Silence fell over the room. Finally, Hodgens said, "can you explain what Beagle Girl is? What does her being an absorber really mean?"

She didn't realize she'd been holding her breath until it flowed out of her. The boys had accepted her honesty.

"Ah, another good question! But I don't have a lot to say on that one. We're going to have to do some research in the books on the shelf," she said as she stood.

They spent the remainder of the evening researching absorbers in the magic texts they had in the apartment. The way they understood it was that Beagle Girl could learn the magic of the creatures around her. But, just like humans she had a limited well of magic. If her well was full, she had to drop a skill to pick up a new one. One thing that wasn't clear was the strength or level of the skill she picked up.

Tenja looked at Beagle Girl, "you still have some secrets, don't you?"

The dog aroofed in response and Tenja laughed.

CHAPTER 20

"Here mom," Conner said as he joined them at the breakfast table. Tenja looked up to see him handing her a newspaper.

"Where did you get this?" She asked him.

"From our front porch. I thought you might want to know what's been going on in the outside world the last couple of days," he told her.

"Did anyone see you?" She worried.

"Oh, I didn't go out there," he responded. "I just magicked it down here."

She let out a sigh of relief. They had been living in the apartment for two weeks now and were nowhere near ready to emerge for any reason. They all continued to work their magic, she honing hers, the boys learning new skills as she taught them. Conner kept exploring what all he could do with this new magic.

"Well, let's see what's been going on," she said as she opened the paper.

The front-page headline stopped her breath.

"Momma what is it?" Hodgens asked as he joined them.

"Graysen get out here!" Conner yelled.

She sat the paper down on the table so they could all see it.

"Prominent local family believed dead. Dwargic and witch missing, believed guilty," Hodgens read aloud.

"Prominent local family? Are they talking about us?!" Graysen interjected.

They all gathered around the paper and read to themselves.

When they had finished, they all sat back and looked at each other. Then Tenja started laughing.

The boys looked at each other. Conner shrugged to his brothers. They watched as Tenja laid her head down on the paper and laughed until she cried. Hodgens got her a glass of water when she finally sat up and started to control herself.

"Want to share the joke?" Graysen asked.

"I'm sorry," she said with one last chuckle, "it's just so absurd. This whole thing. The events of the last couple of months. How did our lives get so turned upside down?"

Graysen burst from his chair, "it's not funny! I miss my old life! I miss my friends, my bed, Friday dinners at the diner. I didn't choose any of this and I wish we could go back to the way things were."

They all watched as he stormed to the bedroom and slammed the door.

"I'm sorry," Tenja whispered, "I didn't mean to upset any of you."

Conner looked at her sympathetically, "it's okay, mom. We've all had our moments being angry about this situation. It was just his turn."

"You know, after reading this article, I think we need to see what is on that jump drive. If there is more information about all of this, we need to see it," she told Conner and Hodgens.

The boys looked at each other.

"And how do you suggest that we get our hands on some technology?" Hodgens asked.

She took a breath and said, "we're going to ask Madi for help."

"We're going to what?!" Conner shot up. "That is crazy! For weeks you've been saying that we can't trust anyone. Now you want to trust Madifen?" He began to pace.

"Just hear her out," Hodgens told his brother. "She's kept us safe so far."

After a couple more passes through the room, Conner sat back down and gestured for her to continue.

"Okay, here's my idea," she began.

#

"Are you sure this is a good idea?" Graysen asked as they all stood in the living room.

"Hun, I don't know if any idea is good anymore until we take the chance," she told him honestly.

"But it's daylight. Someone might see you," Hodgens added.

"We have to risk it," she patted his arm, "we need a computer to look at that jump drive."

"Why does Madifen even have a computer? Only businesses are supposed to have them," Conner added his questions.

"Because of his consulting business that he does outside of his teaching job," she explained. "It's how he submits all of his required paperwork for that business."

Silence as the boys processed her responses to their questions.

Finally, Conner said, "okay, if we're going to do this let's get it over with."

She nodded and slipped her hand in his. In an instant they were in the woods behind Madifen's house. Tenja cloaked Conner and they walked out into the clearing. She sent a stream of magic that hit his shields.

I knew it! She thought to herself. I knew he'd have shields up now.

Less than a minute passed when Madi hastily rolled out onto his porch.

"Tenja!" He yelled so she could hear him across the expansive yard. "Tenja come here! Let me see that you're okay! Where are the boys?"

"We need something from you," she raised her voice, "if you really care about us, if you want to help us."

"I do, Tenja. I always have!" He quickly responded. "You know I can't get out there. Come here, just to the deck."

She shook her head.

"I need a computer," she told him.

"What?" he asked, shock in his voice. "You come here, I haven't seen you or heard from you in weeks and you want my computer? No, Tenja."

"Fine," she said and turned to leave.

"Wait! Just wait," he said, defeated.

It took a few minutes, but he returned with a computer bag.

"I don't know what you need with it, but here. If it will help, it's yours. Tenja, I care about you," he added, "and you know I love the boys."

Tenja held out her hand. The bag disappeared from Madifen's hand and appeared in hers.

"What the...Tenja the boys. Just tell me. Are they okay?"

"They're fine, Madi. We're all fine," she told him. She started to turn and then said, "thank you, Madi."

She turned and whispered to Conner, "take us to woods where we met Farlege."

Madifen watched as Tenja put out her hand - and it disappeared. He gasped audibly. "Tenja!" He yelled as she disappeared.

"Damnit, Tenja!" He exploded as he wheeled back into the house. Ensuring he was safe he erupted from the wheelchair and began to pace.

Someone was with her, he thought to himself. It had to be Conner. He'd seen what Conner did with Hodgens on the stage that night at the showcase. It had to be him who had disappeared Tenja. What are you guys doing?

He took a deep breath. Then another. Once he was calm, he dropped into the wheelchair and readied for his next move.

#

Once they landed in the woods Tenja cloaked them both and dropped to a sitting position. Conner followed suit.

"What are we doing here?" He asked.

"Madi put a locator spell on the computer. We don't have much time," she explained. "I didn't want to take us back to the apartment and reveal its location."

"Wow," Conner said, his mouth hanging open, "how do you know all of this stuff?"

Without looking up she patted his hand, "I've read and heard a lot of stories. Mostly, I'm running on gut instinct and suspicion."

She shoved the jump drive into the computer and opened the file stored on it. Clicking the right arrow button, she quickly moved through images on the screen. With each image her brows moved closer together.

"What is it?" Conner asked.

"Nothing new unfortunately," she told him. "It's just pictures of the," she trailed off and continued to move through images.

He gave her a minute and then as she started flipping back and forth, he couldn't help it, he had to interrupt her. "Mom what is it?"

"This painting, it's not the same," she stuttered out.

"It's not the one from the gallery?" He asked.

"No," she said slowly, "it's the one from the gallery," she stammered, "but it changed again. It's - oh god," she looked up at him. All of the color had drained from her face. "We have to go," she jumped up. "Now, Conner!" She yanked on his arm. "Take us home now!"

Moving as fast as he could he got his feet under him and grabbed her hand. Before she could utter another word, they were standing in the living room. Graysen and Hodgens bolted out of their seats.

"We -" Hodgens started to say something as Tenja pushed past him and ran to the wall filled with pictures of the painting from the gallery. Her hand flew to her mouth and her knees buckled. Graysen caught her before she hit the floor and Conner slid a chair behind her. As they eased her into it, she dropped her hand to her lap.

They boys watched helplessly as Tenja dropped her head between her knees. Hodgens stood looking at the painting, straining his eyes to try to see something different than what they had been looking at for days.

Turning back to his brothers he shrugged and said, "I don't know. I don't see anything different."

"I don't think the issue is something in those pictures," Conner finally said. "I think Mom saw something in the pictures on the jump drive."

"What? Where?" Graysen asked.

Conner told them everything that happened up until Tenja got agitated and almost passed out. By the time he was done filling his brothers in Tenja was sitting up. Some of the color had returned to her face and she was once again staring at the painting.

Hodgens knelt in front of her, "what's going on? You're scaring us."

She looked at him and a moment passed before he could see her eyes actually focus on him. Then he watched as she physically shook herself, as if a cold chill had coursed through her body.

She grabbed him and held him tight. Conner and Graysen looked at each other with concern.

"I'm sorry," she said as she let him go. "I'm so sorry, boys."

"Sorry for what?" Graysen asked.

She got up and looked at all three of them, "let's go sit down," she gestured toward the couch and chairs. Once they were all seated, she shared with them what she believed she'd learned.

"I believe that there was information on the jump drive. There were more images of the painting. Only, they were different," she told them.

"What do you mean they were different?" Graysen asked.

"In that image," she pointed toward the wall, "Easpach is in ruins and Draiocht is glowing, implying that it is thriving," she swallowed hard. "But, what we didn't realize was that the picture was still transforming. It wasn't done evolving to its final state."

The words caught in her throat, and she struggled to them out.

"In the images on the jump drive, Draiocht was also in ruins. It was as if it exploded," she finally managed to say.

The boys all stared at her with their mouths hanging open.

"What does that mean?" Hodgens finally managed to ask.

"The story that I was told had been passed down from generation to generation. Scholars believe that if the link between Easpach and Draiocht was ever broken, the creatures in Easpach who had magic would die. But, in that picture, more than magical creatures were dead, entire worlds looked to be annihilated. In the final images on that jump drive there weren't just dead incants in Easpach. Easpach was gone. Draiocht was gone. This is all different than what I had been told," she explained.

"But how do we know that was the final stage of the painting?" Conner asked.

"Yeah, couldn't there be more to the story?" Graysen added.

"If there is more to the story the painting doesn't tell it. In the last images the painting faded to an all black wall," she finished.

"I don't understand," Hodgens finally whispered. Everyone looked at him.

"What don't you understand?" Tenja asked.

He looked at them like a deer caught in a flashlight beam. She assumed he hadn't meant to say that out loud.

"It's just that Momma Raben left us to fix this, right? She went to be a part of the solution. If she's now sending us signs of impending doom for EVERYONE, then why did she even bother to go? She could have stayed here, and we could have enjoyed the time we had left together," he said, already resigning himself and them to death.

"Wow, okay," Tenja said, "where to even start with that," she sighed. "Yes, Raben went to be a part of the solution. And for all we know she has been. What if her going bought us the last ten years so the rest of the solution could be found? Perhaps it isn't as cut and dry as what we're thinking it should be. You all know that magic is complicated," she said gesturing to all of them. "It's not as simple as 'if this then that'. I can't even imagine what Raben has been dealing with for the last decade. And for all we know she's been doing it alone. We've had each other."

The boys looked at the floor, at each other, around the room. Basically, anywhere but at her.

"She's trying to preserve a future for all of us. I know it's hard for the three of you to trust this, to trust her. But I KNOW her. We can't know why all of this is happening. But it is and she's doing what she can to help us. I trust her. I need you three to keep trusting me," she leaned forward and extended her hand.

After one more glance at each other they all put their hands on top of hers.

"On three," she told them.

They raised and dropped their hands. On the third time they all said, "triplet strong!" And it sounded like they meant it.

"Now, let's go to bed and get some sleep. We've got more work to do tomorrow."

As they all stood up she said, "I love you my favorite little people," and was met with three genuine smiles.

CHAPTER 21

Farlege's office phone rang. He stared at it as it rang a second time. Few people had his direct number. Realizing what it could mean, he scrambled to grab the receiver before it stopped ringing.

"Captain here," he spoke into the receiver.

"She was here," the voice on the other end sounded full of anguish. "She was here, and I couldn't get to her, Farlege."

"I'm on my way!" He said as he jumped up. "Catch me on the radio if you need me," he said to Beth as he ran out the door.

#

Madifen met him at the door, not letting him into the house.

"Get me to your car," he said as he wheeled past Farlege. "I'll explain on the way."

"Madifen, I don't -"

"The car, Farlege!"

Once they were in the car, Madifen told him. "Drive to the park. The main entrance."

"Why?"

"Just drive!"

Farlege threw the car into gear, flipped on the sirens, and tore out of Madifen's driveway.

"Talk!" He ordered as he drove.

Madifen told him about Tenja showing up at the back of his property, being careful to stay outside of the boundaries. He explained what she wanted and Farlege muttered something.

"What?" Madifen asked.

"Nothing. Go on."

"So, I put a tracking spell on the computer, the case, pretty much everything I gave her. They are in the park."

"Wait, they?" Farlege looked at him

"Yeah, so I thought she was alone. But, when she turned to leave, she reached her hand out and a split second before she disappeared, her hand was gone. So, I assume she had Conner cloaked and he was doing the traveling."

"You're sure it was Conner?" Farlege asked.

"Well," Madifen paused and looked at him, "no I can't be one hundred percent sure. I can only assume."

"Maybe she has help," Farlege stated.

Madifen shook his head, "no, remember what you said to me? The only people she trusts right now are the boys. If she had someone with her it was Conner."

Farlege nodded, "yeah, you're probably right."

He parked the car and got Madifen's wheelchair. Madifen took off so fast Farlege had to run to keep up. Not far down the paved trail Madifen stopped and turned toward the woods.

"Shit!" He exclaimed. "I hate this damn chair!" And the thing was, he was serious. It had served a purpose but now he wanted to ditch it, get up and walk, be damned who knew. But instead, he took a deep breath and pointed into the woods. "They are about half a mile that way," he told Farlege.

"Madifen, you know they aren't going to be there. Tenja is too smart for that. She would have assumed that you had a tracking spell on the stuff you gave her."

Wish I would have thought of doing that, he thought to himself. I'm a guardian for magic's sake and I didn't think of doing that!

"Just humor the guy in the wheelchair, Farlege. Please?"

Farlege threw up his hands, "fine, fine. I'm going." He ran straight into the woods for about 6 minutes and stopped. He knew where he was going and veered off to where he had met up with Tenja. Sure enough, he found the computer, the bag, and, as he suspected, the jump drive. He stuck the jump drive in his pocket, put the rest of the stuff into the bag and headed back to Madifen.

"Here," he said as he handed the computer bag to Madifen. "No one was there."

"Did you see anything suspicious?" Madifen asked.

"Like what? Footprints? It's not like they walked out of there, Madifen. Conner took them out of there just like he brought them in," he grumbled as he ran his hand through his hair. "How do one woman and three boys stay at least two steps ahead of us?" He pointed at Madifen, "you're a professor! I'm the Captain of the Police Department, a trained detective!"

Madifen actually chuckled.

"What's so funny about this?" Farlege asked angrily.

"Nothing," Madifen responded, "everything. I mean, come on. We're being outsmarted by Tenja and her boys. If you had told me that was possible, I wouldn't have believed you."

Farlege looked at him, unamused, "they are in trouble, Madifen. There is nothing funny about it."

"Really? They seem pretty in control to me," Madifen retorted.

"Go to the car!" Farlege yelled at him, "I'm done with this wild goose chase."

They said nothing to each other on the way back to Madifen's house. Before Madifen wheeled up his ramp Farlege finally said, "uh, thanks for calling me, Madifen. At least I know she's alive."

Madifen stopped briefly but didn't turn around to look at the man who had retrieved his computer. Instead, he grinned to himself and headed into his house

#

Madifen plugged the computer into the power cord and waiting for it to boot up. He knew Tenja would not be where the computer was. The trace wasn't about finding her. It was about getting the computer back so he could see why she needed it. Every action taken on this computer was tracked. One of the joys of the computer restrictions

176

imposed by the government. Of course, he could get around them and would clean off whatever she'd done. But for now...

He watched as the images loaded onto the screen. At first, he saw nothing new, nothing worth risking her exposure. But then, about twenty images in he realized that the painting had changed. He backed up a few images and looked carefully.

"Ah well, damn," he said as he stared at Draiocht burning.

#

Farlege tossed the jump drive on his kitchen table and dropped into a chair. Until today he hadn't known if she'd seen the images of the painting. Now she had, and he wondered if it would change anything. Would she reach out to him? Would she finally accept that this was about more than just an assault on her family? He needed her to realize how much was really at stake.

#

Praelox sat up when he came into the house. She'd been lying on the couch, bored as usual, as the days dragged on and on.

"Where have you been?" It was a question that demanded an answer, not a friendly inquiry.

He looked at her, ignored the question, and asked his own, "where are your friends?"

"They aren't my friends," she replied lazily and propped her feet on the table.

He knocked her feet off the table, "have some manners," he told her. "This isn't your place."

"Whatever," she shrugged, "it's all going to burn anyway."

"Hey boss," the dwargic said as he entered the room, the big guy following. "To what do we owe the pleasure?"

"She's seen the photos," he told them.

The dwargic rubbed his hands together and giggled, "ooh, ooh, that's good! What do you think she'll do next?"

Praelox rolled her eyes, "you are an idiot."

"I don't know what she will do," he told them. "She has been one step ahead of us since this all started. I thought I could predict her, but it turns out that isn't the case. She's got magic skills I didn't know about, and a creative streak deeper than I realized."

He tossed money onto the coffee table.

"For food," he told them. "Stay on your toes. I'll be in touch."

They aren't the brightest stars, he thought to himself, but the sacrificial goat doesn't need brains.

#

Tenja tossed and turned in her sleep.

Imagine if me and you could find a way.

Beagle Girl whined and pawed at Hodgens' shoulder. Hodgens patted her head and rolled over.

Imagine if me and you could find a way.

Beagle Girl jumped on Hodgens' bed and licked his face. Whined again.

Imagine if.

Hodgens opened his eyes.

Imagine.

He realized that Tenja was talking in her sleep. No, not talking. Singing.

He sat up quietly and listened.

Imagine that the stars aligned.

Hodgens noticed a faint glow coming from the kitchen. Stealthily, so as not to wake anyone, he tiptoed to the doorway.

For you and I to have this night.

Hodgens stared at the table. The jewels were shining brightly and hovering over the table.

To make our way both wrong and right.

"Mom!" He yelled and ran back into the bedroom. Shaking her he said, "mom, mom wake up!"

She rubbed her eyes and tried to focus on him.

"Get up," he tugged at her arm.

"Get up, guys!" He shoved his brothers awake.

When Tenja finally made her way to the kitchen, Hodgens was impatiently pacing around the table. It seemed like forever before Graysen and Conner finally came in.

"Hodgens," Tenja yawned, "it's five in the morning. What is going on?"

"You were talking in your sleep," he finally said to her.

"What?" She gasped. "I never talk in my sleep!"

He shook his head, "you weren't really talking. You were singing."

"I don't understand why that warranted waking us up," Conner added grumpily.

"It was the song!" Hodgens exclaimed.

"What about it?" Graysen asked.

"Mom, you were singing, and the jewels were glowing!"

At that Tenja jumped up. She grabbed Hodgens' shoulders and asked excitedly, "what was it? What was the song?"

"I don't know," Hodgens said, "it sounded familiar, like I'd heard it before. But I couldn't place the lyrics. I just know that when you were singing the jewels were glowing."

Now Tenja paced.

"What can you remember? Any of the lyrics? The melody?" She asked.

"It was like the words in the arrow message. Something about imagine if me and you? Imagine me and you? Yeah! Yeah, that's it! You were singing something like imagine me and you. I do," he tried to sing.

As he did, the jewels took on a faint glow and they all gasped.

179

Tenja ran toward the bookshelf, "Graysen, get your clarinet!" She tossed some sheet music on the coffee table. Quickly she added the jewels and the journal Raben had given them already open to the page with the embedded jewel. The boys joined her, coffee in their hands.

When did they make coffee? She thought to herself and then dismissed the question when Conner handed her a cup.

"Mom, what's going on?" Graysen asked.

"That song. That song was our song. Mine and Momma Raben's," she explained. "I haven't played that song, haven't heard that song, in a decade. Since she left, I could never bring myself to listen to it again. Listening to it made my heart hurt, like it was going to burst from my chest."

"That is why it was so familiar!" Hodgens said, "I have heard it before!"

"Yes," she told them. "We used to play it all the time. In fact, you three used to make fun of us for playing it all the time."

"I remember that now!" Graysen added. He grabbed the sheet music and started to play.

They all sat, transfixed, as they watched one jewel after another begin to glow and then embed itself into the journal. As they did, a path glowed between them. Then other images began to show on the pages.

"What is that?" Hodgens wondered aloud.

Conner stood and walked around the table, looking at the journal from different angles.

"It's a map!" He blurted out.

Hearing that revelation, Graysen stopped playing. When he did, the jewels stopped glowing and all the images, including the path, disappeared.

"Well, that's interesting," Graysen muttered and started to play again. The jewels started to glow again, and all of the images became visible again.

"Oh Raben, you sly devil!" Tenja laughed.

The boys looked at her.

"Share the secret, momma," Conner poked her.

"It's a security measure," she explained. "In order for this to work, you have to know the song and be able to play it. So, if we were to lose the book or get separated from it, someone would have to get lucky enough to figure out how to do anything with it."

"That's -" Hodgens stuttered. "That's kinda genius level puzzle making!"

Graysen stopped playing again and said, "I'm starving."

Without missing a beat Tenja bolted out of her seat and said, "French toast! Let's eat and then we'll figure out our next move."

CHAPTER 22

Stomachs full, they cleared the kitchen table and Tenja set the journal in the middle so everyone could see it. Graysen began to play his clarinet and the pages came to life. They watched as shapes like trees, streams, structures, and mountains appeared. The path wound from jewel to jewel, weaving among the other shapes on the pages.

"So, what are we supposed to do with this?" Hodgens asked. "It's a map, but to where?"

"And where does it start from?" Graysen asked. When the images disappeared, he huffed out, "this is frustrating because I want to talk, too."

Tenja chuckled, "it's okay for you to pause, bub."

"You know, we could make a copy, so we have a static version of it...just in case," Graysen told them.

After thinking about it for a minute, Tenja said, "I don't think we should do that. Raben put the security in place for a reason."

"Yeah, brother, this is just one of the roles for you to play in this adventure," Conner patted him on the back.

Hodgens was flipping the pages of the journal. When he was back on the first page of the map he said, "Graysen, play again. I want to see something."

Obliging, Graysen played, and the images appeared. Hodgens pointed at a shape on the page.

"I think I know what that is supposed to be. Where we are supposed to start," he shared.

"Really?" Tenja asked, "where is it?"

"It's an old water mill deep in the park. I went there on a field trip with my environmental science class one year," he explained.

"Do you think you can find it again?" Conner asked him.

"There are some markers," he said thoughtfully, "yeah, I think I could get us there. It's pretty remote, though, and will take us a while to walk to it."

Tenja got up and paced the living room. The boys watched, letting her have time to work out what was going on in her head. Beagle Girl sat on the couch watching her walk back and forth. When she stopped and just looked around the room Conner finally asked, "Mom, what is it? What are you thinking?"

She turned slowly and looked at them. Her boys. Her young men. The life they knew upended. It was just months ago that they were planning commencement, thinking about their futures, the fun they wanted to have before adulthood officially took hold. Now...? They were growing up. Momma was becoming mom. And their future felt unknown.

She walked back to them and took a seat at the table. Pointing to the first page of the map she said, "this is not a short map."

"No," Hodgens agreed, turning the pages. "It covers about ten pages of the journal."

"What does that mean for us?" Graysen asked.

"I think," she choked up, cleared her throat. "I think it means we have to leave the apartment...and I don't know when or if we'll be back."

Beagle Girl aroofed and silence enveloped the room.

Finally, Conner said, "once we find each landmark on the map, I could travel us back here for the night and we could start again the next day. We don't have to leave - leave do we?"

"These are just lines on a page, Conner," she shook her head. "We don't know how far apart the landmarks are. We don't know what obstacles we'll encounter. There's no way to know what is at the end of the map or how long it will take us to get there."

"Mom's right," Graysen agreed. "Too many variables."

Conner sat back in his chair.

"What aren't you saying?" Hodgens asked her. "There's something there you aren't sharing with us."

He knew her. Too well sometimes.

Sighing she said, "we don't even know if this entire map is in Easpach."

Shocked faces around the table.

"You...you mean we could have to leave this world to follow the map?" Conner spluttered.

"I think we can't rule that out," she agreed. "There's also more risk if we're traveling back and forth every day. If we stay put, stay together, I can cloak us all."

"Plus we stay together all the time," Hodgens added, "if you're traveling us, Conner, then someone gets left alone out there until you come back for them. I don't like that idea at all."

"Good point," Conner nodded.

"So, we need to prepare," Hodgens stated as a matter of fact, "we need to plan and pack. If we're going to do this, then we're all in. To be all in, we need to make sure we have what we need."

"Well, I think that calls for some lists," Tenja said "We'll make our lists now and spend the day getting ready. Then we'll get a good night's sleep here and head out at first light tomorrow. Agreed?"

They all nodded. Her heart filled with pride. Then it sank. She'd keep doing her best to protect them even though she didn't know how much longer she could

#

They ended up with three lists: food, necessities, equipment. Tenja was suddenly very thankful for the hunting lessons she had as a child. Her parents had made sure that, should anything happen to them, she would be able to fend for herself. She could acquire food, construct rough shelter, and find water.

"So, what exactly are we going to do about food?" Graysen asked.

"We're going to pack high protein items. We'll have to forage for fruit. I'll hunt for meat," she looked at them. They had all paled a little.

"I know it sounds hard," she tried to empathize with them, "but we've camped a lot. We can do this," she attempted to sound positive.

"Camping!? You're seriously comparing this to camping?!" Hodgens blurted out. "This will be nothing like camping. Chances are we'll never get to come back home!"

The elephant in the room finally reared its head.

"Momma why is this happening?" Conner started to cry. "Why are we having to do this? If Momma Raben had stayed with us, if she had stayed out of whatever this is, would we still have our life?"

Her throat closed. Tears once again welled. God she was tired of the tears. She reached out and laid her hand on his arm. A young man, and still her little boy.

"I can't answer any of those questions. I wish I could. I wish I knew why all this was happening. I want to know exactly what we're supposed to do. I want the answers," she choked up. "I want to know that we're all going to be okay in the end."

With that thought, Hodgens and Graysen reached out and the four of them held hands. In those moments they all let the tears flow. They spent the next couple of hours reminiscing. Remembering the good and bad times they'd had together through the years. Beagle Girl jumped up on Hodgens' lap and laid her head on the table, not wanting to be left out of the bonding.

When the conversation finally lagged, Tenja sat up straight and said, "we will always have our memories. But we can't go back. Even if none of this had happened, our futures were always uncertain. We lived each day the best we could. That's all we can do now."

Conner wiped his face with his hands, took a deep breath, and said, "okay, so what do we need on this food list?"

#

Tenja made each of the boy's their favorite meal for dinner. They'd get one more favorite breakfast and then it was on to the next adventure. But for this night she had her boys close. They were all safe, warm and fed.

She looked at the bags in the living room. They had each filled a rucksack, being careful not to make it too heavy. They wrapped their sleeping bags in their bivy sacks and strapped them to the top of the packs. Graysen had settled on a recorder as the instrument to take with them to activate the spells in the journal. It required the least amount of maintenance. It was hard for Tenja to watch him make that decision. He had tenderly picked up each instrument. Played them. Considered what he would need to care for them. The sadness in his eyes as he set each one down almost broke her. She made no comment when he placed the recorder in his bag.

She had chosen several of the books that she thought they might need. But the boys wouldn't let her carry them all. So, they shared the weight of them, and each put a couple in their bags. It was hard to choose clothes as they didn't know what they'd need. After a bit of back and forth they decided on thermals, a few layers, and one jacket. There just wasn't room for everything.

Hodgens added some of his spell books and notes. Tenja added the journal to her bag. While the boys were sleeping, she added her paint bottle and brush to a hidden pocket on the inside of her rucksack. Her bow and quiver leaned against her rucksack. They were as ready as they could be for whatever was going to come next.

#

Tenja pushed at the wet nose against her face. It couldn't be time to get up. She tried to pull the blanket over her, but Beagle Girl yanked the blanket out of her hands. The action startled Tenja awake, and she sat up quickly.

"What is it, girl?" She asked the dog.

186

Beagle Girl began to spin in circles and aroof softly.

Tenja jumped up, "we've gotta go don't we? We've got to go!"

Beagle Girl jumped up and down and ran to the living room.

Tenja started shaking the boys, "guys, guys wake up! We gotta go. Get your shoes on! Come on come on! Grab everything and let's go!"

In less than five minutes they were dressed and ready, standing at the closet door. Tenja ran in with a bag full of food and shoved it at them. Hodgens grabbed it before it hit the floor.

Quickly Tenja opened the portal and shoved them all through it. Beagle Girl jumped in last. In the split second between Beagle Girl getting through the portal and Tenja closing it, they saw the ceiling of the bedroom come crashing down.

#

"Sorry, sir," the beat cop told Madifen, "only emergency personnel allowed behind the barricade."

"Get out of my way!" Madifen yelled at the cop.

"Officer Wayland," Farlege yelled, "let him through."

Madifen barely waited for the barricade to be out of his way before he wheeled up the driveway.

"Farlege! Were they in there?" He asked anxiously, "were they in there??"

Farlege looked down at him, "we don't know yet Madifen. You got here fast. We just started taking stock and trying to figure out where we can start."

"I'm sure everyone in town heard the explosion. I had a sick feeling in my gut. So, I headed this way, hoping I was wrong," Madifen told him.

"You should stay here. There's debris all over the yard," Farlege told him. "I'll update you when I know something."

"Wait!" Madifen commanded him. "I want some answers."

"I told you I don't -"

"Not about that exactly," Madifen gestured toward the house. "How did that woman get out of the hospital? How did that dwargic skip out? Where are they Farlege? They disappeared on your watch and now this."

"I can't do everything Madifen!" Farlege returned the anger.

"No, but you hire the people to help you!" Madifen fought back.

Farlege just looked at him and then turned to walk away. Madifen grabbed his arm.

"Madifen, keep your hands off of me!" Farlege reeled on him.

Madifen whispered something so soft that the change of attitude caught Farlege off guard.

Farlege leaned down, "what did you say?"

Madifen repeated, "I know what you are, Farlege. What you really are. What I don't understand is why your shields didn't hold."

Farlege stumbled back. Satisfied, Madifen rolled back to the barricade to wait for news.

CHAPTER 23

Tenja shoved the boys against the wall of the park restrooms while simultaneously cloaking them and throwing up and oral shield around them. They all froze. The boys couldn't gauge how much time passed before they heard Tenja breath.

"Okay," she finally said, "I think we're safe. No one followed us."

And with that, she collapsed to a sitting position on the ground. The boys joined her.

Conner started to cry. Hodgens put an arm around him. Graysen laid a hand on his leg. Tenja rested her head against her sleeping bag at the top of her pack and let the tears silently roll down her face.

When's Conner's sobs finally subsided she said, "does anyone have a watch on?"

"Yeah," Hodgens answered. "It's four-forty-one in the morning."

Tenja stood up.

"The sun will break the horizon soon and even cloaked I don't want to be here. We need to get deeper into the woods and then we'll stop for breakfast. That's what is in the bag you took from me before we went through the portal, Hodgens," she told them.

The boys just looked up at her.

"I know we're all in shock. I know we're scared. We need to process what has happened," she crouched to their level. "But right now, we have to get to a safer place. Right now, we stay alive."

Given the idea of not being alive, the three stood up.

"Hodgens, do you know the way to the old water mill from here? We know that is the starting place. So, we don't need music or the journal to find the beginning of the map," she explained.

"Yeah, I can get us there - if I have light. It's too dark right now, momma. I can barely see my hand in front of my face," he said.

She thought for a moment, two. Then she asked, "is there some place between here and the mill that I would know? Someplace I could create a portal to so we can get away from here?"

Hodgens considered the question, "Um, yeah, actually. The waterfall with the old rickety steps is about halfway between us and the old water mill. From there the path gets harder to navigate. Not many people go past the waterfall anymore."

She nodded, "yes, I know where you're talking about."

The boys watched as she looked around the restroom building.

"Okay," she said after a moment, "here's what we're going to do. I'm going to make a portal using the door of the restroom. It will take us to the edge of the river at the bottom of the waterfall. That will get us away from here and deeper into the forest."

"But," Graysen asked, "isn't that risky?"

"A little," she acknowledged, "but less than staying put until we can really see. It's the last time I'll be able to do this. It's really our only choice."

Beagle Girl aroofed and they all watched as she nodded and turned in the direction of the front of the building.

"We'll go together. But I have to drop the cloak to open the portal. So, we have to be fast. Everyone understand?" She explained.

The boys mumbled and nodded. Tenja led the way around the building. She looked at the parking lot one last time. No one. Not a sound. She dropped the cloak, opened the portal, and they all jumped through. She closed the portal without incident, and they all breathed a sigh of relief.

Tenja cloaked them again and added the oral shield to be safe. They all stood still for a few minutes, making no sound. Finally, Tenja told them, "we're okay. We're okay, boys. Let's get back up in the trees, out of plain sight for now."

"Aren't we cloaked?" Conner asked.

"We are, yes," she agreed, "but it's still never good to be out in the open."

They asked no more questions, simply followed her up into the forest. When she found a spot with some fallen logs she stopped, took off her pack and sat down.

"Sit down," she told them. "Let's eat breakfast and talk while we wait for the sun to help us"

Obliging her, they shrugged out of their packs and sat down. Hodgens opened the bag of food he was holding. Reaching in he grabbed a bottle of milk and started to say, "well this won't be -" and then he stopped and looked at her. "How is this still cold? It's like I just took it out of the fridge!"

This time she just shrugged, "just a little cold spell that I learned a long time ago."

"I am beginning to think there is a lot about you that we don't know," Graysen said quietly.

She looked at them, her boys. Her heart. They were right. There was a lot that they didn't know. Some of it she could tell them now. The rest would have to wait.

"I know, guys. All of this has required me to use some magic that I've not needed in a very long time."

"But even when we went camping you used ice and coolers. Were you using magic too and we just didn't know it?" Conner asked.

She shook her head, "no, other than my art, most of the time I only used magic if I absolutely had to. I didn't use it just to make life easy. I was taught that,"

"You use magic when it is necessary," Hodgens nodded.

"Exactly, and now some of that magic will be necessary. So, I'll be using it more often. And, if you'd like, I will teach you some of the spells, too. It will be necessary to have more people than me able to help with these spells," she told them.

They all nodded in agreement.

"I'm starving, brother," Conner said, "quit hogging the food bag!"

#

They ate and talked until the sun was lighting up the space beneath the canopy. Tenja told them of learning to keep things cold and warm. She began teaching them the basics of the spells. Every little bit helped, and it kept them distracted from the bigger picture. When they could safely see to walk through the woods, she stood and began to pack up.

"Okay, what's the plan?" Hodgens asked once everyone had their packs on and were ready to go.

"I'd prefer to stay in the trees. Is that possible with the direction we need to go to get to the watermill?" Tenja asked.

"Yeah, we can do that," Hodgens nodded.

"Wait, if this stream feeds the mill, how is it secluded? Wouldn't more people know about it?" Graysen asked.

"This stream doesn't feed the mill," Hodgens explained. "The waterfall was between where we started and the mill, but it is not the stream the mill was built on."

"Got it," Graysen said.

"We are going to follow this stream for a little bit. Then it takes a turn, and we are going to make our way in the opposite direction," Hodgens told them. "Once we make the turn into the forest the terrain gets more challenging if I remember right."

"Okay," Tenja acknowledged his leadership in this moment, "then we'll leave it to you and Beagle Girl to lead us onward. Hodgens, do you have any idea how long it will take to get to the mill?" She asked.

"Well, when I hiked it a few years ago it took our group all day. We left after breakfast and got to the mill just before dinner. I imagine the four," Beagle Girl aroofed, "sorry," he acknowledged the dog, "the five of us, will be faster than my class was. So, I expect if we push through, we'll get there by late afternoon," he shrugged.

"So, we're looking at a day of hiking to knock out one page of the map?" Conner asked.

Hodgens just looked at him.

"What?" Conner finally asked.

"Brother, it's going to take a good portion of the day just to get to the watermill - and it's our starting point on the first page of the map!" Hodgens told him.

"Gee, that's encouraging," Conner retorted without attempting to hide his sarcasm.

"It's our current reality, Conner," she patted his shoulder, "Let's go. Stay in a line. Stay close without crowding each other," she gestured to Hodgens.

Beagle Girl turned and took up her place beside Hodgens. Tenja would never tire of seeing that companionship.

The trek to the spot where they turned away from the stream was uneventful. The ground was relatively even and they were able to stay in the trees. Even cloaked Tenja knew it was best to stay under the canopy of the trees whenever possible.

Hodgens came to a stop. Looking around he said, "this is where we veer away from the stream." With his back to the stream, he bent down and looked around at the ground. "This is even less traveled than when I was here a couple of years ago. Looks like no one has been out this way since then actually."

"How can you tell that?" Conner asked.

"Professor Landlover taught us how to read the foliage," Hodgens told him.

"Professor Landlover?" Graysen laughed, "you mean Landover."

"Huh?" Hodgens looked at him dumbstruck.

"You called him Professor Landlover...his name was Landover," Graysen laughed again.

"I can't believe I actually said that out loud," Hodgens started laughing right along with Graysen.

Their laughter was infectious and soon Conner and Tenja joined in. They all laughed so hard they cried.

As they all started to calm down Tenja said, "risking another laughing fit, I have to ask. Where did Landlover come from?"

193

"One of my classmates made it up that year we came out here. Every other word he said seemed to be about the land. A fellow student observed his use of the word and said boy he sure loves the land. And the rest is history," Hodgens explained with a hiccup. "I just can't believe I actually said it aloud."

"Everyone in school calls him that outside of his classes," Conner added to the story.

Tenja wiped the tears of laughter from her face, "okay guys, let's get moving. Hodgens you're good? Know where we're going?"

"Yeah, let me grab my compass out of my bag quick," he told her.

The three of them watched as Hodgens shifted his feet to remove his pack, and then disappeared with a scream.

Tenja grabbed Conner and Graysen and back paced several steps as a hole the size of a tractor tire opened in the ground before them.

"Holy crap! Hodgens!" Conner yelled.

"Are you okay?" Graysen joined in.

Silence followed their questions and Tenja's heart sank to her stomach.

"Shh!" She told them, "I need to hear."

She took off her pack, bow, and quiver and rested them against a tree. Then she got down on her hands and knees and began to crawl toward the edge of the hole.

"Mom wait," Conner stopped her. "Let's tie a rope around you - just in case."

"Yeah," Graysen added, "and we'll wrap it around that tree as an anchor point," he gestured to where she had set down her stuff.

"Good thinking," she said as she eased back and stood up. Once they had her secured, she crawled to the edge of the hole. Turning on the flashlight she'd thought to stick in her back pocket she glanced across the hole at Beagle Girl. The dog hadn't moved or made a sound since Hodgens fell. It was peculiar.

Shining the light into the hole Tenja took stock of what they were up against. The hole wasn't particularly deep. Hodgens was lying on his side about eight feet down.

"Hodgens? Baby can you hear me?" She tried not to sound panicked.

"Uhhh," he moaned.

"Hodgens, open your eyes. Talk to me," she said.

She watched as he opened his eyes and could tell he was taking stock of his physical wellness. He slid off his pack and pushed himself to a sitting position.

"Talk to me, bud," she urged him, "is anything broken?"

"No," he whispered, "nothing is broken. But I do have a problem," he told her.

"What? What is it?" She asked anxiously.

"I'm not alone down here," he informed her.

She started to move her light to see what else was down there.

"No!" He hissed. Don't agitate it.

"What is it?" She asked.

"Some kind of dog," he said, "and it looks like it has been down here for quite some time. It's not looking very friendly."

That explains why you're so still she thought to herself as she glanced at Beagle Girl. And, as if reading her thoughts, the dog nodded.

"Mom, what's going on?" Conner asked impatiently.

She didn't answer but stayed focused on Hodgens.

Think she told herself. Think.

Closing her eyes she quickly ran back her memory to her childhood. She rifled through images and words, experiences from then to present day. There had to be something she could use to help her figure out what to do here.

"A shield arrow!" She finally exclaimed. It had been so long since she'd used one that she had almost forgotten about them.

195

Without turning she said, "Conner, go to my quiver and look for an arrow that has a blue flight with a shield on it. Slide it and my bow over to me. Do not walk out here," she instructed him.

Conner did as he was told. Once she could feel the bow and arrow beside her she said, "Hodgens, I need you to stay perfectly still. I'm going to shoot an arrow into the ground between you and dog. It will create a shield between you that is about as tall as this hole. Then I will have Conner assess the situation and come down and get you. Okay?" She asked for acknowledgment.

He nodded his head and said, "be fast, momma. The dog's getting agitated."

She needed two hands. Committing the image before her to memory she put the flashlight down. Lying flat on her belly she extended her arms with the bow and arrow down into the hole. She took a deep breath and loosed the arrow.

She heard the arrow hit the ground. Heard the dog attack. Heard Hodgens scream. Her brain couldn't figure out which one happened first. Had the shield gone up in time? She tossed the bow to her side and groped for the flashlight. Finding it she shone it into the hole. A cry escaped her when she saw her beautiful boy safe on his side of the shield.

The shield had a limited time span.

"Hold on, Hodgens," she instructed. "We have to be fast. I'm sending Conner down."

She eased back from the hole as quickly as possible. Minutes. They only had minutes.

"Conner," she shoved the flashlight at him, "crawl out there and get a look at where Hodgens is. Once you've got it in your head, get down there and get him and his pack. Be fast. That shield will only hold for a few more minutes."

Doing as she instructed, Conner appeared in the hole beside his brother.

"Hey bro, need a lift?" He said with a smile.

"Seriously?" Hodgens scoffed, "just get us out of here!"

Obliging, Conner grabbed brother and rucksack and disappeared. No sooner had they appeared by Tenja and Graysen when they heard the shield crack and the dog barking insanely and running in circles in the hole.

"Well, that was exciting," Graysen broke the silence.

Everyone just looked at him. Beagle Girl appeared next to Hodgens' face and gave him a few good licks on the cheek.

"I'm okay. I'm okay!" He told her.

"Are you really okay, son?" Tenja asked.

"I am, mom, really. Not even a scrape. It just rattled me," he admitted.

"Well, let's get away from this spot. We'll walk about half an hour and then stop for lunch. I think we could all use a break," she advised.

With that, Hodgens put on his rucksack and navigating them around the hole, headed off in the direction of the old water mill.

CHAPTER 24

He stared at the woman sitting on the couch. Her long red hair flowed in waves down her shoulders. Her bright blue eyes stared back at him unwavering.

"You. Blew. Up. Their. House," he said in a broken sentence. There was no inflection in his voice. He had expected some amount of...what? Regret? Guilt? An emotion of any sort?

The dwargic giggled. The big man held his usual stone-faced expression. Praelox simply rolled her eyes and settled her glare on him.

"Somebody had to do something. The waiting had gone on long enough," she shrugged.

"But you blew it up!" He said with anger this time.

"Oh, get over it!" She exploded out of her seat. "I'm tired of sitting around here waiting on you and whoever else you're working with to make decisions, to take action. We're supposed to all be on the same side, working to restore greatness to Draiocht. I didn't sign up to sit around staring at these two," she gestured to the other men in the room, "and waiting for orders."

"Praelox, sit down," he ordered.

She ignored him, "do you even know who I am?"

"I know enough," this time he shrugged.

"No. No you don't. And because of who I am, I know some things about the Araven house that you don't."

She grabbed some paper and a pen and sat back down on the couch. He watched as she drew boxes on the paper.

"This," she pointed at the largest box on the paper, "is the house as you know it. Two floors and a basement. A front porch. A back deck."

"Okay," he drew out, leaning over to look at her drawing.

"This," she pointed at the smaller box, "was an underground area."

"What?!" He asked, shocked by her words. "How do you know that?"

"I'm an ampnull," she explained, "I attach my magic to another person's and boost that person's power."

"That doesn't explain your newfound knowledge," he said.

"Let me finish!" She scolded him and watched as he actually blushed.

"Big guy over there?" She gestured toward the silent man, "his magic is destructive. So, I decided that it was time to take down the house and to use his power to do it."

"But the shields...how did you get past the shields?" He asked.

"There was one piece of their house outside of the shields," she told him.

"The mailbox!" He exclaimed, excited by the telling of the story now.

She nodded.

"He ran a small stream of his magic into the mailbox, and I pushed it down into the ground. I figured if I was going to find a weak spot in the shields, they would be underground. I found the shields easily and magically searched for a weakness."

He nodded to show understanding of her process.

"What I realized was that the shields were larger than the house I was looking at. So I kept probing. That's when I discovered the, for lack of a better word, underground bunker. That is where I found the weakness."

He leaned back, "okay. You think they were hiding in there this entire time?"

"I'd bet my life on it," she stated.

"Why?"

"Because the shields around that part of the structure were old. Don't get me wrong, they were strong, but they were old."

"Why is that a giveaway?" He asked.

"Because they were made by Raben," she told him.

"H-how do you know that?!"

"I'd know that magical signature anywhere," she explained.

"Why would you know her magical signature? How would you know her magical signature?"

"Because we spent the first five years of her life together. We were born in the same room," she left him wondering for a minute.

"My name is Praelox Draiocht. I'm Raben's first cousin."

He fell back into his seat. His head was spinning. This can't be right, he told himself. Raben's cousin? Praelox Draiocht?!

"I need more explanation," he finally said.

She leaned back now looking proud of herself, the face of someone with leverage, with power.

"What more do you need? I'm a pure blood Draiocht. Raben is my cousin. Ugh, I hate the name Raben. Her name is Gazorel Brena Draiocht. I knew her as Gazorel. Raben is a nice nod to her middle name, though, I'll give her that," she muttered.

Shaking his head and waving his arms he said, "enough! I need details! I need answers!"

She gave him a blank look. Then she laughed and his temper flared.

"What are you laughing at!?" He exclaimed.

"For someone who is supposed to be in the know, leading a branch of the revolution on this side of the barrier, you sure seem to be missing some very pertinent information," she told him.

She could almost see literal steam coming out of his ears.

After a moment's silence she finally said, "okay, okay. My father, Draygar Draiocht and Gazorel's father, Reginald Draiocht were brothers."

The dwargic dropped the glass he'd been holding, and it shattered on the table.

At least I'm not the only one who didn't know this, he thought to himself.

"Gazorel and I," she continued.

"Wait," he stopped her, "your father is THE Draygar Draiocht? The leader of the revolution?!"

"Yep," she confirmed. "Feeling a little less at the top of the revolution now?"

"Arrogance is not a becoming feature on you," he responded dryly.

He swished the drink in his glass for a long minute. Then she saw the realization cross his face and she waited for it to come out of his mouth.

"Wait. Wait a minute," he stammered and stuttered. "If Reginald Draiocht is Raben's father, then she's..."

"Say it," she whispered.

"She's Princess Gazorel Brena Draiocht - the child of the king who died when she was five," he swigged the rest of his drink. "But she didn't die," he paused, "she came to Easpach,"

"And that," she said, "changes everything for you, doesn't it?"

"Do you think Tenja knows?" He was curious her opinion.

"I'd wager that she doesn't. My guess is Raben would have wanted to protect them by telling them nothing. If they know nothing, they aren't leverage against her," she responded.

"You make a good point," he agreed.

"But I plan to use that as my own leverage. I'm going to drive the truth of who Gazorel is between them like a chisel in stone. I'm going to break them," she stated as a matter of fact.

#

"This rabbit is really good, mom. We haven't camped and caught our own food for a long time," Graysen leaned back against a log.

"I still have a hard time believing you can do all of this," Hodgens said.

"I know, right?" Conner added. "It all seems so, so outdoorsy," he chuckled.

"I'm a woman of many talents," Tenja replied.

They sat in silence for a few minutes. Then Conner finally said, "so, what do you think happened at the house?"

Tenja dropped her head and pushed food around her plate.

"I think whoever is doing this to us found the apartment," she told them.

"But it was caving in!" Graysen exclaimed. "How did they do that? How did they get through the protections?"

"Raben's shields weren't impenetrable, Graysen. They were strong. They were old magic. They were..." she stopped mid-sentence; her face frozen with her mouth hanging open.

The boys looked at each other. They gave her a minute and then Hodgens said, "Mom? What is it?"

"The shields, they were old magic," she said.

"Right? You said that," Conner prodded.

"I'd bet my bow and arrow on the fact that only old magic could get through them, take them down," she continued.

"Okay?" Graysen this time.

"That means whoever took them down knows old magic. They most likely weren't born in Easpach, schooled in Easpach," she explained.

"The woman who tried to break in?" Hodgens asked.

"The dwargic who cause the destruction at the school?" Graysen asked.

"Both of them together?" Conner understood what was being asked.

Tenja nodded at them, "yes, I would venture a guess it was them. What I don't know is why. I don't know who they are or what they want."

"Do you think they want to know where Momma Raben is?" Hodgens asked. "If she's trying to fix something, maybe they don't want it fixed. Maybe they want to stop her."

"Yeah, and they think we know where she is," Graysen agreed with Hodgens.

"Maybe," Tenja said, "but it seems like a lot of destruction if they just want to know someone's whereabouts."

"Desperate time calls for desperate measures." Conner told them.

"Perhaps," Tenja said. "Let's get lunch cleaned up and finish making our way to the watermill. I'd like to get there before sundown, make camp for the night."

They worked in amicable silence and started on toward the mill. Beagle Girl continued to walk beside Hodgens. Tenja brought up the rear and kept them all cloaked and oral shielded. Stealth was their weapon. But man was it making her tired. She'd have to consider how to preserve her energy. She considered Beagle Girl. An absorber. It might be time to make use of that magic.

#

The stretch from lunch to the mill held was uneventful. Hodgens was right about the terrain. It was tough in some spots. But, with each other's help they navigated it with little struggle.

When the mill came into sight Tenja said, "hold up Hodgens. Beagle Girl, can you scan the area?"

The dog nodded and stepped in front of Hodgens. She raised her muzzle and sniffed the air. She closed her eyes and, Tenja assumed, sent her magic out into the area. After a few moments she turned around and looked at Tenja and wagged her tail.

"All clear, then?" Tenja said.

Beagle Girl nodded.

"Okay guys," she said and was interrupted by Conner disappearing.

He appeared in the mill and Beagle Girl began to bark furiously.

"I'm going to kill that boy!" Tenja exclaimed as she began to run.

The dog aroofed and took her position at the back of the line. Tenja led the gang across the clearing to the mill. About ten feet from the door, she ran into a shield...and everyone ran into her. Conner was inside the shield, unable to get back out. Tenja felt the shield move away from her and toward Conner.

"Oh no!" She whispered.

"Mom?" Hodgens asked, worried about what was happening.

"Beagle Girl?" Tenja turned around. The dog aroofed and ran to her. "It's a shrinking shield. Do you know what those are?"

The dog nodded.

"Any ideas?" Tenja asked.

She watched as the dog ran around the mill. When she returned, she scratched at Tenja's bow. Understanding what she meant, Tenja readied the bow. But she hesitated, not sure which arrow to use. Then she looked at Conner taking quick step backwards.

"You three," she pointed at the dog and boys with her, "get back. About 20 paces." Then she motioned to Conner to get in the building and shut the door. Once he was safely inside Tenja nocked an arrow and aimed it at the shield. There was a blinding white flash and a kick back that knocked her down.

Beagle Girl came running up to her.

"Did it work?" She asked the dog.

In response, she was rewarded with a wet cheek and an aroof.

Getting to her feet Tenja marched up to Conner, grabbed him by the shirt and, in a calmly scary voice said, "don't you EVER do ANYTHING like that again. Do you understand me?!"

Conner nodded apologetically.

After taking a few deep breaths Tenja said, "everyone into the mill."

They all did as they were told without saying a word.

"Graysen, get out your recorder. I want to check the journal," she directed.

Graysen did as he was told. This time not only did the mill show up on the page, but a puzzle piece.

"Well, well, well," Hodgens grumbled. "Shocker - there is a puzzle."

"Where did you guys get the sarcasm?" Tenja laughed.

"Gee, I wonder," Conner poked her, hoping she had forgiven him.

"Okay, seriously, though. The sun is heading down. Let's see if we can find this puzzle or puzzle piece or whatever it is and get out of here," Tenja said.

"We aren't staying in here tonight?" Conner asked.

"Nope, sitting ducks. Especially after the light show I just created," Tenja shook her head. "We camp under the canopy."

They all started looking around. Raben, what are we looking for? Tenja though to herself.

"If I was Momma Raben, where would I put a puzzle or a puzzle piece?" Graysen asked out loud.

After a few moments Conner started knocking on the walls and posts in the room. When he was about halfway around the room, he knocked on a support beam and stopped.

"Mom," he said, "this beam sounds hollow."

They all gathered around it. Hodgens ran his hands over the post, up and down, back and forth. Then he stepped back and just looked at the post.

"Mom, do you sense magic on the post?" He asked Tenja.

She reached out with her magic and shook her head, "nope, nothing I can sense."

"Okay, give me a second," he told them. They watched as Hodgens closed his eyes and reached his hands out toward the post. He stopped just short of touching it. After a moment a small door appeared in the post. Without opening his eyes Hodgens reached just a bit further and opened the door.

"Holy crap!" Conner jumped up and down.

Graysen reached in and took out the rolled parchment. "Looks like you found it, Hodgens!" He said with delight.

Hodgens opened his eyes and smiled, a genuine, proud of himself smile.

"Well done, buddy!" Tenja hugged him. "Okay, we're outta here. Let's get into the canopy and make camp. Then we'll take a look at that," she pointed at the parchment. "Stick it in my pack, Graysen."

Once again Tenja nocked an arrow. This time she slowly stepped out of the mill. Sounds of the forest. Wind in the trees. Crickets. Animals moving about on their typical routines. Nothing out of the ordinary.

"We're good. Let's go," she headed toward the canopy

The crew followed and within minutes they were safe and sound in the shelter of the trees. The sun was almost down, and it wasn't long before they were once again hidden in the darkness. They set up camp and gathered around the fire for dinner.

"So, I have a question," Graysen said.

"Sure, what is it?" Tenja urged him.

"How do you keep the fire and smoke from giving us away?" He asked.

She smiled, "well, Conner and I figured that out. Our cloaking spell keeps the fire itself hidden from view."

She elbowed Conner, "tell them what you're doing."

"Oh," he nodded, "I'm changing the make-up of the smoke. You see it going up but when it hits momma's cloaking spell, I change the smoke to oxygen. So, there's nothing that can get out of the cloaking spell that would be seen by anyone."

Hodgens and Graysen just stared at their brother.

"That's pretty freaking amazing!" Hodgens finally said.

Conner blushed, "thanks, man."

They finished eating in silence and when he'd finished Hodgens finally said, "okay, let's check out the parchment."

Tenja unrolled the parchment and caught the piece of canvas that fell out before it landed on the ground.

"What is it?" Graysen asked.

Tenja held it up and couldn't believe what she was looking at.

206

"It's an actual puzzle piece," she told them. "Made out of canvas. It has some kind of drawing on it, a piece of some bigger picture."

"Is there anything written on the parchment?" Conner asked.

She handed the puzzle piece to Hodgens and looked closer at the paper.

"Yes, let me see," she said and then started to read out loud. "I had no doubt that you would get this far. I believe in all of you and knew that you would work out how to get here. I'm sorry that it has to be this way, that you've had to get here. But here we are. Keep following the map. Keep collecting the puzzle pieces. I hope, with all that is magic, that we will be together again one day soon. I love you all ~ Momma Raben."

"You were right," Hodgens whispered, "all this time you were right. You said to trust her. You said you believed in her."

Tenja looked at her boys. Their eyes were all bright with tears illuminated by the flickering flames of the campfire. She swallowed hard.

"Together," she told them. "We just keep doing it together."

They all nodded at her.

"Okay," she cleared her throat, "let's put this away now, clean up and get some sleep. The next leg of our adventure begins tomorrow."

CHAPTER 25

Farlege paced around his house. He hadn't slept all night, disturbed by what Madifen had said.

How does he know what I am? Did he mean what I think he meant by that? Does he really know that I'm a guardian?

Pace. Pace.

Should I confront him?

He plopped into a chair and dropped his head in his hands.

How did I let this happen? Everything is so out of control!

It didn't help that he had no one to talk to, no one to work with. He couldn't tell anyone about Tenja because then there would be too much interference in the search for her. Finders were wanted magicians and if it got out what she was there would be a lot of people searching for her for their own gain.

Wait, he thought, if Madifen knows what I am, does he know what Tenja is? Can I find out if he knows without giving it away if he doesn't?

With that thought in mind he steeled his spine and headed to Madifen's house.

#

"Open the door Koarré!" Farlege bellowed. "I know you're in there!"

Five minutes passed. Ten.

Jerk! He thought as he continued to bang on the door. Finally, the door opened and Madifen looked up at him.

"Are you quite finished?" He said in a less than polite tone.

"Are you done being a jerk and leaving me standing out here?" Farlege responded in kind.

Madifen rolled back and nodded to gesture that Farlege could enter. Stomping passed him Farlege made his way to the living room and sat down.

Madifen just looked at him.

"Comfy?" Madifen asked the man.

"What did you mean when you said you know what I am?" Farlege didn't waste time getting to the point.

Madifen just cocked his head and looked at the man.

"Seriously? You know exactly what I meant when I said it. I know what you are Farlege. I know that your magic is old. I know that your skills aren't often seen in Easpach," Madifen responded.

"Spit it out, Madifen. If you think you know something, have the guts to spit it out!" Farlege responded in anger.

In a steady voice Madifen looked Farlege in the eye and stated, "you're a guardian, Farlege."

Hearing the words, Farlege slumped in the chair. He watched as Madifen poured him a drink.

Nodding as he handed Farlege the snifter, he said, "brandy. You look like you need it."

Damn the man, Farlege thought, I want to be angry at him. But he took the snifter and downed the alcohol.

"How? How do you know?"

"How I know doesn't matter," he answered, "fact is that I do know."

"Come on," Farlege urged, "appease my curiosity. Doesn't hurt anything if I know how."

Madifen gave him a long, assessing look.

He's trying to read something into my asking, thought Farlege. So, he shrugged and said, "never mind then. If it's that big of a secret, keep it. Just poor me another snifter," and he handed over the glass.

Madifen took the snifter and poured another two fingers of brandy for his guest. Then he made one for himself and downed it. Handing the drink over he said, "I knew one once, a guardian. It was a long time

209

ago, a lifetime ago it feels like most days. Once you've felt the magic that lives in a guardian you can't mistake it for anything else when you meet another one."

Farlege sat silent and just listened. He watched as Madifen stared at the wall, his eyes unfocused, seeing a different place, a different life.

After a few moments Madifen shook his head and poured himself another drink. "Sorry," he finally said. "Now I'm feeling a bit nostalgic. It must be all that is going on."

"It's okay. I think a lot of us are remembering different times these days," Farlege eased. "I still don't understand, though. In my training, only guardians could identify other guardians. And I can tell, you aren't one."

"There was a lapse in your training, then," Madifen told him. "In rare cases, an offspring can feel that magic in the first years of their lives. For most that sense fades. For a few, it never goes away."

"So," Farlege processed what Madifen was saying, "your father was a guardian?"

"Yes, I am the child of a guardian," Madifen answered, being very careful not to say that his father was a guardian. Half-truths were sometimes the safest way to protect one's self.

"Seriously, though, do you know why your shields didn't hold? That was some old magic you weaved into them," Madifen asked minus the previously accusatory tone.

Farlege shrugged, "You're right. I poured some old magic into those shields. Do you have any idea what could have taken it all down like that?"

"Well, from what I know about magic, it was something at least equal in age to what you set," Madifen rubbed his chin.

"Yeah, I figure as much," he agreed.

With that, Farlege set down his glass and stood up.

"I'll leave you in peace now," he told Madifen. "You'd be doing me a solid if you'd keep this little piece of information between the two of us. I know I can't make you keep a secret, but I'd owe you one if you did."

Madifen considered the man standing before him.

"I'll keep your secret and your IOU," he said.

Farlege got in his car and slammed the door. "Well shit," he said aloud. Then he shifted into drive and hit the gas. He didn't like the fact that Madifen knew his secret, that he had to trust the man with his secret. And now he owed him one? "Shit, shit, shit!" He hit the steering wheel. The only consolation was that he didn't think Madifen knew about Tenja.

#

"You need to let me go check out the house," Praelox insisted.

"You mean the pile of rubble?" He asked.

She threw her habitual eye roll in his general direction.

"Call it what you want, but I need to go there. I need to be close to the spells," she pushed.

"How am I supposed to make that happen? It's not like you can just waltz up to the place. You're a wanted criminal!" He pushed back.

"Wanted for what? They don't have any proof I did anything wrong," she pouted now.

"No proof? No proof?" This time he laughed.

"What's so funny?" She crossed her arms.

"They have you on video turning that poor nurse's memory to mush. She doesn't even know her own name, let alone yours or her family's. If what you did at the Araven house wasn't enough, they've got you dead to rights on the assault on the nurse," he didn't think he really needed to explain it.

She stiffened, "if you want to find Tenja and those brats then I'm your only hope."

He considered her words. She was right. He knew it. She knew it. Hell, the big silent guy probably knew it. She was just such a wild card.

211

Was she though? He wondered. Would you send a wildcard to do such an important job? He let the thoughts and questions swirl around in his mind while he let her stew.

"They are on the run because of you," he finally said. "If you had come to me when you found the underground area instead of blowing up the house, we wouldn't even be in this predicament. You would have fulfilled your duties and we'd all be back in Draiocht."

Now her face flushed. He didn't know if it was out of embarrassment or anger.

"What exactly were you trying to accomplish with that trick?" He angled his head and stared at her. "Because it looked like you were trying to kill them."

"And so, what if they had died?" She blurted out. "Would that have been such a bad thing?"

"But they didn't die!" He yelled at her. "They are," he gestured wildly with his hand, "out there somewhere and we have no idea where! Hell, they could be in Draiocht by now!"

That statement landed like an arrow in a bullseye. All the color drained from her face. She anxiously began to pace and run her hands through her hair.

"Oh my god," she repeated over and over. Finally, she looked at him and said, "what have I done? You've got to help me! Please," she was begging now, "get me to the house. I'll find something. I know I will."

"I'll figure something out," he said in a mild tone.

#

Hodgens held the journal and his compass while Graysen played his recorder. They'd been hiking most of the day, only stopping for a quick lunch. No one had said much, the reality of their situation taking hold of their hearts and minds.

212

At the edge of a clearing Hodgens and Beagle Girl stopped walking. He turned around and looked at everyone. Graysen stopped playing.

"We've covered two pages of the map today. This is the next area where there is a puzzle piece indicated," he told them.

"Let me see the journal," Tenja held out her hand. "Graysen, play for me."

She watched as the images on the journal became visible. On the map were four trees, almost like cornerstones of a building. They formed a square. Tenja looked up and thought Well crap. The puzzle piece is in the middle of the clearing.

"Let's sit for a minute. What time is it?" She asked.

"3:18pm," Hodgens told her.

"We have time before sundown and I have to think," she told them.

"What's wrong?" Conner asked.

"According to the map the puzzle piece is in the middle of that clearing," she said, pointing north.

"And that's bad because...?" Conner asked.

"She hates clearings," Graysen said for her.

"Yeah, even with the cloak we're all totally exposed," Hodgens agreed.

"So how do we want to play this?" Conner asked.

"Give me a minute," she sounded exhausted.

The boys each took a drink from their canteen and waited for Tenja to share her idea. Time ticked by and the boys started looking at each other with worried expressions.

"Do you want me to just take you out there?" Conner finally asked.

"I thought about that, but no. I'd have to leave your brother's here without a cloak. Plus, we don't know who's magic might be needed to release the spell holding the puzzle piece," she shared, "because I assume that there is one."

Just then a movement at the opposite side of the clearing caught Hodgens' eye.

"Shh," he said, even knowing they had an oral shield around them. "Look!" He pointed toward the clearing.

They watched as a young boy walked straight to the middle of the clearing. He pulled out a recorder and began to play. Graysen strained to hear the tune. Closing his eyes he absorbed the notes, committing them to memory. When the song stopped, they all gasped when the boy just vanished.

"Where did he go?" Conner asked.

"He wasn't really there," Tenja whispered.

"What?" The three boys said in unison.

"But we all saw him," Graysen said.

"What time is it?" She asked again.

Hodgens looked at his watch, "it's 3...18," he told her in disbelief.

"That doesn't make sense. Did your watch stop?" Conner asked. "You said it was 3:18 a few minutes ago."

Hodgens tapped his watch. It seemed to be working.

"His watch is fine. We're in a time tunnel," Tenja said, sounding as if she was in awe. "I haven't seen one of these since I was a little girl."

"Seems to be a lot of that sort of thing happening," Graysen said.

"Want to explain?" Hodgens asked.

"We're in a sort of state of suspended animation," she began, "time here doesn't go forward or backward. Whatever time it is when you step into it is the time it stays until you leave it. When you step out, you rejoin the world at the time it is in the world, not when you went in."

"But what if we stayed in here for what is days out there?" Hodgens asked.

"Your watch and your body would be thrust into the current time out there when you reenter it," she told him.

"This is insane!" Conner exclaimed. "For all that I thought I had learned about magic there is so much I don't know!"

"Magic is expansive," Tenja agreed. "There is so much I want to teach all of you once you go through the evolution. Until then, your power reservoir just isn't deep enough."

"Okay," Graysen interrupted, "so what do we do?"

"Well, I think it's safe to continue to the center of the clearing cloaked and oral shielded. Beagle Girl, do you agree?' Tenja looked at the dog who wagged her tail.

"Great. So that part we have covered," she looked at Graysen, "did you recognize the song the boy was playing?"

"It was familiar. But I can't quite put my finger on it," he admitted.

"Can you play it like he did?" Hodgens asked.

"I could, but I don't see the point. I'm sure there's a catch. It wouldn't be that simple," he told them.

"Well, let's talk it through. Maybe we can come up with something," Tenja patted his leg.

"Hmm, well, we're in a time tunnel," Graysen began.

"But music can't stand still. It would only be one note," Conner said.

"And when we leave the time tunnel, we'll be thrust forward to the time it is in our real world," Hodgens said, "so just playing it forwards probably isn't the answer."

"Backwards!" Graysen said excitedly, "maybe I play it backwards!"

"Can you do that?" Tenja asked in awe. "I've never known you to play music backwards."

"Sure, I just have start at the last note and play towards the first note," he shrugged.

"You make it sound so easy," she laughed.

"Let me think about the notes for a minute," he told them and closed his eyes. After a few minutes he opened them wide and looked at his family.

"What? What is it?" Tenja asked, concerned by the look on his face.

"I know this song," he said. "We know the song and I'm not sure if I should laugh or cry."

"What is it?" Hodgens asked.

"Oh no," Graysen told him. "Let's get to the middle of the clearing and I'll share Momma Raben's wicked sense of humor with all of you," he said with a chuckle.

When they reached the center of the clearing Graysen began to play. As they watched a metal cylinder rise up from the ground, they all joined in singing about a lion sleeping in a jungle. Once the next puzzle piece was tucked in Tenja's bag they joined in laughter. With smiles on their faces and warmth in their hearts they made their way to the opposite edge of the clearing to set up camp.

Meanwhile, at the park restrooms, Praelox Draiocht was searching for her next clue.

CHAPTER 26

Madifen stood at his chalkboard. He stared at the three columns he'd drawn months ago. At the top of the column on the left was the word Draiocht. In the middle, Sa Làr. On the right, Easpach. In the Draiocht column was one name: Praelox. In the Easpach column were four names: Tenja, Hodgens, Conner, and Graysen. He stepped up to the board and added another name to Easpach: Farlege with a double-headed arrow between his name and the Draiocht.

You've got ties there, don't you fella? Madifen thought to himself.

He turned and grabbed the brandy from his desk, sat down in the plush chair. Staring at the board he thought, where are you Raben?

There had always been political strife in Draiocht. For as far back as history documented there was a group of Draiochtians who believed that all magic should stay in Draiocht. They thought that sending magic to Easpach depleted the magic that Draiochtians could do. Through the years researchers had studied the magic in both Draiocht and Easpach. The amount sent through the grid was proven to have no impact on the strength of the magic within Draiochtians. But, there were always naysayers, conspiracy theorists who pushed back at the research. They fed their fellow Draiochtians with lies and misinformation. They pushed their anti-grid agenda.

He took a swig of his drink.

The lack of conflict and hostility in Easpach was actually one of the things that he liked most about it. No one was treated differently if they had or didn't have magic. Everyone had the same rights, the same freedoms – within the bounds of the legal system of course. And they set up a vein of the legal system to handle those with magic. Leaving those who have magic to deal with magical delinquencies. Non-magical delinquencies were handled by individuals without magic. It just all made sense. And the two sides were fair when the crime crossed the boundary between magic and non-magic folks. He really couldn't believe it worked and that so much peace prevailed in Easpach. But it did and he liked it.

Focusing on the board once again his eyes settled on Tenja and the boys' names. Where are you four? He wondered to himself. Are you still in Easpach? Did you find a traversable and get out? Are you all still alive?

Surely, they are alive. If one of the boys had died, he firmly believe that Tenja would have come for him by now. After all, she thought he had something to do with everything that was happening. If Tenja had died, the boys had no place else to go. No one to turn to. If something happened to her, he thought for sure they would come back to him.

He got up, poured himself another drink and sat down at his desk. Pulling a leather-bound journal from his top drawer, he took one more look at the board. Then he began to write. He was getting older and wasn't holding details in his memory like he did when he was younger. Though he hadn't expected to experience these lapses so soon after turning forty, he'd learned to work with them. The last thing he did each day was sit at this very desk and commit the day's events to ink. He added his thoughts, feelings, perceptions, whatever came to mind to each fact he could remember.

Memory was about associations. So sometimes he had to describe his lunch in detail to get to the fact that he wanted to recall. But he always got there. And he always wrote it down. He had tried to use his healing magic to repair his memory. But, healing the brain is tricky magic, rarely successful. Without proper training he could leave himself in a worse state than the present one.

No one knew about these lapses. He had slipped up in class a couple of times last year. But, with students it was easy. He just laughed it off as being exhausted or joked about being old. They ate it up. And he protected his secret.

It was important that he not only protect his secret, but that he safeguard his knowledge. He was living in a historical time for Easpach and possibly for Draiocht. What was happening was going to change

218

the course of their futures. He thought about the painting left in the art gallery. He remembered how, in the end of the painting's transformations, everything was burning. Then he considered how he knew about the final transformation of the painting and smiled to himself.

He closed the journal, pulled out a sticky note and pressed it onto the cover. Then he wrote one word: James.

#

Farlege was exhausted. He hadn't slept well in weeks. His meals were mostly grabbed from the freezer and popped in the oven. There hadn't been fresh fruit or vegetables in his house in weeks. Life had never been like this for him. He was a stable person. Dependable. Honest. Wasn't he?

He splashed water on his face and looked in the mirror. This was supposed to be his day off. But here it was, six o'clock in the morning and he couldn't sleep. Toweling off his face he walked into the bedroom and threw himself flat on his back on the bed.

Staring up at the ceiling he thought what exactly am I supposed to do now?

What he wanted to do was put in for a vacation and go on a hunt for Tenja and the boys. He didn't think the chief of police would look kindly on him taking off on vacation when there was a house in shambles because of magic and a family missing, presumed dead. Not to mention the hospital was short a patient and the parole office was short a parolee.

"Ahhhh!" He exclaimed aloud to an empty bedroom.

He was a detective after all. He should be detecting something by now - that's what his colleagues were saying behind his back. He had heard the whispers, seen the looks every time he was in the office or on a call. All of it was driving him just a little bit crazy.

So, he had to do something about it all. He got up, threw on some casual clothes and headed to the diner for a healthy breakfast. He would make this day be different than the last - however many - had been.

#

He felt much better after breakfast. The sun was shining. The air was crisp without being cold. He could almost feel happy. Then he pulled up to what used to be the Araven house. Instead of that cute house with a hint of wear, there were piles of rubble and holes in the ground. Letting out a breath he got out of his car and ducked under the caution tape.

He wasn't happy to see part of the CSI team there. On a Saturday. This early in the morning.

He waved, "hey guys. I'm didn't think you would be here," he told them.

They looked at each other and mumbled a 'hi captain'.

They look nervous, he thought to himself, like I caught them doing something they aren't supposed to be doing.

"I don't remember approving an overtime request for CSI today. Am I just so exhausted I don't remember?" He asked.

After a long silence, the lead forensic investigator stepped out and said, "look Captain, we mean no disrespect. But we can't really tell you anything. You'll have to talk to the Chief."

Farlege was stunned. It was worse than he thought. The whispers, the looks - the Chief was even doubting his abilities. This was not good. But he didn't begrudge the team. They were doing as they were told.

He held up his hands in mock surrender, "no worries, guys. I would like to look around, though. That okay?"

"Sure, Captain. It's still your crime scene," the leader said.

"Thanks," Farlege nodded. "Let me know if you need anything or if I can help in any way." And with that he moved to the location of the underground area. The area that no one had even suspected existed.

A lot had been excavated from what had been determined to be a basement apartment. A ladder stood in the hole for easier access to the area. Farlege climbed down. When he stepped off the ladder he just turned and studied the area, taking stock and trying to acclimate himself to an apartment layout. From what he could tell he was standing in a bedroom. Though most items had been removed he could tell bed frames, possibly bunk beds had been there. He moved through the space identifying a bathroom, kitchen, and living room area.

The living room area was most interesting. He bent down and studied some papers on the floor. They were photographs and it didn't take him long to realize they were the ones he had given Tenja of the painting. Given is a nice way of putting it, he said as he rubbed the phantom pain in his chest and recalled how Conner took the bag from his shoulder. So many changes. So much I don't know.

There had to be something, anything, that would redeem him with the Chief and his men. He couldn't let himself be pushed out of the investigation. He stood and made his way to the kitchen. Refrigerators were amazing inventions. More than once he'd seen them withstand an explosion. Opening the door of the refrigerator he was shocked by what he saw. Apparently, no one had bothered to open the refrigerator, or he would have heard something.

A note hung in the empty space. He put on a forensic glove and grabbed the note. Was Tenja crazy or was she a genius? Either way, this would definitely get him back in the Chief's good graces. He raced up the ladder and sped off toward his office.

#

"Hi Captain," the weekend dispatcher said as he walked in. "Didn't expect to see you on your day off."

"Hey Charlie," he returned the greeting. "I hadn't planned on being here, but I got a lead on the Araven case."

"Oh, that's great news! I hope it pans out."

"Me too, Charlie. Me, too."

Farlege sat down at his desk and was just about to ring the Chief when Charlie raced in.

"Sorry to interrupt Captain, but I think we got another lead!"

Farlege jumped back up feeling the man's excitement, "what is it?"

"Frank from the pizza place just called and said his pizza delivery driver just dropped a pizza off. The man who answered the door was a really big guy who said nothing. But someone in the background yelled for the guy to hurry up and bring the pizza. The delivery guy caught a glimpse of the other guy as the door swung shut. He said the guy was a male dwargic that fit the description of the wanted fugitive!"

"Charlie, you just made my day! Call in the guys. It's time for a stakeout," he responded, giddy with anticipation.

The pizza parlor was happy to help by providing not only the address of the drop off, but a uniform for a police officer to use in the stake out.

When the big guy answered the door the decoy pizza delivery guy said, "Frank said we delivered the wrong pizza to you guys. So, I'm supposed to give you this one and tell you he's sorry."

The man at the door just looked down at him, saying nothing.

"Hey man, I'm just doing what I'm told. You want the pizza or not?" The cop asked.

"Don't stand there with the door hanging open!" The cop heard another voice. "Just take the pizza!"

The big man did as he was told and as he swung the door shut the police officer caught a glimpse of the dwargic. As he turned and walked back down the sidewalk he simply nodded, got in his delivery car, and drove off.

The team descended on the house like a group of kids going after candy. Farlege threw a shield around the house, his team staying just outside of it, magic at the ready.

"Come on out guys!" Farlege enhanced his voice with magic so they could hear him. "We've got you surrounded."

A blast of magic hit the shield but was just absorbed. Another one followed quickly. Then another.

"You can do that all day, but this shield is not coming down," Farlege told them. "Step out here one at a time and my officers will place magic blocking bracelets on you. Let's do this the easy way."

A car in the yard exploded.

Farlege shrugged, "or we can do it the hard way" he thought aloud.

Knowing the drill, his officers hit their stride. Slowly Farlege moved the shield closer to the house, tightening the magical noose around the fugitive and his sidekick. The officers moved with the shield, ready to take down the two men inside the house. They were about five feet from the house when two men ran out and rushed the shield.

"Officers down! Officers down!" Jespen yelled into his radio.

Farlege moaned and tried to move but strong hands held down his shoulders.

"Easy Captain," Jespen was saying. "You need to stay down until the medics get here."

Farlege could see the man's lips moving but couldn't understand what he was saying. All the words were muffled. He cleared his throat but could barely whisper the words, "what happened?"

More lips moving. More mumbling by his officer. Farlege was getting frustrated. He tried again to sit up, but the pain shot through his leg and straight up to his head.

"Hold on, Captain. Just hold on," Jespen tried to reassure him.

CHAPTER 27

Praelox stood in the doorway of the mill. "You left behind too much trace, Gazorel. Did you really think no one would come here looking?"

She was only seven when Gazorel died. But she had never believed the story about Gazorel drowning. Her and the nanny? Too much of a coincidence. Of course, she hadn't heard the story until she was older. At seven she was left out of grown-up talk. All she knew was that Gazorel wasn't around to play with anymore.

Devon took it the hardest. The shock of losing his twin was almost too much for him to bear. He didn't talk for almost two years. He spent most of his time indoors. Gone were the happy play dates and outings to festivals and parks. He'd been too afraid to leave the safety of the castle.

Just shy of her thirteenth birthday her father ripped her out of her life in the castle. He moved the family to a cottage in the forest. She was furious. In fact, she hated him for years. Then she began to understand. Draiocht was just giving away its magic! Some fool decided a long time ago that Draiocht should share its magic with Easpach and allow citizens of Draiocht to even move to Easpach and take their magic with them. As she got older, she realized that her father was on the side of Draiocht and Reginald was leading their world to ruin. If he wasn't stopped Draiocht would lose its magic. And life without magic just wasn't worth living.

But her father had been captured and tried for treason. And Reginald threw his own brother into the dungeon! The mistake the king made, though, was to allow Draygar one visitor before he began his life sentence in darkness - her. During that single visit Draygar told her everything she needed to know. He passed the baton of leadership to her. Now, she was going to end this once and for all.

When she crossed over to Easpach it didn't take long to pick up Gazorel's magical signature. Praelox was two when Gazorel was born, and she'd started feeling the infant's magical signature almost immediately after her birth. Though not a finder by birth, Praelox could always feel Gazorel by her magic. The skill had always puzzled their parents. Gazorel left so many strong spells behind that finding it was like riding a bike. She might as well have put up a neon sign. But there were others on the trail, too. She was supposed to be leading the revolution, but there were others in high-ranking positions that didn't trust her. She'd wanted to just kill those Draiochtians but figured that wouldn't earn her any points with the rest of the revolutionaries. So, she'd focus on finding Gazorel. Once she had Gazorel as her prisoner she would have the best bargaining chip.

Shaking her head, she forced herself to come back to the present. She walked into the building and looked around. It didn't take long for her to see the hole in the beam. Laughing she thought, thanks for leaving a trail for me to follow Tenja. Obviously Gazorel was the brains in that relationship. Relationship. She had to admit that she was a bit shocked to learn that Gazorel had married a woman and given birth to triplets. Those were two events in Gazorel's life that she hadn't expected.

She reached with her magic to test the hole in the beam. There had been something there. A letter? Some kind of instructions?

Dust started to fall from the ceiling. Looking up she could see cracks forming in the wood. She ran out of the mill as fast as she could, barely making it through the doorway before the entire building collapsed right where she'd been standing. A trap she thought to herself. Well played, cousin. Well played.

She turned with her back to the pile of rubble and imagined herself exiting the building after finding the item in the beam. To her left was the direction she'd come from. They wouldn't have gone back that way. She had three different directions to choose from. In the end she decided to continue in a somewhat straight line for now and headed into the forest.

"Are we even close to the next symbol?" Graysen asked Hodgens.

"Yeah, we've been on this part of the map for two days," Conner added.

"I told you guys, there's no way to tell how far apart things are. We find it when we find it. Before we get to it we have to cross a -" his words were interrupted by the distant sound of a river.

"The river!" Conner jumped up and down.

"Easy," Tenja grabbed Hodgen's arm. "Where there's water like a river there might be people. Beagle Girl, reconnaissance please."

The dog obliged and trotted ahead a little way. She came back quickly shaking her head no and urging them all to move back.

"Show us," Tenja told the dog who led them up a small hill.

They all stood in a tight group behind a tree. Tenja drew the boundary and oral shields tightly around them. As they stood there, they watched a group of men come into the woods from the direction Beagle Girl had been.

"You sure you saw something over here Isaac?" One man asked.

"Well," the man they assumed was Isaac scratched his head, "I thought I saw a rabbit or something."

"A rabbit? We need more meat than a rabbit to feed the five of us!" Another man exclaimed.

"Come on, let's keep going. There's gotta be some game somewhere in these woods," yet another man told his group.

Tenja and the boys watched as the men moved on and out of sight. But they didn't move until Beagle Girl indicated that it was safe. They wouldn't have survived this without her and Tenja was pretty sure Raben had known that would be the case.

"We've seen more people in this forest than I expected we would," Hodgens told her.

"I'm with you. I didn't expect we'd be dodging people almost every day. It's nerve wracking," she agreed. "We must assume that every person is an enemy. It's how we continue to survive."

When they got to the river Tenja was dismayed to see how swiftly it was moving.

"I was hoping we'd be able to just walk across it," she admitted.

"Yeah, that's not going to happen," Conner shook his head.

"What are your thoughts here, mom?" Hodgens asked. "After the river we head on to the next symbol on the map."

"Why don't I just travel each of you?" Conner asked.

"We can't travel cloaked," Tenja told him.

She looked at Beagle Girl.

"Beagle Girl, I've tried not to ask, but we need you to help us here. Can you drop magic and then absorb my cloaking and Conner's traveling?"

The dog nodded. They watched as she laid down and closed her eyes. After a moment she stood up and wagged her tail.

"Great. Are you able to travel a human? Like, could you take Hodgens across the river?" She asked the dog and was again answered with the wag of a tail.

"Okay, here's how we're going to do this. I'll uncloak us. Beagle Girl will take Hodgens. Conner will take Graysen. You go at the same time and when you get there, Beagle Girl will cloak all of you."

"But what about you?" Conner asked.

"I'll recloak myself after you four leave. Then you come back for me."

The boys looked at each other.

"I don't like it," Graysen told her.

"What other option do we have?" She asked.

"We could find another way to cross," Graysen told her.

"You want to spend more days trying to find the next symbol? We could walk for days up or down this riverbank before we find a bridge or some way to cross. And once we find it there will likely be people

227

there. This affords us the protection of the canopy on the other side of the river immediately once we get there," she told them all.

"But we'll all be exposed," Hodgens added to Graysen's concern.

"Only for a few seconds at most," Tenja assured them. "I'm good at this, guys. You should trust me with it by now."

Beagle Girl nudged Hodgens' leg as if to tell him it would be okay.

"Fine," he told her. "Let's just get it over with."

She looked at Beagle Girl and then at Conner, "I'm going to count and on three I'll drop the cloak. You go when I say three. On the other side, Conner, you count to three. Beagle Girl, drop the cloak on three. When Conner's gone you put it back up."

She counted and they went. As soon as they disappeared, she threw up her cloaking spell. She saw the flash of color on the opposite bank that told her the four had landed. But Conner didn't come back. That's when Tenja heard the voices.

"Isaac, you keep saying you see things, but you never do. Why are we following this guy again?"

"I really saw something this time. I swear!"

Tenja put a tight oral shield around herself and moved behind a tree near the river's edge.

"Let me go, Hodgens!" Conner insisted. "And call off your dog!"

"Beagle Girl, can you do an oral shield?" Hodgens asked his companion. The dog responded with a nod as she continued to hold Conner's ankle with her teeth.

"You can't go," Graysen told Conner. "You have to wait."

"But mom's over there alone!" Conner told them.

"We know, but we have to trust her," Hodgens said. "We'd be exposed for you to leave, and you'd be exposed when you get there. We can't risk it."

"Fine," Conner said, "fine! Let me go!"

They did as he asked, and they all watched the events on the other side of the river. They couldn't hear what the men said, and they didn't know where Tenja was. All they could do was watch and wait.

"This is pointless Isaac. Let's all just go home."

"Wait, I feel something here. It's weird, like there's some kind of spell," another of the me said.

Tenja nocked an arrow.

"You're losing your mind, man. I'm going home. I want to drink."

She watched as the man who thought he felt something stared straight at her, unable to see or hear her. After a long minute the man turned and hurried after the other members of his group. Tenja let out a sigh of relief and put the arrow back in her quiver.

When she could no longer hear voices or other noises that told of people close, she dropped her cloak. Beagle Girl did the same and Conner traveled her back to the group.

"That was way too close," Hodgens told her.

"Tell me about it," Tenja said, "he was so close I could smell him. Let's find this next symbol."

#

They only had to walk for about twenty minutes when Hodgens stopped and closed the book.

"There's something here. I can feel it," he told them.

Stopping with him they all began to look around. Graysen said, "hey I've got a stack of rocks over here."

"There's one here, too," Conner said.

Upon further inspection they found four rock sculptures.

"What does this mean? What do you think we do with them?" Hodgens looked at Tenja.

"I'm not sure. Let's each touch one with our magic and see if we feel anything," she suggested.

When they did, three of the sculptures simply fell. They all gathered around the one still standing. Tenja reached out with her magic.

"Nope, I got nothing," she told them.

Hodgens stepped back so he could look at the sculpture. He walked around it, thinking.

"When you first look at it," he said, "it seems like the rocks are all the same size. But there are subtle differences in the circumferences of the rocks."

"They look the same to me," Conner said. Graysen agreed.

Hodgens sat down facing the sculpture. "Give me a couple of minutes," he told them.

They watched as all of the rocks were suddenly floating in air. One remained on the ground, like a base. Hodgens couldn't budge that one. He began stacking the rocks back up. When he put the last rock back on top nothing happened.

He frowned, "I was sure that was the answer."

"What did you do?" Conner asked?

"I stacked them from largest at the bottom to smallest at the top."

Tenja shook her head, "too easy. Someone might be able to do that without magic. Flip the stack over and hold it with your magic," she encouraged.

He did as Tenja said, and they watched as the rocks began to transform.

"It's done," Hodgens told them when he felt the magic fade. He reached out and grabbed the scroll that was now standing where the rocks had been.

"That was amazing!" Graysen murmured.

"It was some interesting magic," Tenja agreed, "come on. Let's get away from here and make camp. Then we can see what's on the scroll."

Hodgens tucked the scroll into his bag, took out the journal and pointed them in the direction indicated on the map.

#

"So, what does this puzzle piece look like?" Graysen asked when they finished eating.

Hodgens pull out the scroll and Tenja retrieved the other pieces of the puzzle. They laid them on the ground next to the fire.

"It's definitely a picture of some kind of box," Conner pointed out.

"Do you think we'll have to find it after we find all of the pieces?" Graysen asked.

"I'd hazard a guess that yes, finding the box is important," Tenja said.

"Does it look like anything you've seen before?" Hodgens asked her.

She shook her head, "nope. It's not familiar."

Hodgens scooped up the pieces and handed them to her.

"Hey mom?" Hodgens asked.

"Yeah?"

"There's something I've been wanting to ask you," he said.

"Sure, what is it?" She sat down and looked at him.

"How is it that you use arrows from your quiver, but you never run out of arrows?" He pointed at her bow and quiver lying on the ground next to her.

She picked up the quiver, stood it in front of her.

"Magic," she told them. "This quiver was made especially for me and will work with no one else's magic. It regenerates three types of arrows: hunting arrows, defensive arrows, and offensive arrows. Hunting arrows are as you'd expect. I can use them to get food. Defensive arrows create shields. Offensive arrows will tear apart whatever they hit."

"Even living things?" Graysen paled.

She nodded, "yes, even living things. I've never had reason to use one."

"Who made it?" Hodgens asked.

"My father before he and my mother disappeared when I was ten."

"What do you think happened to them?" Graysen asked.

231

"I don't know," she replied sadly, "it's a question that I hope to answer some day."

They all stared at the fire and finished up their tea.

"Let's get some sleep. Final leg of the puzzle adventure tomorrow," she told them.

CHAPTER 28

Farlege opened his eyes slowly. Where am I? He thought to himself. Slowly realization crept into his conscious. He was lying in a hospital bed. Pain shot through his leg, and he let out a small cry. Farlege looked down to see his left leg in traction. Well crap!

A nurse came running into the room, "Captain, nice to see you awake," she said.

"Pain meds," he hissed, not wanting to sound demanding.

He watched as the nurse pushed a button on a small handle next to him. Then she handed it to him.

"You've got morphine for the pain. Just push this as you need it. If doesn't seem to be enough, let me know and I'll contact your doctor."

"What happened?" He asked.

"Your leg was shattered. It took the doctors hours to put it back together. You've got a long road of recovery ahead of you," she told him.

"How? When?"

"Well, you've been out for two days," she began.

"Two days!?"

The nurse nodded, "as for the how...well, I'll let the Chief explain all of that." She patted him on the shoulder. "You rest. I'll call the Chief and let him know that you're awake."

He didn't know how much time had passed before he heard the clomp of police uniform shoes in the hallway followed by voices that were mumbles to his ears. Then he heard the Chief take a seat next to the bed.

"I'm awake," he told his superior as he opened his eyes.

"Glad to hear it," the Chief replied. "How are you feeling?"

"Like I got hit by a bus," Farlege told him.

Nodding the man said, "from what I've been told that is a pretty accurate description."

"What happened?" Farlege asked.

The Chief recounted the events of two days prior as they'd been told to him by the surviving officers. The dwargic and big man had set off two large bombs. It just happened that one was on each side of Farlege's shield. The bomb inside the shield killed the two men. The bomb on the outside did the damage to him. Bartray was in serious condition. The doctors didn't know if he would make it. Lancaster was dead.

Farlege moaned, "how did it all go so wrong?"

The Chief patted his shoulder, "you didn't now they had bombs in the yard, son. There was no way you could have been prepared for that attack."

Farlege just turned his face away from the Chief. He looked out the window to find a storm raging outside and thought how appropriate.

The Chief cleared his throat and stood up, "I'll let you get some rest. You call me if you need anything."

Farlege listened to the footsteps fade as the Chief left. He looked down at his leg. What the hell am I supposed to do now?

#

Hodgens stopped and looked around. Looked down at the journal.

"What's wrong?" Tenja asked as they all gathered around him, Graysen continuing to play the recorder and illuminate the pages.

Hodgens flipped a page in the book and then turned it back again.

"This is really weird," he said. "There's a gap in the path."

"Let me see," she said holding out her hand.

Hodgens handed her the book and she took a few minutes to study it as he had. She flipped back a page, forward a page.

"Hmmm," she finally said handing the journal back to Hodgens. "Point me in the direction we're supposed to go. I will lead for a little bit."

"Are you sure that's a good idea?" Conner asked.

"It is the best option," she told them. "Beagle Girl, you take up the rear. Form a line behind me. Whatever this is, I go in first."

Tenja took two steps forward and disappeared from the boys' view. They immediately started yelling. Beagle Girl started barking. They all started running - and ran into her.

"Good grief guys," she said in confusion, "what is wrong with you?"

"You disappeared!" Graysen exclaimed.

"What do you mean I disappeared?"

"You took two steps and then we couldn't see you. You were just - gone," Conner explained.

"It was really freaky," Hodgens added.

"Huh," she muttered, "you four stay here."

"Momma!" Hodgens reached for her but not fast enough. They watched as she walked back the way they had come and disappeared again.

"Ugh!" Conner let out an exasperated sigh, "was that necessary?"

Tenja looked around. Yep, it's where they had come from. It was exactly what she saw when she had turned to head this direction. Then she turned toward the boys, except they weren't there. She reached out with her magic and one signature met hers, Raben. A portal and boundary spell weaved together? Well, isn't this interesting, she thought. She should be more concerned because of the portal, but the boys had come through exactly to where she was. Not quite understanding what had happened, she walked back through the spell and rejoined her family.

"It's a portal and boundary spell weaved together," she told them, "Raben made it."

"You can weave those things together?" Hodgens asked in curiosity.

"I've never seen anything like it," Tenja told them.

"We've not encountered a portal or spell like this at any other time on this adventure," Graysen wondered aloud. "Why now?"

"I don't know, but I'm going to continue to lead," Tenja said as she moved through the group. "Line on me again," she told them and watched as Beagle Girl took up the rear.

This time Tenja got about ten steps and then made a sound that could have been laughter or tears, maybe both. The boys came around to each side of her and just looked at what she saw.

After a moment Conner said, "with all that is magic, is that real?"

Beagle Girl let out an excited aroof and began to dance around in front of them.

"Based on her behavior," she pointed at the dog, "I'd say yes, what we think we see, we actually see."

"But," Graysen stuttered. "B-b-but how? It looks just like our house in Easpach!"

"Apparently a lot can happen in ten years," Hodgens spat out. "If she was building a house, how could she have time to be saving us?"

No one seemed to notice his question, or, if they did, they didn't seem to care about the answer.

"Do you think it's the same on the inside?" Conner asked.

"I guess we'll have to go in to find out. Head on in, I want to check on this boundary spell to see what is protecting us," she told them.

As the boys headed toward the house, Tenja reached out with her magic and could feel oral shields, defensive shields, and one like what Farlege had placed on their house, to prevent anyone on the outside from noticing magic being done inside the boundary. Only the spell was slightly different. She couldn't exactly tell how it was different, but all the spells felt threaded with love and protection. For the first time in weeks, she felt like she could breathe, like they were safe as long as they stayed within the boundaries.

She entered the house and heard footsteps in three different directions. Leave it to her boys to check out every nook and cranny. She walked through the foyer, curious about the room on the left. In the Easpach house there was no doorway there. What she saw when she turned stopped her, stole her breath. A den. Their den.

Hodgens joined her in the doorway. "It's a nice addition don't you think?" he asked.

Tenja couldn't speak. A memory had closed her throat, preventing words from escaping.

"Mom? What's wrong? Don't you like it?" He turned to her, a concerned look on his face. Then he watched as she turned and walked out of the house. Following her he stopped when she dropped to her knees and began to sob.

He turned and ran back into the house, "guys, guys! Come here, now!"

Conner and Graysen came running.

"What is it? What's wrong?" Conner asked.

Hodgens led them outside to where they were needed. They all sat in a circle around her, laid a hand on her, and let her weep. They didn't know how long they had sat there when she finally began to breathe normally and sat down cross-legged in the grass.

"It wasn't supposed to be like this," she told them.

"It's okay, mom, we've all had our moments," Graysen said.

"No, I mean ALL of it. None of this was supposed to happen. Raben and I were supposed to live happily ever after. Then you three were born and the five of us were supposed to live together through that happily after. She and I were supposed to raise you together," she paused, took some deep breaths.

"Then she left, and it felt like me against the world. I was lucky," she smiled meekly, "you three were, for the most part, easy to parent. But that doesn't mean it wasn't hard, that there weren't hard times, lonely times," she was brutally honest with them.

"But she was my one true love and the thought of trying to love someone else made me feel, well, nauseous," she let out a laugh.

The boys chuckled nervously, still not knowing if they should say something or what it should be if they did.

"What I never saw coming was the four," Beagle Girl had joined them and nudged Tenja's hand, "sorry, the five of us, having to go on this epic quest."

"Epic quest?" Hodgens laughed now.

"Hey," she said, "we moved past adventure when you fell in that hole, buddy!" She poked him in fun.

He smiled at her, "can I ask? What was it about the den that broke the dam?"

Her smile was gone, her shoulders slumped.

"We were going to add a den. We had talked about it just after you guys turned six and were really getting into reading on your own. We thought it would be nice to have a den with a fireplace where we could all sit around and read stories, either separately or have a family story time," she explained.

"But you never added it," Graysen whispered.

She shook her head, "no. We had the plans all drawn up. Had even talked to a contractor. But then she left and every time I thought of adding it, of being in that space and enjoying that space with you three - without her - my heart broke a little more. So I burned the plans and forced myself to stop thinking about it."

Silence fell. She looked up at the sky.

"The sun is going to be gone soon. I'm starving. I'll go hunt something up so we can -"

Conner interrupted, "don't have to. The fridge and cupboards are stocked."

"What?" Tenja asked in shock.

"All of our favorites are there," he shrugged.

"But...how?" She stammered.

"I don't know, but let's eat!" Conner jumped up.

So, they did. As they cleaned their plates, feeling full for the first time in a long time, Tenja sat back and wondered how Raben had pulled it all off. She had to have help. This was all more than even she could learn to do. But who? Raben had been gone from Draiocht for

238

so long, who could she possibly know that would be willing to help her to this extent? Who could she know that she could trust this deeply?

Her thoughts were momentarily interrupted by the boys cleaning up their dinner dishes. But she quickly fell back into her confusion and awe. Running water. Indoor plumbing. Electricity. It just didn't make sense in the middle of the forest.

"Mom!" Graysen said.

"Huh? What?" She shook her head and looked at him.

"Where were you?" He asked.

"Sorry, I'm still trying to figure out how she made this house," she admitted.

"At this point, I don't care," Conner said, "I just want to sleep in a bed for a night."

"Agreed," Hodgens nodded.

"We're exhausted. Going to call it a night," Graysen told her.

"Okay, I'll be up in a little bit," she said.

As she watched them head toward the stairs, the moment felt very normal. So, she had to say it, "goodnight my favorite little people. I love you."

Three laughing voices replied, "I love you, too, mom."

#

Praelox came up to the clearing.

"Really, Gazorel? In a clearing? Are you trying to get them killed?" She said to no one.

As she stepped into the clearing, she felt something shift. The leaves in the forest had started to turn colors over the last couple of days. But as she looked around the plants were green. The sun was high in the crisp, blue sky. And it was warm. She took a step back.

Chilly air brushed her skin, and the leaves were a greenish brown color. Fall was around her. She took a step forward.

And she was in summer.

"Well, I'll be," she said, "a time tunnel!"

As she walked toward the center of the clearing, she spotted a hole in the ground. But a few strides in she also noticed the clearing was shrinking. The left and right sides were getting closer to her. Then she looked straight ahead and saw that with every step she took the length of the clearing got longer.

She'd heard stories of people getting trapped in time tunnels. When she was a kid her father had told her that they were once used for criminals. Once the criminal was locked in, the magic would make the time tunnel infinite, never allowing the person to reach an end and get out.

Think, Praelox, think! She yelled to herself.

She stopped walking. When she did, the time tunnel stopped changing shape.

Okay, she thought, if I walk forward the time tunnel shrinks and gets longer. So going forward isn't an option.

Without changing direction, she took a step backward. The tunnel widened and shrunk. She took another step back. Same result.

"Gazorel, you're a tricky one, aren't you?" Praelox laughed. "It's about time I had some competition."

She continued to walk backward until she felt the chill against her skin and saw the greenish brown leaves. A few more steps back and then she sat down and took a breath. She would never admit it to anyone, but the thought of being trapped in a time tunnel scared the magic out of her.

"Well played, again, Gazorel. You bought them some time since I have to go around this magic," and she started her trek around the boundary of the time tunnel.

CHAPTER 29

Madifen rolled into the hospital room. Farlege was propped up reading the newspaper.

"You look like crap," Madifen said in jest.

"I'm not in the mood for you, Madifen."

Madifen considered the man lying in the bed. His leg must have been a mess based on the amount of traction holding it together. He'd given a lot of thought to this moment. He'd had several drinks while he contemplated the action he was about to take.

Turning his wheelchair Madifen rolled to the door – and closed it.

Farlege dropped his newspaper, "what in the hell do you think you're doing?"

Madifen turned and looked at Farlege, "you're not the only person in Easpach with a secret."

Farlege tried to sit up straighter. He glanced around the room frantically, thought about pressing the call button for the nurse.

"Madifen, I'm warning you. I will protect myself against attack."

"Oh relax. I'm not going to attack you. I'm going to heal you."

"Y-y-you're what?" Farlege stuttered.

"I'm a healer, Farlege. Old healer magic type healer."

"But you're symbol..."

"Your symbol isn't that of a guardian," Madifen tipped his head. "People go to great lengths to protect their secrets."

Positioned next to Farlege's leg Madifen placed his hands over the leg and closed his eyes.

"Wait!" Farlege grabbed Madifen's arm. "Is this going to hurt?"

Madifen opened his eyes, "yes, it's going to hurt. You'll want to push that green button a few times before I get started. But, if I don't do this, your leg will take months to heal, even with what magic healing the doctors here can give. And then it might never get back to normal. If I do it, it will be like it never happened."

Farlege stared at him, "are you serious?"

"I don't joke about a healing. You're going to want to put a boundary spell up to prevent anyone from coming in. Add an oral shield to it so no one can hear you scream. Once I start, I can't stop and I'm sure they will check on you before I can finish. They'll try to stop me."

"But if you do this, everyone will know your truth."

"Yes, they will. And they might not trust me again," he nodded to Farlege, "but you, you will owe me one."

"What does that mean?"

"It means that you and I are on the same side."

"We are?"

"We're both trying to find the Aravens, to get them to safety. We've been butting heads trying to make that happen, working against each other instead of together. I get this leg healed and that changes. We work together. No secrets. Deal?"

Farlege thought about the offer before him. Tenja hadn't trusted Madifen, at least not completely. But he was hitting some walls in his attempt to find them. Perhaps an alliance would pay off in the long run.

Farlege nodded and put a boundary shield at the door. Then he pressed the green button four times.

"Do it."

Slowly, meticulously, Madifen began healing Farlege's leg from the top to the bottom. He healed the leg from the inside out. As the bone and muscles healed, he guided the healing to push out the traction bars. It took hours. He lost track of how many times Farlege let out a scream, how many times he pushed the green button. He tried to block out the man slipping between conscious states. Focus Madifen, he thought to himself, you've got to get it right.

After six hours of healing Madifen sagged in his wheelchair. Traction pieces were scattered all over the bed and the floor. He rolled back from the bed and contemplated how life as he'd known it was about to change.

As he came awake Farlege wiggled his toes. No pain. He opened his eyes and looked down at his leg, saw the traction bars scattered around. Then he looked over and saw the man asleep in the wheelchair.

"Madifen," he said, and again a little louder, "Madifen!"

Startled awake Madifen's leg jerked. The men stared at each other.

Damn it, Madifen thought to himself.

Farlege watched as the man picked up his leg and repositioned it in the wheelchair.

"Involuntary muscle movement," Madifen said, "it happens sometimes when I wake up or stretch my upper body, get startled. Things like that."

"I didn't know you had any feeling in your legs," Farlege stated curiously.

Changing the subject Madifen wheeled over to the bed, "speaking of legs, how's yours?"

Farlege sat up straight and reached down to feel his leg.

"It's a little stiff, but there's no pain. None at all."

"Some stiffness is to be expected. You're going to want to start using it as soon as possible."

"Like right now?"

"Sure, give it a try. Stand up slowly – and I mean very slowly."

Farlege did as Madifen said and stood, without pain or discomfort. He took one step, two, and felt the tension in the muscles ease. Within minutes it was as if the leg had never been broken.

"Madifen, this is amazing!"

"Old healing magic is pretty incredible," Madifen agreed.

"They are beating against my shields," he looked at the man who had just restored his future. "Tell ya what, you go over into the corner. I'll open the door and go out into the hallway, distract them. Maybe you can get away."

"It's okay, Farlege. I mean what are they going to do, arrest me? I just healed the Police Captain. I'm tired of hiding so much truth about myself. Just let them in."

#

Tenja sat bolt upright when she realized she'd awoken in a bed. Every sense went on alert, and she surveyed her surroundings. Her room? Her bed? This wasn't right. They were on a trek...they...oh yeah. The house. She rubbed her eyes and swung her feet over the side of the bed. She glanced at the clock, ten in the morning and then she heard the voices downstairs. This house is freaky, she thought to herself.

As she padded downstairs, she realized the boys were talking about the map.

"Hodgens, I think it means we go to wherever this is and then come back here," Graysen said. He had learned to play the song on the recorder and be able to converse with them at the same time.

"But we've never backtracked like that," Hodgens pointed out.

"We also never had a safe place like this until now," Conner added.

She poured herself a cup of coffee, grabbed a pastry, and took a seat at the table where the debate continued.

"I don't believe Momma Raben went to all of this work for a house we'd only stay in one night," Graysen argued.

"That's a good point," Conner agreed.

Hodgens looked at Tenja, "what do you think?"

She shook her head, "uh uh, no thinking or decision making before the first cup of coffee is gone. But, I get that you think we just keep going but your brothers think we come back here after we find the last piece."

"Yes," he agreed, "exactly."

"Okay, light it up while I eat and drink. Let me look at it for a few minutes," she told them.

So, Graysen played and she examined the book. She flipped forward and looked through the last pages. When her coffee cup was empty she said, "I think Graysen and Conner are right."

"Ha! See!" Conner tapped Hodgens on the shoulder who returned the gesture with a glare.

"Why? We've never gone back to a place," Hodgens questioned her answer.

"Because of the compass. If you watch it closely, it turns on the pages where we reach a marker. And then the next break in the map is a blank space like when we found the house," she told him.

Hodgens took the book from her and examined the pages closer.

"Huh, you're right. I didn't notice that the compass turns," He conceded.

"You would have when you were leading us," Tenja said.

"Like Graysen, I also don't think Raben would have gone to the trouble of this house if we were only going to stay in it one night. She planned for us to live here, at least for a while," she added.

"You say that like we're not going to stay here," Conner looked at her, a puzzled expression on her face.

She shrugged and just said, "we don't know what each day holds. We'll use it as long as is possible." She stood, "for now, let's get this leg of the journey over with. I want that last piece of the puzzle so we can see what's next. I'm really kind of tired of searching for puzzle pieces."

"Me too," Conner agreed.

"Yeah, I'm glad there are only four pieces to this puzzle," Graysen said as he grabbed a anish.

Beagle Girl met them outside, ready for this part of the quest. The morning went smoothly and soon they were stopping for lunch.

As they ate in amicable silence Graysen started laughing. The others looked at each other then at him. Beagle Girl even cocked her head and stared at him.

"Want to share the joke, brother?" Conner asked.

"A memory just popped into my head," he told the group. "Do you guys remember when we were about eight and decided that we could use our magic to peek at the Christmas presents?"

Hodgens laughed and spewed a drink of water, "what made you think of that?" He laughed.

"I don't know, maybe this whole quest we're on. We're each having to use our magic to solve problems. That's kind of what we were trying to do then."

"And exactly what was your problem then?" Tenja poked him.

"The problem was that we didn't know what was in our presents!" Conner chuckled.

"They were wrapped so pretty, just sitting around the tree," Hodgens agreed.

"I mean, really mom, they were begging us to peek," Graysen leaned into her.

"It wasn't our fault that Hodgens couldn't rewrap them just the way they'd been before we messed with them," Conner said. "I got them to our room one at a time."

"Yeah, and I played my music to distract you," Graysen added.

"Hey! I was only eight years old. I didn't know wrapping the presents back up would be so hard!" Hodgens laughed again.

Tenja laughed, "I shielded the tree the next year. Those packages weren't going anywhere."

They reminisced for a few more minutes, sharing funny stories of their childhood. It warmed Tenja's heart to know they had such fond memories of growing up together. She hoped they maintained that camaraderie as they got older.

"All right let's get this done and get back to the house," she finally said.

The path took them into a dense part of the forest. About an hour into this part of the journey Hodgens stopped abruptly and threw his arms out so no one would go around him. Then he slowly stepped back.

"What is it? What's wrong?" Tenja asked as she stepped up beside him.

Then she saw it. A trench about ten feet across ringed an area of land ahead of them. On that patch of land was a column that stood about twelve feet tall.

"Flashlight," she said and held out her hand.

Graysen handed one to her and she shined the light down into the trench.

"I estimate that is about fifteen feet deep," she told the boys.

"Well, this is interesting," Conner said flatly. "There's not room on that small spot of land for all of us to travel over there."

"Okay, let me think for a minute," she said and looked around.

After a few minutes she said, "Beagle Girl, you stay here with Hodgens and Graysen, keep them shielded."

The dog aroofed.

"Conner, I'm going to drop shields and you'll travel us over. Then we'll recloak."

"Sounds good," he told her.

"On three like usual," she told Beagle Girl who nodded in acknowledgement.

Tenja dropped the shields and Conner grabbed her hand. But they didn't go anywhere. He tried a second time but couldn't move. He looked at Tenja in confusion.

Tenja cloaked them and asked, "what's wrong?"

"I – I don't know," Conner told her. "I can feel my magic and draw on it like I usually do but nothing happens. It's like I can't travel us over there."

Tenja tapped on Beagle Girl's shields with her magic. The dog yielded and Tenja surrounded them with her own shields.

"Well, we should have known that would be too easy," she told them.

"I'm sorry," Conner sounded defeated.

She put her hand on his back, "no, Conner, it's not you. The old magic used here is too strong. You can't penetrate it and that's okay. We just have to find another way across."

They all turned and looked at the situation.

Hodgens noticed rocks strewn around the edge of the trench. They looked big enough to walk on and it gave him an idea. Using his magic, he began moving a rock. He placed it at the inside edge of the trench right in front of him, and he held it there.

"What are you doing, son?" Tenja asked.

He didn't answer, just grabbed another rock and placed it on the other side of the first one, making a line toward the land with the column. When he realized his plan might work, he brought the rocks to the grass beside him and sat them down.

"Okay, here's what I think we do. I'm going to bring these rocks over and use them to make a bridge. Then I'll hold them there and walk across the bridge to the column. I'll inspect the column and we'll go from there," he told them all.

Tenja thought about his plan for a minute. Beagle Girl aroofed.

"I don't know, Hodgens. You've never stood on something that you were suspending in mid-air. It doesn't sound safe," she said.

"We could do the rope trick," Conner said, "tie a rope around him in case he falls. Then at least we've got him."

Tenja shook her head, "the rope won't work across cloaking spells, but that was a good idea."

Hodgens weighed Tenja's concern.

"Let me test it out," he told her and raised one of the stones into the air. When he stepped up onto it, the stone remained suspended in mid-air.

"Huh," Tenja said, "your magic has gotten stronger. Okay, you can do this, but you can't be exposed for long. Can you hold the rocks up for Beagle Girl to follow with you?" She asked him.

"I can do that," he agreed.

"Beagle Girl, I know we haven't tried this, but since he'll be walking and not traveling, can you walk behind him and try to cloak him?" She asked the dog.

Beagle Girl nodded and walked up to Hodgens. He turned and began to work his magic. Now that he knew what he needed to do, and truly believed that it would work, it only took a few minutes to construct the rock bridge. He and Beagle Girl walked across without even a wobble. Once they had crossed, he moved the stones back to the grass so he could easily access them to return to the group.

When they reached the column, he felt the magic in it. It was as if the magic in the column was calling out to his magic. He placed his hand on the smooth stone. Momma Raben, he thought, I feel you.

He pulled his hand back, closed his eyes and sent his magic to the column. The magic in the column drew his inside. There he found a switch of some sort. Using his magic, he turned the switch and heard a loud click above him. He pulled his magic back and looked up. Two pegs, about four inches long, now stuck out from opposite sides of the column. Unfortunately, they were about seven feet up. There was no way he could reach them.

He crossed his arms. Circled the column. He looked for other pegs or stepping spots. But he found nothing.

He looked down at Beagle Girl, "let's go back to the others and tell them what we've found."

Hodgens reconstructed the bridge, and they walked back across the trench.

"Did you get it?" Graysen asked.

He shook his head, "no, not yet. There was a switch in the column. I turned it with my magic, and it made two pegs appear on the column. Only problem is they are about seven feet off the ground."

"What kind of pegs?" Tenja asked.

"They looked like ones that loggers use to climb a tree," he described what he had seen to them.

"But there's nothing else to climb?" Conner asked.

"Nope, nothing."

"I wonder if, once I'm over there, I could travel up to the pegs. I wouldn't be trying to cross the trench. I'd already be there," Conner shared his idea.

"That might work," Tenja agreed. "Hodgens can you make that bridge again?"

"Yep, I can do that," he told her.

"Beagle Girl, go with Conner this time. Keep him cloaked," Tenja instructed.

Once at the column Conner looked up and studied where he need to land, "could you have made this any trickier, momma?" He said out loud.

He had one shot to get this right, he could feel it in the magic around him. Feet on the pegs, arms around the column. Feet on the pegs, arms around the column. He repeated the instructions to himself several times as he stared at his destination.

Tenja grabbed Hodgens' and Graysen's hands, took a breath, and held it.

Beagle Girl watched as Conner disappeared from beside her and reappeared seven feet off the ground. Feet square on the pegs. Arms wrapped around the column. She aroofed and bounced up and down.

Conner looked at the flat top of the column. There was a circle about the size of a silver dollar carved into the stone. He pressed on the circle, and it popped up like it was spring loaded. He took out the parchment and put it in his pocket. Then he traveled back down and stood beside Beagle Girl.

"Let's get out of here," he said to the dog who nodded in return.

Then, as they turned toward the stone bridge they watched in shock as the stone fell to the bottom of the trench.

"What the hell!?" Conner exclaimed, looking around.

"Hodgens? What happened?" Tenja whirled to look at him. "Put the bridge back up!"

"I can't! I don't know what's happening, but the stones just stopped letting me use them. They just stopped," he blurted out.

"Well crap," Graysen said, "what do we do now?"

Tenja reached for her magic. She couldn't feel it. Panic rose up in her.

"Can you guys feel your magic?" She squeaked out the question.

She watched as they each closed their eyes.

"I don't feel mine," Hodgens answered as his brother nodded in agreement.

"Is this like at school? When the magic went away?" Graysen asked.

"I don't know," she admitted. "I guess."

She paced beside the trench.

"What are we supposed to do?" Conner asked the dog.

The dog shook her head.

Tenja looked around. There had to be a log or something they could move so they could get back across.

"What are we supposed to do?" Hodgens asked.

"Shh," Tenja told him. "Give me a minute."

Just as she spotted a fallen tree that she thought they might be able to lift, she felt her magic swelling inside of her. It grew so fast it made her chest hurt. Her breath caught in her throat. Then, as fast as it has rose, it settled into its normal rhythm inside of her.

She looked at the boys. They stared back at her.

"What just happened?" Graysen asked.

Without saying a word, Tenja sent her magic out into the expanse – and felt nothing.

"He can travel through now," she mumbled half to herself.

"What?" Graysen asked.

"I don't feel the magic that was there before," she spoke louder. "I think he can travel back now."

"But he doesn't know that," Hodgens said.

"He'll figure it out. I know he will," she said and willed her son to come back to her.

Conner looked at the trench, at the dog, and then across the trench where his family waited for him.

"Well, what do you think? Do we take down the cloak and try to communicate with them," he gestured toward the bank where everyone else waited.

Beagle Girl shook her head no. Before Conner could process what was happening the dog grabbed his ankle and they were standing next to Tenja and his brothers. Tenja threw her arms around him.

"Well, that was exciting," Conner said. No one laughed.

"Can we just get out of here?" Hodgens asked.

"Yes," Tenja nodded. "Conner and Beagle Girl, can you two travel us to just outside the house boundary spells?"

They both nodded.

"Excellent. The four of you go first. Conner, come back for me. Beagle Girl go with Hodgens and Graysen inside the house."

They all did as they were told. Once they were all in the house, they laid the four puzzle pieces out on the kitchen table. Then they watched in amazement as the pieces slid together and the individual pieces became one whole image.

"What is that?" Conner asked.

"Some kind of box?" Hodgens guessed.

"But it's like it keeps shifting shapes," Graysen observed.

Tenja looked at the image, "well, I guess it's just the next piece that we have to find."

"There's only one more leg of the map," Hodgens said.

"Well, we finish the map and then we'll see what's next," she told them.

Tenja rolled up the picture and stored it in her pack.

"No more today," she said, "let's rest and we'll begin the last part of the map tomorrow."

"Okay, mom," Graysen said as he stood up. "I'm going to go into the studio and play some music. I've missed having my instruments." His brothers wandered off to their various activities.

252

Tenja got a glass of water and sat back down at the table. She was staring at her glass when Beagle Girl jumped on the table.

"Hey!" Tenja exclaimed. "I know we're not in Easpach, but the no dog on the table rule still applies."

Then she realized the dog hadn't been in the kitchen with them since they got back from the trench.

"Where have you been?" Tenja asked.

The dog held out her paw. Tenja just looked at her. Beagle Girl gestured for Tenja to put out her hand. Hesitantly, Tenja held her palm up. Beagle Girl pressed her paw into Tenja's palm. Then she pulled it back and waited.

Tenja looked at her hand, read what she saw there "2am, P<T>B. What in the world does that mean?"

Beagle Girl jumped down and tugged at Tenja's pant leg. With a sigh, Tenja got up and followed the dog. She was so tired of this quest. This was not the life she had hoped to have. For a while it had been more than she ever dreamed. Now...

Beagle Girl disappeared beyond the boundary spell. Tenja stopped. Then she saw the dog stick only her head back through the spell.

Aroof! She barked and disappeared back beyond the boundary. This time Tenja followed her.

The dog was standing just beyond the boundary spell, before going through the portal. Tenja walked up to her. Beagle Girl nudged her hand.

Tenja looked at the writing again, "2am, P<T>B." This time she read it slower.

"2am, I get that. It's a time," she saw the dog nod.

"P?" She asked Beagle Girl. The dog turned toward the portal. "T?" The dog nudged her leg.

She gasped and knelt. Looking into the dog's eyes she said, "it's a message from Raben isn't it?"

Beagle Girl jumped up and down.

Tenja continued, "she wants to meet me at 2am between the portal and the boundary spell?"

This time the dog licked her cheek.

#

Praelox looked at the three piles of rocks. "What do you have them chasing, Gazorel? It seems like a wild goose chase to me."

She examined each pile of rocks. Faint traces of magic. As she knelt looking at the last pile, she realized that the ground was disturbed nearby. Upon examination she found a strong magical residue.

"So, the prize was here," she said.

When she first started tracking Tenja and the boys she thought they were just trying to get away, to get somewhere safe. While they still may be trying to find someplace safe, they were also finding things along the way. There was no way for her to know what they were finding, though. The magic protecting the items was strong and the residue it left after being triggered didn't reveal the contents.

She had to admit, all of this was more intricate than she expected when she decided to come to Easpach. How had Gazorel managed to pull all of this off? She couldn't possibly be working alone. She had to have a network of others helping her.

Studying the grass and undergrowth around the area she easily identified which direction they had taken. Most people wouldn't see it, but she'd discovered they were trying to cover their tracks with magic. That magic was giving them away.

#

"Are you coming up to bed, mom?" Graysen asked.

254

"In a bit," she told him. "I think I'll sit and read in the den for a bit. It's been a long time since I've got to relax and enjoy a book."

"Do you want company?" Hodgens checked on her.

"No, no," she waved them off, "I'm fine, really. I know you three are tired. Get some sleep," she told them.

"Okay, night," Conner said,

"Good night my favorite little people," she smiled.

"We're not little anymore, mom," they smiled back and then headed up the stairs.

Tenja struggled to not stare at the clock. Each minute felt like an hour. She did pick a book off the shelf, but after reading the same page three times she gave up. Sighing, she headed into the studio.

Once there she set an alarm on the clock on her desk. She had always needed an alarm when she painted. Too many times she had fell into her work and lost track of time. The feel of the brushes and paint in her magic were like home. She let her worries slip away and played with color.

The alarm went off at one forty-five in the morning. She turned it off and cleaned up her brushes. Then she stepped between the boundary and the portal and waited.

Only a few minutes had passed when Raben appeared in the space between. They looked at each other. Then they ran to each other and held on tight.

"Baby, I don't have a lot of time," Raben finally said. "There are things that I need to tell you, important things."

Tenja stepped out of the embrace and really looked at Raben. She'd lost weight, cut her hair. There were dark circles under her eyes. She looks horrible, Tenja thought to herself. The last ten years have aged her twenty.

"I figured," Tenja finally said, "why else would you be here?"

"Well, I'd like to be coming back to you and the boys," her eyes were sad, "but I can't. Not yet."

"We miss you," Tenja said.

Raben sighed, "I can't even begin to put words to how much I miss all of you. How are they?"

"They are amazing, Raben, really amazing," she said proudly.

"I can't believe they are only six months away from their evolution," Raben shook her head.

Tenja started to say something and then stopped.

"What? What is it?" Raben asked.

"Conner already evolved," Tenja told her. "He bent his magic to save Hodgens and forced the evolution."

"When?"

"About five months ago now. Not long after his seventeenth birthday," Tenja said.

"What is his new symbol?" Raben asked anxiously.

Tenja looked around, grabbed a stick and did her best to draw Conner's symbol in the dirt.

Raben knelt and looked at the symbol.

"No," she whispered, "no, no, no."

"Raben?" Tenja asked worriedly.

"I need the journal. Where's the journal?" She asked angrily.

Tenja ran into the house and grabbed the journal from her pack. She handed it to Raben who opened it to the last page of the map. She laid her hand on it and closed her eyes. After a moment she handed the journal back to Tenja.

"Okay, I've adjusted it to fit the current status of things." Raben told her.

"What does that mean, Raben? What is happening?"

"I can't just tell you. The magic won't let me just tell you," she paced, frustrated. She pointed at the journal, "read the opening poem again. Read it and think about Conner. That's all I can say about that."

Tenja furrowed her brow, "fine, I will. Raben, you're scaring me. Like I'm not already scared enough."

"There's good reason to be scared, Tenja. There's a revolution happening in Draiocht and it's come to Easpach."

"What?!"

"The magic, it was failing. I was right about that ten years ago. What I didn't know at the time was that the group of people who believe magic should stay in Draiocht had organized, gotten stronger. They want to destroy the tapestry. They want to stop Draiocht from sending magic to Easpach."

"The painting," Tenja said, "the final transition of the painting showed the destruction of Easpach. The destruction of Draiocht."

"What? What painting?" Raben asked.

Tenja frowned, "you didn't send the painting?"

"I don't know what painting you're talking about Tenja."

So Tenja told Raben about the events surrounding the painting. And once again she watched her wife pace.

"There's more going on than I realized," Raben finally said.

"Raben. how are you doing all of this? Where are you leading us?"

"Where? I'm not certain now. I thought I knew, but Conner's evolution changed something. And when one thing changes events like this, there is typically a domino effect."

"I don't understand," Tenja shook her head.

"Oh, Tenja," Raben took Tenja's hands in hers. "There is so much I wish I had time to tell you."

"Can't you stay? Even for just a few hours?"

"I wish I could, but I've already stayed too long. I need to get back."

"Back to where?"

"Tenja. I have to tell you two things that are very important. I need you to listen carefully."

"Okay?"

Raben took a deep breath, "My birth name is Gazorel Brena Draiocht. I'm Princess Gazorel."

"Princess Gazorel?" Tenja asked.

Raben watched as confusion, then recognition, and then anger filled her wife's eyes. Tenja dropped Raben's hands.

"I don't understand. What are you saying to me right now?" Tenja spat in anger.

"You know what I'm saying," Raben simply stated.

Tenja shook her head again, "no, that girl died years ago. I remember the story. She drowned."

This time Raben shook her head, "no, the story was that she drowned. What happened was that a visionist came to the castle when I was five and foretold my death and the fall of Draiocht if I stayed at the castle. My father, King Reginald, took visionists very seriously. So, he devised a plan."

"He sent you to Easpach when you were five? I thought you said you came here when you were eleven. Was that a lie, too?"

"No that wasn't a lie. My nanny became my mom. She changed my name to Raben Araven and hid me in Draiocht until I was eleven. Then one day that same visionist showed up. She had found us deep in the woods. She said I had to get out of Draiocht. So, again, I was forced to leave what I knew to be home. That time, though, I had Madifen, and we came through together. The rest you know is all true."

"Why Raben Araven?"

"What?"

"Why did your nanny choose the name Raben Araven?"

"Raben is just a rearrangement of my middle name, Brena. To get me far away from the castle my nanny joined a caravan. When they asked what our names were, she had to come up with something on the spot. So, I assumed Araven came from the word caravan," Raben shrugged.

There was a moment of silence and then Tenja asked, "so everything we're having to go through right now is because of who you are? Because someone knows you're Princess Gazorel and that you're alive?"

"And they obviously know about you and the boys."

"The boys!" Tenja exclaimed. "You have sentenced the boys to a fate they don't deserve! You've passed on the Draiocht name, responsibilities, and magic. They are turning eighteen soon and they don't even know who they are! Yet there are people after them for exactly that reason!?"

"You can't tell them, Tenja," Raben pleaded, "please, don't tell them."

"Why not? Because it will put them in danger? Look around, Raben! This house is nice, but it is an illusion of safety. We're not safe anywhere right now!" The anger flooded out of her. The pain and resentment bubbled up inside of her.

Raben had no response.

"What was the other thing you needed to tell me?" Tenja asked, "tell me and then go."

"Tenja," the name caught in Raben's throat.

"Tell me, Princess, what do you need me to know," Tenja saw the jab hit home and watched Raben's eyes fill with tears.

"I have a twin brother," Raben said. "That's who brought me the message ten years ago. His name is Devon William Draiocht. I don't know where he is yet, but I know that if we find him, he will help us. He would never turn his back on me. Not ever."

"And what? You want me to find him?" Tenja crossed her arms.

Raben shrugged, "I'm not saying you should go looking for him right now. I just wanted you to know that there's an ally out there if we can find him. I have other allies now, but he is the one I would, without a second thought, trust with my life."

Another moment of silence passed.

"Tenja, I have to go."

"I know. You told me. Leaving again."

The verbal slap shattered Raben's resolve, and she began to sob. The sound of her wife suffering broke Tenja's determination to be angry. She gathered Raben in her arms.

"I'm sorry," Tenja whispered. "I know you didn't ask for this. It's just all so much."

Raben straightened and wiped her eyes, took a breath. Placing her hand against Tenja's cheek she said, "I'm sorry, too. I love you."

"I love you, too, Raben. I always will. But I need some time with all of this."

Raben leaned in and kissed her. Then she laid her forehead against Tenja's.

"I really have to go now."

"Will you be able to come back?"

"I don't know. I have no idea when we will see each other again," Raben told her honestly.

Tenja hugged her one more time. Then she turned and walked through the boundary spell toward the house. This time she would do the leaving.

#

Tenja sat at the table with a cup of tea. It was three o'clock in the morning and she couldn't sleep. The time with Raben had rattled her. Raben? Gazorel? Who are you, really? She thought to herself.

She read the poem again, this time making notes in the margins.

"The shimmer and the glimmer are fading from the sky. That's easy, magic isn't as strong. The fraying tapestry is the grid that sends magic from Draiocht to Easpach. Got it."

She took a swig of coffee, "creatures born of fire? Dragons?" She wrote down the word. "Relic in the dark...hmm. She looked at the image the puzzle pieces had created. Perhaps?" She wrote the words puzzle picture with a question mark next to that stanza.

"This makes my brain hurt," she said to Beagle Girl who had joined her around two thirty.

"The one who can seek their help bears the origin mark," she read slowly. "Origin mark," she repeated the phrase over and over. Then she heard Raben's voice, "read it and think about Conner." Tenja gasped, "the origin mark! Whatever this task was, Conner has to do it.

And he has to seek out the help of dragons? I don't think I like this at all, Beagle Girl."

The dog had no response. Tenja didn't like that either.

"Don't try to save the one who's lost. Raben?" She wrote in the margin. As she did, a new stanza appeared.

Three is magic it's been foretold

And enough to save the world

Three together, three to find

And a flag of peace unfurls

"Three of something will solve the problem, evidently. Three together - the boys? Three to find. We don't know what we're looking for yet. Still a question there. Flag of peace? Could this all really end in peace between Draiocht and Easpach?"

She patted Beagle Girl on the head, "well wouldn't that be nice."

CHAPTER 31

Praelox stared across the trench toward the column.

"Was all of this really necessary, Gazorel?"

She was so tired of the game. It had taken her hours to walk around that stupid time tunnel. She looked at the column on the small area in the center. She walked around the trench looking for a way across. Nothing.

"Traveler?"

Studying the column, she saw the pegs just a little over halfway up. Yeah, someone had to have been able to travel there. She walked around the trench once more, this time looking for the trail that would tell her which way to go to follow them to the next location. Again, she found nothing. So, she went back to the spot where they had come upon the trench.

She couldn't find any indication that they had went back the way they came into the area.

"The only possible answer is traveling" she said aloud. Then she reached out with her magic.

#

"Rise and shine, guys," Tenja knocked on the boys' bedroom door. "Let's get this last part of the map over with."

She headed down the stairs and started the coffee. The boys all joined her within thirty minutes. By the hour mark they were fed and out the door. Hodgens led them around to the side of the house and into the forest.

The air was cold. Not quite biting, but fall was in full swing. She was glad they were walking because it helped her stay warm. The further they walked, however, the colder it seemed to get. They could see that the forest stopped ahead of them.

"Where in all that is magic are we?" Hodgens asked sounding shocked.

Tenja walked up beside him and looked out at the ocean.

"Well, I'll be," Tenja exclaimed.

"Is that really the ocean?" Graysen asked.

"Well, it's an ocean," Tenja said. "We know the outer spell at the house was a portal."

"So, like Hodgens said, where are we?" Conner asked.

"I have absolutely no idea," Tenja told them.

"I have some bad news," Hodgens said.

"What?" Conner and Graysen asked at the same time.

Hodgens pointed, "you see that island out there, I think that's where we have to go."

Conner groaned. Graysen took off his pack and retrieved his telescoping eye glass.

After a moment he said, "it looks like there is a cave on the island."

"Let me see that," Tenja grabbed for the telescope.

"Geesh, mom," Graysen said as he let go.

She looked through the glass and after a moment sighed. Handing it back to Graysen she looked at Conner and said, "we need to all talk. Let's make lunch and I'll tell you what I know."

While the boys ate Tenja told them about the poem.

"Conner, I believe that you are the bearer of the origin mark," she told him.

"What?" He almost choked on his food. "What does that even mean?"

She shook her head, "beyond you having to complete this task, I don't know. We'll have to try to find out more about that later."

"What else, momma?" Graysen asked.

"Well, I wasn't sure what it meant about the relic being in the dark until you noticed the cave. I figured the relic was the image the puzzle turned into. The part about being in the dark was confusing, though," she confessed.

"So," Conner began. "Creatures born of fire? Any thoughts on that one. It doesn't sound good to me."

She looked at him with an odd expression on her face, "I think it means dragons."

He jumped up, "Dragons? Dragons!? Are. You. Serious!?"

Hodgens and Graysen just looked at each other, then at Conner.

"Conner, sit down," Tenja urged.

"Do you know anything about dragons?" Conner asked her. "Anything?"

"Only what Raben told me years ago, and what I've read in books," she told him. "The way I understand it, dragons only attack under two conditions. Either they feel threatened, or they've been trained to attack."

Conner threw his hands up in the air, "oh is that it? Only then? How will they know I'm not a threat? What if I go in there and they are trained to attack?"

"Then you get out," Tenja said. "You come back here, and we think of a different plan."

He just looked at her.

"I don't know what else to do, Conner. I don't like it. I don't like it at all. But I also don't believe that Raben would knowingly put us in danger like that. She certainly wouldn't send any of us to a slaughter," she tried to reassure him.

Resigned to his role in this task, he sighed and said, "fine."

"What about the last part?" Hodgens asked.

"More details we'll have to figure out later. Raben and I used to refer to you three as being magic. So it might mean the three of you?"

"Three together," Graysen said in a whisper.

"Three to find," Conner added.

They all sat in silence as they finished their lunch. Once they had packed up, they stood looking out across the ocean.

"You know," Graysen said. "On any other day I'd enjoy being at the ocean."

264

"Right?" Tenja agreed. "Maybe someday we can come back under better circumstances."

"I think we should go down to the beach," Hodgens told them.

"Hmm, I don't know," Tenja rubbed the back of her neck.

"I know it's a lot of open space," Hodgens said. "But I think it would be best."

"Beagle Girl," Tenja looked at the dog. "What do you think? Do you agree with Hodgens?"

The dog looked down at the beach, then back up at Tenja, and nodded.

"Okay then," Tenja said. "To the beach."

On the beach, they all sat down their packs. Tenja kept her quiver on and bow in hand just in case. Conner took the telescope from Graysen and studied the island and the cave entrance.

"So, it looks like there is plenty of room for me to stand by the cave entrance. I want to go there and wait a few minutes. Check things out and see if anything happens before I go into the cave," he told them.

"I think that's a good idea," Tenja agreed. "Beagle Girl, will you go with him for cloaking?"

The dog nodded but nudged Conner.

"What?" Conner asked.

"Do you not have his power anymore?" Tenja asked her.

She aroofed.

"Can't you just absorb it?" Tenja inquired.

Beagle Girl shook her head no.

"Okay. Conner, you're going to have to travel her with you," Tenja told him.

"No problem. You ready?" he asked the dog.

When she agreed he picked her up. Tenja dropped the cloaking spell around the two of them and they were gone. She watched through the telescope to see them briefly appear by the cave. She saw Beagle Girl, but not Conner. Beagle Girl didn't cloak herself. Instead, she started barking, going crazy at the cave entrance. Tenja watched as she tried to run into the cave, but the little dog couldn't get in. Then Tenja saw Beagle Girl sit down and howl in anguish.

Tenja dropped to her knees, "what have I done? Damn you, Raben! What have we done!?"

"Mom!?" Hodgens and Graysen dropped beside her.

"What is it? What's wrong?" Hodgens said ripping the telescope from her hand.

"Conner didn't travel to outside of the cave. Somehow, he ended up in the cave. Beagle Girl can't get in and she's upset. Something has gone horribly wrong," anger rose within Tenja as she looked out across the ocean. "Damn you, Raben!" She yelled.

Graysen put an arm around her, "let's give it some time. Give Conner some time. He has a habit of doing the unexpected."

So, they sat. And they waited.

"It's getting cold," Graysen said, "we need a fire."

"Can't," Tenja stopped him, "we don't have Conner to handle the smoke."

So, they huddled together for warmth under their sleeping bags. And they waited. They passed the telescope around until the sun was far enough down that it was too dark to see anything.

"Mom, you need to eat," Hodgens said as he pushed a bag of granola at her.

"We also won't make it through the night without a fire," Graysen said. "I know it's a risk, but freezing is a certainty."

She said nothing. Just ate the granola. Drank some water. She didn't stop Graysen from starting a fire. She just stared out at the island.

"This is ridiculous!" Hodgens jumped up. "I'm going to build a raft. We have to get over there!"

"It will take you too long to build a raft. Besides, that water is too choppy for something like that,' Graysen told him.

Ignoring his brother Hodgens began bringing wood down to the beach. After about thirty minutes he gave up and sat down.

Shrugging he said, "yeah, I guess you're right, Graysen. That idea won't work."

They took turns sleeping. One of them was always watching their surroundings and the island. As soon as the sun began to light the sky Tenja awoke and looked through the telescope. No change. Beagle Girl sat staring at the cave opening.

"Isn't there anything we can do?" Graysen said as he put out the last of the fire with sand. "Don't you have any spells up your sleeve that could help?"

"No, Graysen, I've got nothing. If I had something I would have used it last night."

They ate breakfast and continued to sit in silence. Tenja hated this feeling of helplessness. Sure, as a parent she'd felt it before. But in the last six months she'd felt it for more life and death moments than she could count.

"What is he doing now?" Graysen pointed at Hodgens.

His brother had five rocks about the size of his fist. He had extended them over the water like he had the big rocks over the trench at the column. He was trying to stand on them to no avail.

"Uh, Hodgens?" Tenja said.

"He saved my life," Hodgens responded. "Saved it. Now he's alone, in a cave and none of us are helping him. I have to help him!"

She walked over and took him by the arm.

"I know you're worried, we all are. But this," she pointed at the rocks, "will only serve to put you in danger, too."

"Why don't we go back to the house?" Graysen asked. "Maybe he went there."

"If he had went there, I think Beagle Girl would know he wasn't in the cave," Tenja pointed, "she's still staring at the cave like she wants to get in there or wants him to come out. She's not ready to give up on him. So, I'm not ready to give up on him."

"We're just supposed to sit here and keep waiting?" Graysen asked in anger.

"Yes, Graysen. We wait," Tenja stated.

"What about the journal?" Hodgens asked. "Do you think there is anything in there that would help us?"

She sighed, "you can look if you want."

Graysen pulled out his recorder and Hodgens grabbed the journal. They spent the morning scouring the journal trying to find something that might help them bring Conner back to them. As lunch time drew close, they gave up and put it all away. Tenja admired their desire to save their brother. She just wished there really was some secret that would help. Unfortunately, it was just a waiting game.

Tenja looked through the telescope. Beagle Girl was lying down now, still facing the mouth of the cave. Tenja had to believe that meant two things: Conner was still inside, and he was still alive. If either one of those wasn't true, she just knew Beagle Girl would get a message to her somehow. The little dog was nothing if not resourceful.

So, she would wait. She would eat, keep up her strength. She would stretch and be ready for whatever came next. After all, they were on the right side of a revolution. They may not be face to face with the enemy, but they were still in the battle. And she'd make damn sure she did everything she could to ensure her boys stayed alive to have a life when this was all over. If Raben could sacrifice for their boys' futures, then she could, too.

#

Praelox loved it when a plan came together. It had taken her hours to sort through the magic in the air to identify Gazorel's blood line in a traveler's magic. She was having to work too hard for this and it was making her hungry. Being hungry made her grumpy. But, in the end she had found what she was looking for - and it made her giddy.

"Today's the day, Gazorel. Today I find your wife and your offspring. By tomorrow at the latest I will have you."

She let out a hysterical laugh and began to follow the trail of magic. She just needed to find the right tree branches to set her final plan in motion.

CHAPTER 32

Graysen paced back and forth, glancing across the ocean at the cave entrance. Finally, he said, "mom, it's been a long time. Isn't there any way to get over there? Can't Beagle Girl come back and get one of us? Take us over there?"

"She can't," Tenja shook her head.

"It's been almost 24 hours since he went in that cave!" Hodgens exclaimed. "Why can't she help us?"

"Because she isn't holding Conner's power anymore. We knew that before she went over" Tenja told them.

"What do you mean she isn't holding his power anymore?" Graysen asked.

"Limited well of magic, remember? She had to let it go at some point. I don't know when," Tenja explained.

"Ahhh!" Hodgens yelled. "This is crazy. We have to -"

He was interrupted by Conner slamming into him and knocking him to the ground.

"Conner!" Tenja jumped up and grabbed him before he fell on Hodgens.

Graysen helped her ease him down to the ground. Hodgens righted himself and before the anger escaped his lips, he looked at his brother.

Conner was covered in dirt, his jeans torn at the knees. There were scrapes on his arms. But in his hands, he held a box of sorts.

Tenja knelt in front of him. She placed her hands on each side of his face and raised it so she could look at him.

"Oh, my sweet boy," she whispered.

He was shaking and exhibiting signs of shock.

"We need to get you warmed up," she said. Graysen grabbed a blanket. Hodgens grabbed a cup to make some tea.

But before they could do any of those things a large, winged creature swooped down and deposited Beagle Girl on the ground near them. They all turned and looked at the dragon, mouths' hanging open. Without missing a beat Beagle Girl began to bark and tug at Tenja's shirt. Having learned not to disregard the dog, Tenja asked, "what is it? What's wrong?"

She watched as the dog ran from her toward the direction back to the house. She did this several times, barking as she did.

"We've got to go!" She yelled at the boys.

"I'm so tired, momma," Conner began to cry.

"I know, baby," she said sympathetically, "but we can't stay. Something is wrong or someone is coming. I don't know what, but we've got to go."

"Can't we just travel there?" Graysen asked.

"No, Graysen. No time. Conner's depleted. Beagle Girl doesn't have that magic anymore. We. Have. To. Go," she insisted.

Hodgens grabbed the box in Conner's hands and shoved it in his pack and strapped it on. Then he picked up Conner's. Tenja and Graysen gathered their things and helped Conner to his feet.

"I've got him," Graysen told her. "Lead the way back."

Beagle Girl took up the end of the line and together they began to make their way back to the house. It had taken them a day to get to the cave. We'll never make it back before dark Tenja thought to herself. What are we going to do? she tried to brainstorm a way out of their current situation.

Then she saw it. Two trees forming what looked like a doorway. She ran toward it.

"Mom, what are you doing?" Hodgens asked anxiously. "That's not the way -" and then he watched her create a portal. Through the portal he saw the area around the house.

"You're a genius!" Graysen exclaimed.

"Let's go!" Tenja urged them to follow her through.

The portal had brought them a few hundred feet from the first boundary shield. Her heart began to slow down. Her pace slowed.

"Nice try, Tenja. You're not the only person with portal making magic," a voice said. They all turned around and saw a woman standing at the edge of the forest.

"Run!" Tenja told them as she nocked an arrow.

"But mom!" Hodgens pleaded.

"Run!" Tenja yelled it this time, and they obeyed. Even Conner put his feet to the ground as fast as he could.

"I don't know who you are, but you need to stay back!" Tenja yelled at the woman.

"Oh, I'll tell you who I am. I'll tell you who your wife really is," the woman enhanced the volume of her voice.

"Last warning," Tenja said. "Don't take another step."

When the woman did take a step, Tenja let the arrow fly. As she watched it soar through the air she felt her magic drop away - again. And she watched her arrow fall to the ground.

Anger rose in her.

"You! You tried to kill my sons!"

The woman waved her hand in the air, "kill is such a negative word."

Tenja hated to do it, but she felt as though she had no other option. Humans were just a type of animal. She'd taken down large game before. This wouldn't be any different. Acting as quickly as possible she reached into her quiver and nocked a hunting arrow. Then she let it fly right toward Praelox's heart.

Praelox flicked the arrow aside like it was an annoying bug. Tenja's heart caught in her throat. No one had ever been able to do that to her arrows.

Tenja couldn't hear the boys running anymore. That meant they had gotten within the boundaries. But how are those spells still up when I can't feel magic? Then she realized that the woman was an ampnull. She was draining the power from the people but couldn't take it out of the world. Realizing what was going on, Tenja turned and ran.

She heard the footsteps behind her as the woman tried to catch up to her. But then, like magic, when Tenja crossed through the first boundary spell the sound of the woman's footsteps was gone. Tenja's magic slammed back into her with a force that knocked her to the ground. She looked back to see no one. She was alone between the two spells.

#

Praelox slammed into a wall and fell to the ground. Blood spurted from her nose as she rolled onto her hands and knees moaning.

"What the hell!" She mumbled, wiping the blood from her face.

She got to her feet and looked around.

"Noooo!" She yelled when she realized she was standing at the park restrooms. She was right back where she had started in her search for Tenja and the brats. When her eyes finally focused, she saw a note hanging on the wall. Nice try cousin, she read. She let out a scream and watched the note go up in flames.

#

Tenja ran into the house, dropping her pack, bow, and quiver as she crossed the threshold. Conner was flat on his back on the floor. His brothers were kneeling over him talking to him, shaking him.

"Let me in!" She ordered. Hodgens and Graysen backed up.

"The woman?" Hodgens asked.

"Gone," Tenja told them. "Conner?"

Graysen shrugged, "he just collapsed once he got in here."

She felt Conner's forehead. Normal temp. She checked his pulse. Normal heart rate.

Then he snored. Graysen and Hodgens couldn't tell if she was laughing or crying.

"Mom?" Hodgens asked quietly.

"He literally fell asleep," she said, wiping her eyes. The brothers laughed.

Beagle Girl came over then. Using magic, she lifted him gently from the floor and placed him on the sofa in the living room. Tenja covered him up and kissed his forehead. When she entered the kitchen, she found Hodgens and Graysen at the table, the box Conner had retrieved in front of them.

"We have questions," Hodgens began.

"Join the club, buddy," Tenja retorted, "join the club."

She plopped in a chair and gestured for them to talk.

"First of all, who was that woman?" Graysen started.

"Easy one. I don't know. Next?" Tenja said plainly.

"What did she mean when she said she'd tell you who your wife really is?" Hodgens asked.

Tougher one, Tenja thought to herself. She got up and grabbed a glass, filled it with water. When she sat down, she took a long drink from the glass and considered what she should tell them. Screw it, she finally thought, they're who they are because of who she is.

"Your Momma Raben came to me several days ago," she began.

"What?! When?" Hodgens erupted.

"The second night we stayed here. We met between the barriers in the middle of the night. She's how I knew to look at the poem when we were completing the last task on the map," Tenja was honest.

"What did she say?" Graysen asked.

"A lot in a just the few minutes before she had to leave. We're caught in the middle of a revolution. There are a group of people trying to overthrow the Draiocht government. They don't want Draiocht sending magic to Easpach. They want to keep it all," she tried to explain.

"What does that have to do with us?" Hodgens prodded when she paused.

"Because of the truth of Momma Raben's past," she sighed. "Apparently Momma Raben is actually Princess Gazorel Brena

274

Draiocht. Her father is King Reginald Draiocht, the current King of Draiocht."

No words. Just blank shocked expressions. The boys looked at each other. Looked at her.

Then Graysen started laughing, "we're freakin' royalty, brother!"

Hodgens looked at him, "what?"

"If Momma Raben is a princess, and we're her boys, that makes us princes. Prince Hodgens Draiocht. Prince Graysen Draiocht. Prince Conner Draiocht," he said.

Hodgens turned to Tenja, "is he right?"

She shrugged, "well, I hadn't thought about it, but yes. You would all be princes."

What does that make me? She wondered.

Graysen pushed his chair back, "I'm exhausted. I'm going to clean up and call it a night."

Tenja and Hodgens watched as he left the room. Hodgens picked up the box and turned it over in his hands.

"It's not just a box," he finally said, "it's a puzzle. It's familiar, like I've seen it before."

Tenja took the box from his hands, "tomorrow, bub. We can rest for a night." When he didn't get up, she stayed in her seat.

"So much has changed in the past six months," he said getting up and heading toward the den.

She followed and watched as he started a fire. He poked at the logs until he had the fire burning the way he wanted. Then he sat in a chair staring at the blaze. Feeling like she should, she joined him.

"You're right, a lot has changed. But not all the changes are bad," she said.

"True," he said, eyes on the dancing flames.

Beagle Girl curled up in front of the fire and quickly fell asleep. Hodgens smiled lovingly at her.

"She's one of the best things to come out of all of this for me," he nodded at the little dog.

275

"I know," Tenja agreed, "Raben sure hit the mark with her."

He let out a sigh, "the four of us, we've left a lot behind, things, people, our lives."

"Yes, we left everything and everyone we knew, except each other," Tenja said hesitantly wondering where he was going with this line of thinking.

"I thought I'd be at veterinarian school right now. Instead, I'm six months away from my evolution and every day I wonder if I will live to experience it."

"That's a heavy burden for a young man."

"Momma Raben, she'll always be Momma Raben to me no matter what her given name is," he gave Tenja a side long glance. "She risked a lot to get us this far."

"She did," Tenja rocked in her chair.

"She came and left you, again," he continued.

Geesh kid, rip out my heart here, Tenja kept the thought to herself.

"That couldn't have been easy for either of you. Did you know she was a princess? Did you know who she really is?"

"No. I only ever knew her as Raben," Tenja admitted.

"Are you mad at her for not telling you?"

"I'm a lot of things. I do feel anger that she didn't tell me. It's all confusing and my emotions are complicated."

He didn't know what to say to that, so they sat in silence for a long time. The flames danced and turned the logs to ash. Tenja had decided to sit with him for as long as he needed.

Finally, he asked, "do you think that Momma Raben kept her identity a secret to protect us?"

"As much I hate to admit it, yes, Hodgens, I think that is exactly why she did it."

"Do you really believe she risked everything to ensure that we would get to grow up?"

"I do. I really do," she looked at him. As she watched the last flickers of the fire casting light on his face, she could see him

276

changing. In those moments she saw her son grow from a teenager to a man.

"Then maybe it's time I forgive her for the leaving."

To Be Continued...

Pronunciation Key

Easpach: eee-spa

Driaocht: dree-oct

Sa Lár: sa lair

Farlege: far-le<g>

Koarré: co-are-ray

Praelox: pray-locks